JOHN HOWARD AND THE UNDERLINGS

John Howard Tudor Series Book 1

J.C. JARVIS

WHERRY ROAD PRESS

Get a Free Book!

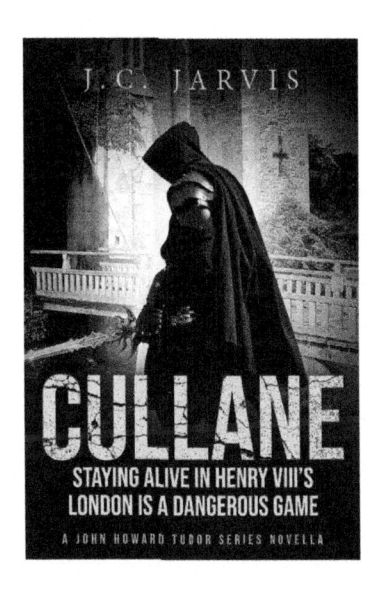

Before John Howard found sanctuary on the streets of London, Andrew Cullane formed a small band of outlawed survivors called the Underlings. Discover their fight for life for free when you join J.C. Jarvis's newsletter at jcjarvis.com/cullane

To my wife, Glenda, who is my biggest supporter and my bedrock. Without her support and encouragement none of this would have ever happened.

Copyright

WHERRY ROAD PRESS

John Howard and the Underlings

John Howard Tudor Series Book 1

© 2022 by J.C Jarvis

Edited by https://melanieunderwood.co.uk/

Cover Design by http://www.jdsmith-design.com/

This book is a work of fiction. Names, characters, businesses, organisations, places and events, other than those clearly in the public domain, are either the product of the author's imagination, or are used fictitiously. Any resemblances to actual persons, living or dead, events or locales are purely coincidental.

No part of this book may be reproduced, stored in a retrieval system, or transmitted by any means without the written permission of the author and publisher.

John Howard And The Underlings

by J.C. Jarvis

Quotes

"The boy who is going to make a great man must not make up his mind merely to overcome a thousand obstacles, but to win in spite of a thousand repulses and defeats."

Theodore Roosevelt

Foreword

Early on in my research, I made the decision to write my books in modern (British) English. If I'd kept it wholly original, nobody would have wanted to read it. So to make it applicable to today's young adult population, I kept the Tudor period words to a minimum.

I used a few to help with the atmosphere of the novel, such as the terms rascal and knave. Even though they don't illicit the same reaction today, the words reach back throughout history to a time when words such as these carried more power and demanded more attention than they do in the modern world.

To keep things authentic, I kept the street names in their original spellings, including the term 'strete' instead of street.

The one thing I didn't change was history itself. Any authentic events I describe are as historically accurate as possible, and when using real characters from history, I didn't have them doing anything they would have found impossible to do.

I described Anne Boleyn's coronation procession

Foreword

through the eyes of a fictional character. Although John Howard's immediate family are fictional, the events they witnessed are not, and I described the event accurately as it happened on the day.

I hope you enjoy the epic adventures of John Howard and the Underlings…

J.C. Jarvis

Coronation

29 May 1533

Thirteen-year-old John Howard's chest juddered faster than an out-of-control carriage on a rocky hillside as the Howard family made their way along the already crowded River Thames towards Billingsgate.

This was a historic morning. John clapped his hands together, unable to control the tingling in his neck as horses clattered along cobbled stretes, their shod hooves echoing across the water.

The air crackled with excited shouts from men, women and children trying to force their way through bustling crowds, all heading in the same direction towards the bend in the river between the Tower and Greenwich, where they would get a good view of Anne Boleyn gliding regally down the mighty river on her big day.

John looked over at his equally giddy eleven-year-old sister, Sarah, who was busy prodding their mother in the ribs and yelling in her ears, trying to make her voice heard over the explosions of sound going on all around her. Wind whipped around the flags flapping freely in the wind, and John watched their mother pull a face that said she couldn't hear a word. He had never seen Sarah so happy in all her life.

She was excited. So was he. Who wasn't? The greatest coronation procession ever held in England was about to set sail down the mighty River Thames, and they were going to be a part of it. It was especially exciting when your father was the one who made it all happen.

Their father, Robert Howard, was one of the most powerful men in England. Not only was he a member of the prestigious Order of the Garter, but he was also the head of the King's Privy Council. As a result, he had the ear of the king, and this gave him extraordinary levels of power and influence at Henry's Royal Court.

Barges of all descriptions crowded the great river as the Howard family made their way towards Billingsgate docks. No wonder Father had us leave so early, John mused as their barge struggled to get around the slower vessels blocking their path.

It took longer than normal, which was why their father had had them leave their London home on the Stronde as soon as it was daylight.

Once they reached Billingsgate, Robert led them to the fleet of magnificently decorated barges lined up ready for the procession. Robert's high status bestowed on him the honour of organising the event, and he made sure the Howard family took pride of place on the first barge at the head of the procession. John looked back, breathless at the majestic view laid out before him.

Barges decked out with flags and bunting stretched as far as the eye could see. Gold foils reflected the early morning sun in a splendid array of colours, overwhelming his senses in every direction he looked.

John waved to his uncle Thomas on the shimmering barge behind them. Thomas Howard, the Duke of Norfolk and John's favourite uncle, waved back. Every aristocrat in the land was present this day, and John was at the head of them all.

"How many are there?" John asked, turning back to his father. The wind from the river roared in his face. It blew his hat far out into the murky waters of the Thames, his long, wavy black hair blowing wildly behind him.

John laughed. He didn't care. This was the best day of his life.

"Fifty barges," his father said, smiling from ear to ear. "A modified wherry is carrying something very special. Wait until you see what that does. You will love it."

"What's a wherry?" John asked.

"It's a kind of boat that carries cargo, or sometimes passengers, up and down the Thames. We have changed this one to look like a…" He paused. "You'll find out soon enough. I don't want to spoil it for you."

John couldn't wait. His heartbeat thundered like the cannons lined up on the banks of the river, ready to explode at any moment. What a day this was!

"Where are all these barges going?" he asked for the tenth time. He already knew the answer, but listening to his father's words made it even more exhilarating.

"The king has arranged four days of celebrations for Anne's coronation," his father explained patiently. "Today is the first when Anne Boleyn is to be escorted along the Thames to the Tower of London, where she will stay at the royal apartments for the next two nights."

"What happens next?"

"Tomorrow will be royal court rituals, which would be utterly boring to a thirteen-year-old boy looking for adventure." Robert playfully prodded John, making him laugh so loud his insides hurt.

"And then what?"

"On the third day, Anne will be escorted by road through the city. This will take all day because they will pack the roads with people from all over England, Scotland, and even Europe."

Robert was referring to the six places in London that coronation processions traditionally passed through. Henry VIII had added three more, making nine finely decorated places in total, ensuring that Anne's grandiose procession exceeded that of his former wife, Katherine of Aragon, during her coronation as England's queen in 1509.

Henry also made sure that he equalled, if not surpassed, the great pageants of Charles V, the Holy Roman Emperor and King of Spain, the most powerful monarch in Europe, in 1522.

Henry VIII declared Anne's to be the greatest coronation of all time.

"Will we see any of this, Father?" John asked.

"No. There will be so many people that I swear the rest of the country will be empty. You won't get close enough, and even if we got near to one of them, you wouldn't be able to get to any of the others."

"What about the last day? Is that when she becomes Queen Anne?"

"Yes. On the fourth day, Anne will enter Westminster Hall as the Marquess of Pembroke and will leave as Queen Anne. We will all be there for that stately occasion."

John turned back towards the water. After what felt like hours, the resplendent procession began. At precisely one o'clock in the afternoon, the great barges pulled against the tide on the River Thames.

With the fierce wind blowing in his face, John had

never felt more alive than he did in this moment. He imagined himself as one of the brilliant navy captains leading his ships off to war.

"Forward ho!" he yelled at the top of his lungs.

Their barge was at the front of the grand procession. Like the other forty-nine, it was huge. "How big are these barges?" John yelled above the roaring wind, not caring that nobody could hear him.

The monumental view of the barges stretching out behind him was a sight John would never forget. Each one was about as big as the tallest tree in the grounds at the rear of their house on the Stronde. He couldn't count how many times he and Sarah had climbed to the top of it so they could view almost all of London from their secret treehouse. He always felt like he was standing on the roof of the world whenever he was up there.

He shook his head, marvelling at the magnificence of Henry VIII.

All the barges had covered tops to protect the occupants from the poor English weather. Today was a sunny day though, and the gold bunting shimmered in the afternoon sun and reflected off the water. John thought it the most wondrous sight he had ever seen.

He couldn't take his eyes off the sights behind him, so he ran to the back of the barge, almost knocking his mother, Jayne Howard, into the river as he barrelled past her.

"Steady, John, or you'll have us all in the river."

"Sorry, Mother," John shouted way too loud.

The mighty river held back the putrid smells that always accompanied any trip to London, and the fresh winds cleared his nostrils of the earlier stench from the crowded city streets.

Music blared out from the mayor's barge as musicians

played trumpets and other instruments. John couldn't make out, and everywhere he looked was awash with colours, streamers, shields, and coats of arms. Bells rang out everywhere, joining in, and then getting lost in the cacophony of joyful noise.

"John." His father pointed to the spectacle playing out in front of the procession. "Hurry, or you'll miss it."

John ran to the front of the boat, narrowly missing his mother once again. She shook her head, laughing as he raced past. His jaw dropped when he saw what his father had referred to earlier. He nudged Sarah, who stood next to him.

"Look," he yelled, pointing at the shapes in front and to the sides of him.

"Wow!" Sarah's mouth dropped open in awe.

Deep, guttural rumblings shook the sole wherry leading the procession, softly at first, before exploding into a hurly-burly wall of sound that felt like a cannonball detonating in John's ears.

A mythical creature writhed and moved in the wherry, flames erupting from its mouth as it tilted towards the water, bowing in deference to the great king.

"Look!" Sarah shouted. "It's a dragon!"

Another great roar almost split John's head open. Flames belched from the jaws of the dragon and lit up the Thames like never before in its long history.

They had turned the wherry into a mechanical dragon! John had never seen such a sight, and from the looks on the faces of his family, they hadn't either.

Nobody had. How mighty was Henry VIII to do such a thing? John couldn't take his eyes off it.

A safe distance behind the roaring, fire-breathing dragon, several other wherries resembling all kinds of "monsters and wild men" as his father described it, threw out hideous noises and cast fires of their own into the water.

John ran to the rear again, for once remembering to watch out for his mother along the way. There were boats everywhere. "How many are there?" he asked. There were far too many to count.

"Fifty barges, around a hundred and twenty other large vessels, and around two hundred smaller ones." His father beamed. "This is my crowning glory, John. I hope you like it."

"Like it? Father, I love it." John squeezed his father's arm.

He looked for Queen Anne. He saw boats carrying the coats of arms of both Henry and Anne, but not the king and queen themselves.

"Where are Queen Anne and the king?" he asked.

"They're setting off later in the afternoon, once all our boats have reached Greenwich."

"Will we be able to see them?" John asked.

"We should. We'll be right behind them."

"I can't wait," John said. He didn't know where to cast his eyes next. Boats and barges stretched out before him in a blaze of deep colours and differing shapes. There and then, he decided he wanted to be a famous sea captain when he grew up.

Rowing against the tide towards the North Sea, it took the barges over two hours to reach Greenwich and reverse order. Once the boats anchored off the palace steps, everyone waited in great anticipation for the appearance of Anne Boleyn.

Finally, in mid-afternoon, Anne began the four-day journey that would end with her being crowned queen of England. Sarah dug her fingers into John's side when she saw the marquess's majestic entrance.

"Look!" she shouted above the winds. "Do you see that?"

John nodded, his eyes wide. Anne's barge was the picture of everything he imagined whenever he thought of kings and queens. It was extraordinary.

His father described it as "sumptuously decorated". John thought the description didn't do it justice. They'd decorated her barge with gold and the finest silks from around the world. Another wherry off to the side carried her family emblem, which was a crowned falcon sitting on a bed of red and white roses.

Anne Boleyn made her way to the waterfront and climbed onto the barge along with her principal ladies-in-waiting, the picture of elegance and royalty.

"Where is the king?" John asked, straining his neck to search for him. "Isn't he travelling on the barge with the queen?"

"No," his father shouted so both John and Sarah could hear. "Do you see the two empty barges behind Anne's?"

John and Sarah nodded.

"This is Anne's big day, so she's travelling in the first barge. The rest of her ladies are going in the second one, and the king will travel behind them in the third, along with his personal guards and court musicians."

"Surely this is something nobody will ever forget," John shouted to his father, who waved back to him in agreement.

The flotilla followed behind the royal barges. This time they rowed with the tide, so they made substantial progress. All along the route, cannons roared continuously, nearly deafening everyone on board when the boats passed by. John thought his ears would never recover.

Eventually, the barges reached the Tower of London. To the great roar of the cannons, Anne disembarked to carry on the festivities and rituals within the walls of the Tower. Robert was to remain, but Jayne and the children were to return to the Stronde until Sunday the first of June when they would be present at Westminster Hall to witness the coronation itself.

John watched as his parents said their goodbyes, then he climbed aboard the family barge nearby. The grand procession grew smaller and smaller as he and Sarah and their mother headed inland, with the tide in their favour, towards their home on the Stronde.

"What a day." John settled down next to his sister.

Jayne Howard

East of Temple Bar and the River Fleet, the Stronde was an area reserved for the aristocracy. Meandering alongside the Thames, several large houses lined the quiet, tree-lined strete. Extensive gardens backed up to the river, allowing their privileged owners access to the barges moored to their private docks.

Robert Howard owned the largest of them all.

Still excited from the day on the river, John tore towards their home the moment the boat docked. Sarah was right behind him, racing through the enormous gardens that produced the household's seasonal fruits and vegetables. Tall trees separated each section of the gardens, reaching for the stars.

One tree was noticeably bigger than the rest, and John and Sarah slowed their pace as they approached it, exchanging guarded but excited glances. The majestic tree held a secret. A year earlier, one of their groundsmen had built a large, covered treehouse for them way up in the sturdy branches. Hidden from the house, they played there for hour after hour whenever they were in residence.

The groundsman had died shortly after completing the treehouse, so John and Sarah were the only ones who knew their secret hideout existed. They'd vowed to each other to keep it that way.

They walked under the enormous tree without looking up so as not to give it away, but they couldn't wait to climb it again.

Evans, the trusty steward, led them past the stables where the grooms were busy preparing the horses and carriages for Anne's coronation a few days hence.

They entered the rear of the house, where their father was having the east side of the ground floor re-worked and rebuilt. He needed a new, larger study for his work in London, and the entire east side of the bottom floor was to be his private domain. He allowed nobody to enter that part of the house.

The children ran up the rear stairway to the second of the three floors. Long, narrow corridors branched off to the left and right. John turned right to the family rooms. The first two doors belonged to their father and mother. Sarah's door was opposite her mother's, and John's was next to Sarah's.

His room was a lot cleaner than he'd left it earlier, but he was too preoccupied to notice as he flung open the divider door that led to Sarah's room.

"I can't wait to go to the treehouse, although we may not get to it this time around."

Sarah wrinkled her nose. "I know, but we have the coronation instead. That makes up for it. Maybe we can sneak down there early one morning before anyone wakes up."

"Perhaps," her brother said, drawn to both the thrilling spectacle of the coronation and the comforting retreat of the treehouse. "But if we can't," he added, reassuring himself as much as his younger sister, "we'll have the rest of the summer to play there."

A terrible wailing sound disturbed John's dreams of warships and roaring cannons. Half awake, he thought it was a cannon blasting away beside him. Voices were calling his name in the distance.

Sarah shook him, sending his dreams to the recesses of his mind. Another gurgling sound followed by a frightful howl ripped right through him.

"John," Sarah was yelling at him. "Wake up! That noise is coming from Mother's room. What is it?"

Squinting in the dim morning light, John lurched out of bed and gathered his senses. Another cry of someone in obvious pain came from beyond his bedroom door.

"It does sound like Mother," he said, hurrying toward the door with Sarah close behind. "Where is Father? Is he here?"

"I don't think he is allowed to leave the king until after the coronation."

John burst open his mother's door and was met with a sight that would haunt him for the rest of his life.

Jayne Howard was on her knees, holding her stomach, rocking back and forth, gurgling and howling while vomiting all over the floor.

John ran to her. "Mother, what ails you?"

His mother grabbed for John's arm, sending him reeling backwards in shock at her cold and clammy grip on his skin.

"Get Evans, and fetch a doctor," his mother gasped, before lurching forward again.

John held her until her retching had finished and then

helped her onto the bed. "Stay with her," he ordered Sarah. "I'll find Evans."

He hurried out of the door, shouting "Evans" as loud as he could while bounding down the stairs three at a time. "Evans, where are you?" He nearly collided with the steward at the bottom of the stairs.

"I'm right here, Master John. Please be careful or I fear you will break your neck jumping down the stairs like that. What can I do for you, sir?"

"Mother is sick," John panted. "She is vomiting, and her hands are cold. Get a doctor immediately and send someone to clean up her room."

Evans nodded and hurried away. John knew he would carry out his duties swiftly. Besides his father, Evans was the most dependable man he knew.

John ran back upstairs. His mother was on the floor, writhing in agony.

"What is wrong with her?" he whispered. He and Sarah exchanged frightened glances.

"I don't know." Tears streamed down Sarah's face. "She was fine earlier." She ran to John, weeping.

Servants rushed in and helped Lady Jayne back onto her bed before cleaning up the floor. Jayne lay there, her face as pale as the winter moon. Her hand felt like ice in John's own warm hands.

"Evans is getting a doctor, and a rider has left to inform Father. Everything will be good, Mother. Perhaps you somehow got a mouthful of that dreadful water from the river in your stomach yesterday. That's enough to make anyone ill."

A watery smile creased the lines of Jayne's pale face. She stroked John's wrists as if to reassure him she was going to be fine.

The doctor arrived shortly and cleared the room while

he examined her. John and Sarah hovered, their ears close to the door, straining to listen to what he was saying.

After what seemed an eternity, the doctor emerged with a grim look on his face. He almost fell over John and Sarah, who were crowding the doorway.

"Lord Howard needs to be informed that Lady Howard is suffering from the bloody flux and is gravely ill," he said. "I have bled her and given herbs to calm her stomach, but the symptoms are ravaging her body. I am sorry, but I have done all I can for your mother. Her fate is in God's hands now."

Tears fell down Sarah's face, and John closed his eyes as they filled with moisture before they too, released rivulets of tears down his cheeks in sorrow and fear.

"But she was perfectly fine yesterday," was all he could say. He was almost speechless.

I'm sorry," the doctor said. "The flux attacks us swiftly."

Evans looked as pale as John felt.

"No." John roared. "Mother is fine. She is suffering from that terrible river water she somehow swallowed yesterday. She will be fine again tomorrow, just you wait and see."

Sarah gripped John's arm so tight it caused his fingers to tingle. "No," was all she could say before burying her head in his shoulder, sobbing for all she was worth.

"Master John." Evans touched John lightly on the head. "Is there anything we can do for you and Lady Sarah?"

"Please hurry and fetch my father," John tried to control his heaving chest. "He'll know what to do."

Evans hurried off, but not before stopping to speak with the servants lined dutifully along the narrow corridor.

John pushed Sarah back so he could look into her eyes.

"I'm not leaving Mother. Not until I know she's recovered."

Sarah's eyes, reddened and swollen from her grief, tore into John's soul. "I'm not leaving her either," she sobbed.

John and Sarah took turns reading their mother's favourite books to her all night long. While one slept in a nearby chair, the other read and mopped Jayne's brow, holding and supporting her as she retched and heaved in convulsive agony in the dim light of the candles.

After carrying out his household duties, Evans returned to stay with them, doing his best to comfort both mother and children. Servants came and went all night, cleaning up after Lady Jayne as best they could.

It was the longest night of John's life.

As daylight broke, Jayne Howard lurched over the side of her bed, coughing up blood and moaning softly. John went to grab her so she wouldn't fall to the floor, but Evans was already there. The doctor, who had arrived back at the house a short time earlier, beckoned John outside the room.

"It might be best if you and Lady Sarah stayed away from now on. Your mother is very ill, and it must be upsetting for you both."

"We will do no such thing," John retorted. "Father will be here soon, and Mother will be just fine. We're staying with her until she recovers."

The doctor sighed. "I wish you wouldn't, but I understand. We are all praying for her soul."

John returned to his mother's side.

On the morning of the third day, Evans called John and Sarah to the hallway. "Your father has sent word. The king will allow him to return following the queen's coronation today. In the meantime, he ordered you both to stay away and allow the doctors and servants to take care of your mother."

"We are not leaving Mother," Sarah spoke before John could even open his mouth. "She needs us now more than ever."

"We're not leaving her, Evans," John said. "We don't care what Father says."

"I understand, sir," Evans said. "At least allow your mother some privacy while we give her a change of clothing. The one's she has on are heavily soiled and need to be changed."

John nodded, taking Sarah's hand. "Let's get some food and go for a walk around the grounds to clear our lungs."

Sarah reluctantly agreed. "We'll be back, Evans. Please tell the servants to take good care of her."

Evans bowed his head in acknowledgement.

After a good meal and a much-needed change of clothing, they hurried back to the door of their mother's bedchamber. The doctor stood outside her door, his face pale and lined with pain. He looked at John and Sarah and just shook his head before heading down the stairs, unable to speak.

Sarah was shaking and crying, although she tried to hold back her sobs by putting her hand over her mouth. John hesitated for a moment in stunned silence before leading the way into his mother's room.

At his mother's bedside, he heard footsteps running up the stairs, and his father's voice getting louder as he shouted at the doctor. When Robert Howard entered his wife's bedchamber, John was holding his mother's lifeless hands in his own.

His father had arrived too late. Lady Jayne Howard was dead.

Margaret Colte

June 1535

Steam rose from his horse's nostrils in the chill morning air as fifteen-year-old John Howard galloped home at full speed through the Forest of Arden.

Wind, leaves, and branches whistled past his head in a blur. The heavy thudding of the horse's hooves on the soft forest floor vibrated through his body. He waved as he galloped past his father, then kicked his horse on as they raced past St Michael's Church and thundered down the narrow lane towards Broxley Hall in the distance, his long hair flying in the wind.

"Aye!" John shouted at the top of his lungs. After the grief and sorrow of recent years, this was the best day John could remember having.

The magnificent house loomed larger and larger as he got closer. Surrounded by a double moat, it always reminded John of an old mediaeval castle where knights would roam the land and protect it from fierce invaders. John loved it.

Broxley Hall was no castle, but it was an imposing estate. It had been in the family since 1485 when his grandfather had fought alongside Henry VII at the Battle of Bosworth. The estate in Warwickshire, in the English Midlands, had been his grandfather's reward once Henry took the crown.

John pulled back on the reins as he got near the narrow drawbridge that allowed access across the moat. He struggled to hold back the eager horse that seemed to have enjoyed itself this chilly morning.

"Halt, boy," he yelled as he pulled hard on the reins, barely stopping before reaching the drawbridge.

He dismounted, patting the horse's neck. Evans, the steward, and Harris, the master of the stables, stood to the side of the drawbridge waiting for them. Four stable boys were waiting farther back to take the horses to the stables.

"Congratulations, Master John," Evans said, "Very well done, sir."

John's eyes shone. He loved Evans, who had been a beacon of strength and compassion when his mother passed away two years earlier, and John had felt gratitude and respect for him ever since.

"What do you think of that, Evans?" John burst with pride as the deer he'd hunted was lowered to the ground in front of them.

Evans counted the number of points on the deer's antlers and whistled. "A hart of ten, no less." Evans nodded. "Not bad. Not bad at all, sir."

As John followed Evans and Harris over the drawbridge, his father caught up to him. "Well done, son." He clapped John on the back. "I'm proud of you. You are learning well." He walked off before John could reply.

The smell of freshly baked bread from the bakehouse

made John's stomach rumble. He hurried to the great hall to get some well-deserved breakfast.

Sarah was already there, waiting for him. "Hurry, John, I'm starving," she said.

John smiled down at her and ruffled her dark, shoulder-length hair. "I hunted a deer all by myself this morning," he said. "You should call me Sir John from now on."

Sarah slapped him playfully. "I heard. Mother would have been proud of you. I am too."

John hugged her. They both missed their mother dearly and spoke of her often.

Servants brought them fresh fruit and wholemeal bread fresh from the bakehouse. Sarah was about to say something when their father burst through the doors.

"I'm very proud of you today, John. You are growing into a smart young man. This will all be yours one day, and I can't think of a finer son to pass it down to."

"Thank you, Father." John puffed his chest out. "I do have the best teacher."

Robert Howard smiled. "But today isn't just about your hunting skills. I have received word that Lady Margaret Colte will arrive late this afternoon. As you know, she accepted my proposal of marriage. She and her son, Mark, are coming here to meet you today and to get used to Broxley. They will stay here from now on."

John's smile turned into a scowl. He gripped the side of the table. Sarah looked down with large tears in her eyes.

"Father, we don't want another mother." John clenched his jaw. "We miss Mother, but we are perfectly fine as we are."

"This isn't about you. Either of you. I need a wife and she is a fine woman. You will be ready to greet her when she arrives, and you will look delighted. You will treat her with respect and congratulate her on the wedding. Is that clear?"

"We have German lessons with our tutor, and then I have sword lessons with Philippe," John complained. "Can I not greet her later?"

"They are cancelled for today. She comes this day, and you will be there to greet her. We will feast on the deer you killed. It's a proud moment for all of us."

John stared at his father. Although he was of an average build and height, Robert Howard cut a very imposing figure. Perhaps it was his bright, piercing eyes or his sharp mind that stood out. John didn't know, but he knew not to cross him. He had learned that at an early age.

"Very well then," their father said. "Be in the courtyard to greet them when they arrive."

He turned and left the great hall.

John and Sarah strolled around the large spring-fed pond that fed the moat around the house. Their father stocked it with fish that served both the manor house and the local villages.

The many acres of hunting grounds were teeming with wild game for hunting, and alongside the sizeable gardens where they grew fresh fruit and vegetables, Broxley Hall was self-sufficient and thriving.

"What are we going to do?" Sarah asked.

"There's nothing we can do," John said. "We have to make sure we are kind, and welcome them into our family. We can't give her any reason not to like us."

"I don't want another mother," Sarah protested.

"I don't either, and she won't be. Father needs a new wife for their functions with the king. We won't see much of her, anyway. Our tutors won't change, and Father will still take care of us. Nothing will change for us."

Sarah smiled and shook her head.

Bells rang out, and shouts were heard. Margaret was here! John thought there would be less fuss if the king himself was standing at the front door.

He wore his finest clothing, reserved for aristocratic functions such as this. Fine-quality woollen breeches sat over a white silk shirt that flowed down below his knees. His royal blue velvet jerkin was embroidered with gold thread, and over that he wore a long cape. Large feathers adorned his oversized velvet hat. He looked every part the heir to a wealthy earl. He ran down the stairs and out into the courtyard.

"You look magnificent," he said to his sister, ignoring the stern look his father gave him for being late.

"Thank you, kind sir." Sarah smiled and curtseyed. She wore a dark blue gown topped with a French hood trimmed with glass beads.

"Here she comes." John pointed towards the drawbridge. Four horses pulled a carriage that John recognised instantly. It belonged to his father, and he had ridden in it many times. Two long seats faced each other, and the sides were open to the elements. The red roof protected the occupants from both rain and sun.

By the time he had finished admiring the carriage, it had pulled to a stop in front of them. The servants bowed and placed wooden steps for the occupants.

John saw Margaret for the first time. Her beauty was obvious, and he could understand why his father was so attracted to her. She was the prettiest lady John had ever seen.

Her hat covered most of her head, but John could see her blonde hair tucked underneath it. Her high cheekbones and green eyes made for a stunning sight.

John's heart beat hard in his chest. He glanced at his

father, who was smiling from ear to ear. He hadn't seen him this happy since the queen's coronation.

Even Sarah was silent for once. John watched as she stared at Margaret, weighing her up like a cat staring down a mouse. He elbowed her in the ribs.

"Stop staring like that. You'll put her off before she even gets here."

Sarah giggled and ran to her father's side.

Behind Margaret, a young boy about Sarah's age waited to get off the carriage. This must be Mark, Margaret's son from her first marriage. From what their father had told them, her husband had died prematurely, leaving her a widow at a very young age.

Mark was thirteen, the same age as Sarah. He was tall, skinny, and had long hair hanging down to his shoulders. His nose was long and thin, and John smiled to himself as he thought it way too big for his face.

Once they exited the carriage, the servants got to work unloading their heavy packing trunks. Robert Howard kissed the outstretched hand of Margaret Colte before turning to face his family.

"Lady Margaret, may I introduce to you my children, John and Sarah Howard."

Sarah curtseyed while John bowed. Margaret smiled at them. "Good day to you both. I've heard so much about you two. Your father never stops talking about you."

Mark stepped out from behind his mother. "This is my son, Mark. You and he are the same age, Lady Sarah. I hope you all get along together because you will soon be brothers and sisters."

John shook hands with Mark. His father had told them he had been a sickly child, but he looked healthy enough to John.

After introducing them to the staff, his father took them

on a tour of the manor house, leaving John and Sarah to their own devices.

"I hope she's kind and gentle like Mother was," Sarah said.

"I don't want anyone replacing Mother," John replied.

"Father said we have to love them like a mother and brother."

John shrugged his shoulders. "Life's still the same for us. I'll treat her the same as she treats me."

Later that evening, after the banquet, Robert and Margaret wandered around the grounds of the estate, leaving John and Sarah to get to know Mark.

"So, what do you think of our home?" John asked. "Do you like it? If Father allows, I will take you around the grounds tomorrow in daylight."

"I love it," Mark replied. "It's a lot bigger than our home. It's even bigger than Saddleworth House, where we lived before father died."

"You will love it even more tomorrow after you have seen it all," John said. "Tell us about Saddleworth and your life there. What happened to your father?"

Mark cleared his throat and stepped away from John and Sarah. "Father and I both caught the sweating sickness. He died, and I didn't. That's all there is to say."

"Why did you leave?" Sarah asked. "Where is Saddleworth, anyway?"

Mark licked his lips before answering. "It's in Sussex. I was only four years old when it happened, so I don't remember hardly anything about it. Mother doesn't like me talking about it, so I don't."

"Why did you leave?" Sarah asked again.

"I told you, Mother doesn't like me talking about it."

"Why can't you talk about it?"

"Because I…"

Mark spun around and ran back to the house, leaving John and Sarah staring after him in disbelief.

"What was that all about?" John wondered.

"I don't know," Sarah said. "But I don't think I like him very much."

Problems

When Robert Howard left for London to attend the king, Margaret took over the wedding arrangements at Broxley Hall. Outside the grandeur of Henry VIII, this was to be the grandest wedding of the year. Margaret was running the staff ragged.

John grabbed his longbow and walked outside to practise. Sarah hurried after him, as eager to get away as John was. As they emerged into a small clearing that was John's favourite place to practise, he sensed a slight movement behind the row of trees.

"Who goes there?" John shouted, pulling his longbow into the ready position. The Howard family had no enemies that he was aware of, but there was always the possibility of a rogue from one of the villages wandering around hoping to steal something.

"It is I, Mark. Put the longbow down." Mark emerged from the trees with his hands in the air.

"Put your hands down and don't be silly," John said. "You know I'm not about to hurt you."

Mark dropped his hands and glared at John and Sarah laughing at him. "It's not funny. Mother said you might not like me and might want to hurt me."

John stopped laughing and walked towards Mark, who pulled back towards the tree line. He noticed that Mark's eyes were splotchy and swollen, as though he'd been crying.

"What ails you this day?" John asked, lowering his longbow and moving it behind him so as not to frighten the poor boy any further.

"Nothing. I am fine."

"You don't look it," Sarah chimed in. "You look as if you've been crying. I don't think John is that scary, even with his longbow aimed at you."

Mark pulled his face. "I wasn't scared," he said.

"So what's wrong then?" John asked.

"I'm fine," Mark said again. "It's just, well, Mother was angered at me this morning. It's nothing."

"Why?" John asked. "What did you do to anger her?"

"Not much. She gets angry at me all the time. I don't want to talk about it."

John shrugged. "Have you ever used the longbow before?" he asked.

"A little. Mother always told me I was too sick to be outside, so I was never any good with it."

"From what Father told us, you were lucky to survive," Sarah said.

"Did the doctors attend to you?" John asked.

"Mother took care of me and gave me medicine. She said it was good for my health."

"What medicine did she give you?" John asked.

Right then Margaret appeared from out of the trees. "What were you thinking, aiming that longbow at my son?" she demanded. "You could have killed him."

Mark's face turned sullen again. "He didn't do it on purpose, Mother. He didn't know I was there."

"Be quiet," Margaret snapped. "I saw what happened. You are lucky I was here, or you could have been seriously injured."

"Lady Margaret, I did no such thing," John defended himself. "I saw a movement behind the trees and didn't know what it was. I would never hurt another person, let alone a member of my own family."

"Get back to the house and don't go near this boy again without my permission," Margaret snapped. "And you,"—she pointed at John—"You do not go anywhere near Mark again with that longbow in your hands. Do I make myself clear?"

"Perfectly." John scowled, "But you are misunderstanding what happened, Lady Margaret. Mark was sneaking around behind the trees and I didn't know who it was."

"My son does not sneak around anywhere. You are banned from teaching him anything. It does not interest him to learn from you."

"We were doing what Father told us to do. He told us to be friendly to Mark," John said.

"Your father isn't here, is he? I am in charge. Mark wants nothing to do with you."

"He won't if you don't give him a chance to get to know us," John fired back, flames dancing in his eyes.

"You will do well to remember who is in charge here, John Howard. This isn't the start to our relationship I was expecting. Your father told me you were gentle and kind, but all I see is a defiant boy who wants to challenge me."

"I'm not defying anything," John said, exasperated. "I didn't do anything."

"Keep away from my son. You cannot be trusted."

Margaret grabbed Mark by the arm and dragged him, protesting, towards the house. John stared after them before turning to Sarah.

"What a vile woman," he said. "She isn't anything like Mother. I don't like her at all."

Margaret stopped dead in her tracks and spun around. "I heard that. You are an insolent boy, John Howard. Your father will hear of this when he returns."

"Be sure of it," John fired back. "I shall tell him myself that you are rude and nothing like our mother."

Margaret's face turned red. "How dare you speak to me in this tone? I won't forget this conversation."

She marched off, pushing a protesting Mark in front of her. When she was out of earshot, John turned to his sister.

"What was that all about?" he asked. "I didn't do anything to her. I didn't mean to scare Mark, but he shouldn't sneak around like that."

"I don't like her," Sarah said. "We need to tell Father when he gets home."

John shrugged in agreement. "I hope it isn't going to be like this from now on. I couldn't bear the thought of it."

For the remainder of the time their father was absent, John avoided Margaret as much as he could. Mark was jolly and happy during their regular lessons with the tutors, and he excelled at languages, especially German, where he helped John understand the language much better than he had before.

He also excelled at mathematics and other matters of academia, and both John and Sarah learned to enjoy his company.

"You are an excellent scholar, and I am learning a lot from you," John told him. "I would like to repay you by teaching you the weapons of the sword and longbow, which is where I excel."

"I'm not much good at those," Mark conceded, "but Mother would be angered if I took lessons from you. I fear she doesn't like you much, although I tell her I find you to be the best friend I have ever had."

John's mouth dropped open. "Well, thank you, Mark. I like you as well."

"So do I," Sarah interrupted, "but I wish your mother would act kinder towards us, especially John. She has barely spoken to him since the longbow thing."

"She finds it hard to trust people," Mark explained. "She means nothing by it."

"I hope not," John said, "because she isn't very nice to us right now."

"It'll get better," Mark said. "At least I hope it will."

"Do you want to learn some sword fighting?" John asked.

Mark grinned and nodded. "I love swords. They're my favourite weapons."

John led the way out of the grand house towards the extensive grounds. As they ran down the steps, the door opened and Margaret appeared from nowhere.

"Where do you think you're going?" she asked, looking directly at Mark.

"I, erm, we, erm…"

"We were about to do some sword play together," John said. He saw no reason to lie to her. After all, they weren't doing anything wrong.

Margaret gave Mark a withering glare, which made him lower his head to the ground. John watched as he walked behind his mother, his face pale and sullen once again.

"What did I tell you about teaching my son those dangerous weapons?" Margaret stared at John.

"I wasn't teaching him anything," John replied. "We were just going to play with them."

"Playing, teaching, it's all the same thing," Margaret said. "Mark can get hurt. The last time I caught you with weapons, you were aiming a longbow at him. The Lord himself knows what you would do to him with a sword. How many times do I have to tell you to stay away from him with any of your weapons?"

John lowered his head. "I'm sorry, Lady Margaret, I thought we were allowed to have fun together."

"I will not tolerate your insolence," Margaret said. "I haven't forgotten the last time you spoke to me in this manner."

"Lady Margaret," Sarah started, but was waved off by Margaret's hand. "When I want your input, I will ask for it. Until then, remain silent and speak when you are spoken to."

"I will not have you speaking to my sister in this manner." John's nostrils flared. "Once again, we are doing nothing wrong."

"I am tired of you," Margaret said. "It is enough I have to tolerate you for the rest of my life, but I shall not tolerate your sharp tongues as well."

"You are not our mother, and when it comes to tolerance, you are the one that is rude and intolerable," John said sharply.

Mark took a loud intake of breath and ran inside. Sarah looked at John with surprise on her face. He had never spoken like this before in front of her. John stood his ground and looked Margaret in the eyes, watching her face turn redder and redder. He knew he had overstepped the line.

"Go to your room immediately and don't come out until you can display better manners."

John thought better of saying anything else, so with one last glance at his sister, he walked past Margaret with his head held high and went to his room.

Wedding

The atmosphere at dinner on the eve of the wedding was sombre. Robert, who had returned to Warwickshire two days prior, put it down to wedding nerves, but John knew better. The tension between himself and Margaret was evident by the glares she engaged him with. He kept his head down, waiting for the inevitable lecture from his father later.

Without warning, Evans ran up to Robert and whispered in his ear. Robert smiled. As soon as Evans stepped back, he rose from his chair to address the small gathering.

"I have just received delightful news. The king has graciously allowed some very important family members a leave of absence to attend our wedding. They have arrived and are waiting to join us at dinner."

The door to the great hall opened, revealing two men John recognised instantly.

Robert greeted them with warm handshakes and pointed out two empty places at the large table.

"Uncle Thomas!" John shouted. "I am so glad you could—"

"Please allow me to introduce two very important members of the Royal Court." Robert Howard gave John a stern look before turning towards Margaret. "My cousin, Thomas Howard, Duke of Norfolk, and to his right, Viscount Rochford, otherwise known as George Boleyn, brother to our new queen. Gentlemen, it is a pleasure to welcome you into my humble home as guests of honour for our wedding tomorrow."

"It delights us to be here," Thomas Howard said. "Lady Margaret, it is a pleasure to see you again." He took her offered hand and kissed it. "You look stunning as always."

Margaret smiled and feigned modesty. John had worked her out by now. He knew her every move.

"The pleasure is all mine, Sir Thomas."

"Lady Margaret," George Boleyn said. "Likewise, it is a great honour to attend your wedding tomorrow."

Margaret once again offered her hand as they exchanged pleasantries.

"I am shocked," Robert said. "We weren't expecting the king to allow anyone to leave London right now."

"The king and queen send their warmest regards to you and Lady Margaret," George Boleyn said. "He also instructed us to take you back to London the day after the wedding as there are many important matters to discuss."

"How generous," Margaret blurted out.

George Boleyn raised his eyebrow. "Would Lady Margaret like me to convey her feelings to the king?" he asked.

"Lady Margaret meant no harm," Robert said, breaking the awkward silence.

Margaret smiled and bowed her head. "I meant no disrespect, sir."

"Good," George said. "Let us eat then."

As much as John didn't want his father to leave, he couldn't help but smile to himself. He had enjoyed watching Margaret being put in her place by George Boleyn.

"Lady Margaret," Thomas Howard spoke after dinner. "I am surprised to not find any of your family members here for your big day."

Another awkward silence.

"I don't have any family left. My parents died when I was young, and I have no siblings. My former husband, Thomas Colte, died when Mark was just four years old. The Lord has blessed us to find such a kind and generous man as Earl Howard and his adorable family."

John almost threw up. He bit his tongue as he kicked Sarah's leg under the table. Adorable family? She hated him and made no secret of it.

"The blessings are all ours," Robert said. "I never knew such a beautiful lady existed."

"The stories of your beauty are not exaggerated," George said. "The whispers in the Royal Court are not untrue. Robert has done very well for himself."

George Boleyn and Robert Howard exchanged an uneasy stare. John could feel the tension between them. Even at his young age, John knew of the jealousies and rivalries at the Royal Court for the king's attention. As a member of the Order of the Garter and having such close ties to Henry, many other high-profile lords didn't like Robert. George Boleyn, it seemed, was one of them.

"I bumped into Sir Henry Colte a few weeks ago." Thomas Howard's eyes never left Margaret's. "Wasn't he your former husband's brother? He was surprised when I told him you were marrying the Earl of Coventry. He sends his regards."

Margaret's face turned a shade of green John had only ever seen when someone was about to throw up.

"Sir Henry?" Margaret said, her voice shaking. "I haven't heard from Henry in a long time. I hope all is well with him."

Thomas Howard remained silent, but he never stopped looking at Margaret, whose face had now turned ashen. She looked anywhere but at him.

After a long pause, Robert broke the silence.

"Come, let us enjoy the evening," Robert said, rising from his chair. "We have the finest wines in England in my study. We have much to discuss, and we have a very important day ahead of us tomorrow."

Margaret stood in the way when John, Sarah, and Mark tried going to their bed chambers. "Mark, I need you with me. You two go to your rooms."

She grabbed Mark and strode off, giving no further explanation.

"Did you see her face when Uncle Thomas mentioned Henry Colte?" John asked. "What was that all about? And why did Margaret drag Mark off so he couldn't talk about it?"

"I don't know who he is, but it's funny that Margaret has never mentioned him. And the look she gave Uncle Thomas was frightful," Sarah said.

The next morning passed in a blur. Everyone was busy getting dressed in their finest regalia, and the house was a hive of activity. The great hall, decorated with banners and buntings of blue, gold and red, made John wonder if it looked as good as Westminster Hall during Anne Boleyn's coronation.

The explosion of colours made everyone stand back in amazement. The only colour absent was purple because that was reserved for royalty.

At twelve thirty their carriage took them the short distance to St Michael's Church, which the owner of Broxley maintained as a part of his estate. Like the great hall, they had decorated the small church in a vast array of colours that demonstrated the earl's wealth and power.

Everyone in the earl's employ outside of those working the wedding had the day off to celebrate. They packed the narrow lane from Broxley as they cheered the Howard family towards the church. The women were all eager to see Lady Margaret in her wedding attire, which they were sure would be the finest clothes they had ever seen.

John and Mark waited in the church, along with the small number of other dignified guests. Sarah was a bridesmaid, so she had spent the entire day with Margaret. George Boleyn and Thomas Howard were the guests of honour right at the front. Their fine silk and wool clothing showed their positions. John had never seen such a well-dressed group of people outside of the rare royal functions he'd attended.

Mark took his seat. He had been quiet all day. John almost felt sorry for him having such a cruel mother.

At exactly two o'clock, his father entered the church. He was smiling, and John could see the happiness in his eyes. He walked down the aisle, accepting the greetings from those present as he walked past.

Musicians played behind the altar, and the priest stood there, ready to perform the marriage ceremony. All they lacked now was the bride and her entourage.

As was tradition, the bride entered the church late. They had set the wedding for two, and the doors opened shortly after. Everyone craned their necks to get a glimpse of quite possibly the most beautiful woman in England. Even John admired her, and he hated her.

Margaret sauntered down the aisle, her long floor-length blue gown brushing the floor with an elegance John had rarely seen. Even Anne Boleyn wasn't this elegant, and she was the queen.

The gold embroidery on her dress shimmered in the candlelit interior of the church, and the deep colours of the jewellery reflected off her perfect, unblemished skin. Pearls adorned her French hood, and her long earrings sparkled. Her beauty transfixed everyone.

John caught sight of Sarah walking behind Margaret, helping to keep the long train of her dress straight as she walked towards the altar. John thought Sarah looked as pretty as he had ever seen her, and he made a mental note to tell her when he saw her later.

The priest began the ceremony once Margaret reached the front of the church. Robert and Margaret stood in front of the altar and made their vows. Much of it was in Latin, which was okay for John, as he knew it from his tutoring lessons. He enjoyed hearing it spoken and followed along with it.

When it was over, Margaret and Robert led everyone out of the church. Tremendous cheers of congratulations filled the air from the estate workers as they celebrated their Lord on his big day.

The exquisitely decorated carriages took the family and their guests back the short distance to Broxley, where they continued the celebrations in the great hall.

"You look magnificent today, easily the prettiest lady anywhere in the whole of England." Sarah beamed as John told her.

"Stop it, silly," she said. "Margaret is the prettiest lady in England. I'm just the prettiest girl." She smiled as she spoke.

"You are the prettiest girl in England." Mark joined the conversation. It was the first time he'd spoken all day.

Sarah looked surprised. "Well, thank you, Mark," she said.

The adults got drunker and louder as the celebrations carried on. "So how do you two feel about having Margaret Colte as your new mother?" Thomas Howard addressed John and Sarah.

Silence fell all around, and John could feel the awkwardness in the room. For some reason, neither his uncle Thomas nor George Boleyn seemed to like Margaret, and John would love to have known why.

"I love it," John said sarcastically. "It's the best thing that ever happened to us."

Margaret's stare burned through John like a flaming arrow. His father tilted his head for a moment before turning around and steering the conversation towards a happier subject.

Shortly after, Robert and Margaret left to enjoy their wedding night, but not before Margaret gave John one last deathly stare.

John left shortly after. He wanted to read in solitude. He wasn't looking forward to his father leaving, because Margaret was always much nicer when he was home.

Eventually, everyone went to their rooms, and Broxley Hall fell quiet. A new era was dawning, and John knew it would be difficult from now on.

Two days after Robert went back to London, Margaret summoned John to her study.

"Robert and I are very disappointed in you, John. You continually bait me and refuse to accept me into the family. Whether or not you like it, I am here to stay, and your father gave me permission to punish you as I see fit."

"I doubt that." John rose to his full height. "Father was too busy with the wedding to consider punishing me for your entertainment."

Margaret's face turned bright red. "We decided you need to learn some humility."

"Why didn't Father tell me any of this himself when he was here?" John demanded. "Or is this something you decided for yourself? He had plenty of time to talk to me had he so desired."

Margaret snorted. "Your father is far too busy to bother with insolent boys like you. He left it to me to deal with you."

"Haven't I been punished enough?" John asked. "You force me to stay in my room for days on end for nothing more than spending time with Mark. Even worse, you seem to enjoy it."

"I don't like you, John Howard. I never have. Having to tolerate you is the price I have to pay for marrying your father."

"And I don't like you either," John retorted. "It's punishment enough having you as a stepmother."

"Enough of your insolence." Margaret slammed her hand on her desk. John stood his ground, looking Margaret straight in her eyes.

"I can't win with you, can I?" John asked. "No matter what I do, it is wrong. I bet Father doesn't even know you are punishing me again."

"You never learn, do you?" Margaret said. "I have arranged for you to work with the stable boys for a while. Perhaps they will teach you some manners."

"Lady Margaret," John started, but a wave of her hand quieted him.

"I am in charge here, John Howard, and you will do well to remember that. Tomorrow morning you are to report to Harris in the stables. Maybe working with the horses will teach you some manners."

"Lady Margaret, I will do no such—"

"Yes, you will." Margaret leant forward in her chair. "You will do as I say, or I will send Sarah in your place. Is that what you want me to do?"

John stared at her in disbelief. "You will threaten me with my own sister? What kind of woman are you?"

"One that will make you do as you are told. Now get out of here and report to Harris at first light tomorrow morning."

"One day, when I'm the earl, you will regret this, Lady Margaret."

"Are you threatening me? What will you do when you are the earl?"

"You will be barred from all the estates and disinherited from anything my father wills to you. I shall see that you die penniless and broken."

Margaret's icy stare burned straight through John as he slowly backed out of the room, his eyes never leaving hers.

"You will live to regret those words, John Howard."

Stables

The normally forthright Harris couldn't look John in the eye when they met the next morning. "Lady Margaret told me it was for your own good, Master John," he said. "I'm sorry, but I'm merely carrying out my orders."

"It's not your fault, Harris," John reassured him, "but remember, I am the son of the earl and I shall not be demeaned in this manner."

Harris bowed his head. "I am sorry, Master John, but Lady Margaret instructed me to take you to the stables, and that is what I shall do. Once there, you are free to do whatever you desire. All I ask is that you do not take it out on the stable boys. They are as innocent as I, Master John."

Six stable boys lined up and bowed as John entered the stables. "Good morning, Master John," the lead stable boy said as he walked in. "We don't know why you're here, but we are here to serve you, sir."

"I'm fine," John said gruffly. "Carry on with your duties and pretend I am not here. That is all I ask of you."

"As you wish, sir," the lead hand said. "Let's get to work, boys."

John sat in the rear corner of the stables and watched the young men groom the horses. When the lead hand took one of them out for exercise, he followed him and watched with interest as he put the horse through its paces.

On the way back to the stables, John stopped dead in his tracks when he heard a low shout.

"Hey, John, over here."

He looked towards the sound and saw Mark and Sarah hiding behind a low wall.

"What are you doing here?" he asked.

"We brought you some bread from the bakehouse," Sarah said. "We thought you would be hungered by now."

"I am, thanks," John said, taking the bread graciously from his sister. "What are you doing out here so early?"

"I overheard your argument with Mother yesterday," Mark said. "I told Sarah, and we agreed to meet with you every morning and give you bread. It's the least we can do. I am sorry Mother is so cruel to you, but you need to be careful. You don't want her as an enemy."

"I fear I have already managed that," John said. "I don't understand why she hates me so much, but I will not back down to her."

"Did she really threaten to send me to work in the stables?" Sarah asked.

"She did," John confirmed. "She knew I would have refused otherwise."

"How long are you here for?" Sarah asked.

John threw his hands in the air. "As long as Margaret demands of me, I guess. But I've written to Father, and I am sure he will put a stop to it as soon as he finds out."

John used his time to study and write letters to his father. The stable boys were careful to avoid eye contact with him, and they tried their best to ignore him and act like he wasn't there. Although he would never say it aloud, he enjoyed watching them work, and he enjoyed being around the horses.

Three days later, John looked up from his German studies to see Harris stride into the stables. The boys jumped up when they saw him, but he waved them away.

"Master John, Lady Margaret has summoned you to her study," he said, trying to avoid eye contact with his future master.

"Am I to be allowed to regain my dignity?" John scoffed at Harris as he walked by him. "Or am I to carry out some other demeaning task?"

"She only sent me to get you, Master John. I'm not privy to her decisions."

John pushed open the door to Margaret's study a lot harder than was necessary, causing the door to slam back against the wall with a loud crash.

"You sent for me?" John asked, ignoring his grand entrance.

"Did you think you could write to your father and I wouldn't find out about it? All correspondence comes through me when your father is not here. I recognised your poor handwriting immediately."

"You will pay for your actions when he hears of this," John said, pulling himself up to his full height. "He would never allow his children to be treated like servants, and our mother would have been horrified at your behaviour."

"Your mother is dead," Margaret said, staring at John.

"How dare you," John said through pursed lips. "You are not fit to be her chambermaid."

Margaret's eyes clouded as she leaned forward. "Your actions always have consequences, and the sooner you learn this, the better it will be for all of us. I will not tolerate your continued defiance, as you shall see."

"What are you going to do, send me to work with the blacksmith? Once Father finds out, he will be furious."

"He already knows, and he supports me completely. I just wanted you to know that your letters are futile. Now get out of here. You smell of horses."

John didn't have long to wait before he discovered Margaret's latest punishment. She walked into the stables with Harris in tow, startling the stable boys and even John himself.

"As you all know, I sent John here to learn some humility. Unfortunately, this has only made him worse. As you were supposed to be teaching him, you are to be punished in his place. Perhaps this way he will learn there are consequences to his actions."

"The workers here have done nothing," John shouted. "At least have the courage to punish me directly. Leave these boys alone."

"You have only yourself to blame," Margaret said. She turned her gaze to the stable boys. "Because of his insolence, you are all to be fined a week's wage. Now get back to work."

John saw the look of horror on the faces of the stable boys. They relied on their meagre wages to support their families. He couldn't help himself.

"I am the earl's son, and heir to his estates. There will be no fines for these men today. If you like, Lady Margaret, I shall write to my father again and explain what I did and why I did it. I am sure he would understand."

Margaret stared at John for what he felt was an eternity. Her eyes were blazing inside her head. She turned to the stable boys. "The fine stands."

John followed Margaret out of the stables. He couldn't let this go.

"Did you have to fine those boys?" he asked. "They didn't do anything wrong. They rely on their wages to feed their families. You know that to be true."

Margaret stopped and turned to face John. "I will not tolerate insolence, especially in front of the workers. They are being punished for your impudence. Remember that, John Howard. It is an important life lesson you just learned."

John scowled. "You sent me to work in the stables like I am a peasant. How is that a life lesson?"

"And I can't even trust you with that. That is why I sent you there. Tomorrow morning you will go to work with the blacksmith, which was your own suggestion if I recall. Perhaps you will learn better manners over there."

John stamped his foot on the ground. "Lady Margaret, I have tried as hard as I can to keep the peace and not anger you. I promised my father I would do all I could to get along with you. I agreed to work in the stables so you wouldn't punish Sarah for what I did. But you are not treating me like a servant. I shall not work with the blacksmith. I am the son of the earl, not a peasant worker."

He moved around in front of Margaret. "I tell you what, Lady Margaret. I'll go to work with the blacksmith tomorrow as long as I am accompanied by Mark. If it's good enough for me, then it's good enough for him."

John watched as Margaret's face turned red. He saw her eyes flash with fury. She clenched her fists.

He waited for a response.

"You are a silly boy if you think you can get between your father and myself," she said after a lengthy pause. "I promised him I would be kind to you and allow you time to accept my presence here, but I am losing patience with you. The fines remain."

Margaret stormed off. John had pushed his luck a little too far, but he couldn't help himself. He heard footsteps behind him.

"John, you really must be careful and stop antagonising Margaret like that," Sarah said. Mark was right behind her.

"Did you hear her?" John asked. "She is treating me like a servant. I have to stand up to her or she will have me cleaning the privies next."

"Be careful, John, or you will find yourself banished from here," Mark said. "She doesn't like you already. I don't want to have to write to you in Norfolk when you're living with your uncle Thomas."

"I hope those words are not a prophecy," John said. He turned and went to his room. He knew this wasn't over.

The next morning, he was up especially early, making sure he could sneak out into the courtyard without being seen. He kept to the shadows, passing the bakery that made his stomach rumble at the smell wafting by his nostrils as he walked past.

He passed the great hall where they held the fancy feasts and evening dinners. The kitchens were coming to life in the early morning darkness. The blacksmith's fires were roaring, and he could feel the intense heat as he passed by the door.

He entered the stables where the boys were already hard at work. They were quiet and sullen this morning, in total contrast to the jovial men he had been used to being around.

They stiffened when they saw John approach them. "I'm sorry you are forced to come here," the lead stable boy said, "but we need our wages to feed our families. We can't be in the middle of this. No offence, sir."

John reached into his pockets. "I haven't come to work here. I'm very sorry that happened yesterday. None of it would have happened if my mother was still alive."

He handed each of them one crown each. Six in total. "I took these from my own money, and I order you to accept them without breathing a word of it. I am responsible for what happened yesterday, and I will not allow you to pay for it."

The stable boys stared at the coins in the early morning half-light. It was the first time any of them had ever held a crown.

"Sir," the lead boy said, "This is way too much. Your kindness knows no bounds, and we are all very grateful to you. This is almost a month's wage for us. We don't know what to say to you, sir."

"The gratitude is all mine. I enjoyed being here, and I learned a lot about horses. Please give your families my best regards and keep this to yourselves. I don't want Lady Margaret finding out."

The stable boys nodded as John backed out into the breaking dawn. He heard yells of laughter and excited voices behind him as he walked away. It made him feel happy and warm inside that he could help in some small way. He had helped feed their families for the next few weeks. If this was the outcome, he would accept admonishment from Margaret all day long.

He suddenly realised that he'd enjoyed being in the stables around the horses. He would never admit it, but he even enjoyed the company of the stable boys.

They were almost friends.

Almost.

Mark Collapses

April 1536

The Dissolution of the Monasteries – a policy forced through Parliament by Henry VIII and his Chief Minister, Thomas Cromwell – meant that Robert Howard spent most of his time in London. His family rarely saw him, so the occasional times the king allowed him to go home to Broxley were more than welcome.

After much discussion, King Henry allowed Robert home to celebrate the birth of his youngest son, Arthur, who was born a week earlier on 18 April 1536.

John, now sixteen, thought he looked more weary than normal when he watched him climb from his carriage.

"Greetings, Father," he said, waiting patiently behind Margaret and Sarah to greet him. "How goes it in London?"

"London is a problem right now," Robert said, giving John an oversized handshake. "There is talk of an uprising against the king, so I can only stay for a few days."

"Why are you involved in the monasteries?" Sarah

asked. "Are you claiming them for the king? Or are you protecting them for the Catholic faith?"

"Neither. I'm keeping out of it. This is Cromwell's department, not mine. All I'm trying to do is to keep the king safe."

"It's a dreadful thing," Margaret muttered. "Henry Tudor will have his day of destiny before God."

Robert stopped and looked around his small family gathering. "Be quiet, woman, and don't ever say that again, do you hear? You'll get us all killed. We all swore an oath to the king, recognising him as the Supreme Head of the Church of England, and as far as we are concerned that is the end of it. Anyone who doesn't, loses both their heads and their estates, just as Sir Thomas More did."

"Enough of this talk." Margaret changed the subject. "We have much to celebrate tomorrow after Arthur's birth. Come, you must be desperate to see your new son for the first time."

"Can you not stay a while longer?" John asked. "We've barely seen you at all this year. And we haven't seen Arthur yet either. Lady Margaret has kept us away from him."

Margaret shot John one of the looks he was accustomed to when she didn't like what he was saying. He ignored her as usual.

"I wish I could," his father replied. "The king isn't happy that I had a son where he could only produce another daughter, the Princess Elizabeth. He reminds me of it every chance he gets. I have to go back so as not to upset him even more than he already is."

"Let us pray that Queen Anne has a son, so the royal lineage may continue," Margaret said. She looked like she was about to say something else, but the look on Robert's face convinced her to remain silent.

Margaret led Robert away from the children, much to

John's chagrin. Like his sister, he wanted to see his father and spend some time with him. With Margaret in charge, he knew that wasn't going to happen.

The following morning the family gathered inside St Michael's Church to give thanks for Arthur's birth and for his continued good health. When the service finished, they all strolled outside for the short carriage ride back to Broxley.

"May I hold him for a moment?" Sarah asked.

"Perhaps, when we get back to Broxley," Margaret said. "The air is crisp this morning, and I don't want Arthur catching anything."

"We would tell you that Arthur is a strong, healthy boy," John said to his father, "but we are never allowed to see him, so we don't know. Lady Margaret makes sure we don't go anywhere near him."

Margaret scowled. "Nonsense. Must you always pick fault when your father is around? Today is a day of celebration, so don't spoil it for everyone."

John shook his head and walked to Mark, who was holding the side of the carriage with one hand, leaning forward as if he was about to throw up.

Mark had been acting strange all morning. One minute he was sweating, and the next he was shivering. He had been quiet all morning and kept staring at his mother with an anguished look on his face.

"Are you all right, Mark?" Sarah asked as they made their way out of the church. "You're awfully pale this morning."

"I'm fine," Mark said. "I just feel a little off."

"You've been quiet the last few days," his mother interjected. "Are you sure you feel all right?" Concern was etched all over her face.

"Mother, I—"

Mark stopped in his tracks and lurched forward on unsteady feet. He vomited time and again before collapsing to the ground. Margaret, who was holding Arthur, looked on forlornly.

Robert, John, and Sarah ran to his aid. John got there first and cradled his head in his arms.

"Are you all right, Mark?" he asked, knowing full well he wasn't.

Mark didn't reply. He was too busy retching and shivering. Robert grabbed him and threw him into the carriage.

"Get him home, fast, and get the doctor from the village," he ordered. "Don't wait for us, we'll be right behind."

Margaret ran to the carriage, but Robert stopped her. "Take care of Mark. If whatever he has is contagious, we have to keep Arthur away from it. Give him to me and you go back with Mark. I'll take care of Arthur."

Margaret almost threw Arthur at Robert before jumping into the carriage with Mark. "Go!" she yelled. "Now."

The carriage took off at a gallop. Robert led John and Sarah on foot.

"Keep away from Mark until we know what's going on with him," he ordered. John and Sarah agreed, too stunned to speak.

Sarah broke the silence.

"I hope he is all right, Father. As strange as he is, I'm quite fond of Mark."

"Me too," John said. "I hope it is nothing serious."

Sickness

Everyone waited outside Mark's room for the doctor to come out. Nobody dared go inside in case it was something infectious.

After waiting for what seemed an age, the doctor emerged.

"Well?" Margaret demanded. "What ails my son?"

"Is it the sweating sickness?" Sarah dived in, looking anxious. "If it is, we mu—"

"Don't be ridiculous," Margaret snapped. "It isn't the sweating sickness."

Robert held up his hand to allow the doctor to speak.

"I have excellent news, Lady Margaret," the doctor said. "While I am not exactly sure what is ailing Master Mark, one thing I am sure about is that it isn't the sweating sickness. The symptoms don't point to that."

"Thank the Lord," Margaret said, holding on to Robert for dear life. "So what is it then?"

"I'm not completely certain," the doctor said, "but I don't think it's anything serious. Mark is already showing signs of recovery and his colour is returning to normal, so I can only surmise that he ate something that didn't agree with him or some such thing."

Margaret gripped Robert. "Thank the Lord," she repeated. "Thank you, doctor."

"To be on the safe side, I bled him a little."

Margaret nodded and entered Mark's room, closing the door behind her. John tried following, but his father stopped him.

"Let him rest, son. He'll be back to normal soon."

John nodded and stepped backwards. "I'm glad he's all right."

"Me too," Sarah said.

"You might take this opportunity to spend some time with your brother," their father said with a twinkle in his eye. "He's with the governess."

John and Sarah smiled at each other and ran to the nursery.

Two days later, Robert was preparing to return to London. Mark was up and about, although he looked pale and withdrawn. He was quiet and barely spoke to anyone.

The family made their way to the front of Broxley Hall to say their goodbyes to Robert. Mark was at the rear of the small procession, and as he reached the carriage, he once again lurched forward and vomited all over the carriage wheel. He collapsed, holding his stomach, and pointed at his mother. His words were unintelligible, but John was sure he heard the word 'help' in there, and he felt incredibly sorry for him.

As before, Margaret rushed to him, while Robert held John and Sarah back.

"Call the doctor again," he ordered Margaret. "You two stay away until we know for sure what ails Mark. This cannot continue. I shall inform the king, and I am sure he will grant me pardon to leave until we find out for sure what it is. He will not want to risk being around the sweating sickness. I shall return as soon as I can."

As soon as the servants had Mark safely in his room, Robert left for London, leaving John and Sarah alone in the library.

"What do you think is wrong with him?" Sarah asked. "It if isn't the sweating sickness, then what is it?"

"I have no idea," John replied. "The doctor will tell us more once he's examined him."

But the doctor didn't know what was wrong with Mark. "I'm convinced it isn't the sweating sickness," he told Margaret. "The symptoms don't add up. Whatever ails him, I'm sure it isn't that."

"Can we go near him?" John asked.

"I'm not sure that's a good idea," the doctor said. "Until we know what it is, it may be wise to keep your distance."

"I have been close to him all this time, and I'm perfectly healthy," Margaret said. "So whatever it is, it cannot be contagious."

"It's up to you, Lady Margaret," the doctor said. "You look healthy enough to me, but I cannot in good faith tell Master John it is safe to go near him until we know what ails him."

"Mark will get all the care he needs right here," Margaret said. "I took care of him before, and I will do so again."

"What was wrong with Mark when he was young?" Sarah asked. "Didn't he have the sweating sickness then?"

"Yes," Margaret said. "That's why I know he doesn't ail from it this time. This is something different."

The doctor left after apologising to Margaret for failing to diagnose Mark's ailments.

"If it is safe to do so, may I read to him during the

evening?" John asked. "I really don't mind, and Mark may enjoy the company."

"I don't see why not? Mark will be thankful."

After Margaret left the room, John turned to Sarah. "That was strange. She usually hates me being anywhere near Mark, yet this time she didn't say a word."

"She must be really worried about him," Sarah said. "I thought it odd too."

That evening, John took his favourite book to Mark's room so he could read to him.

"I am thankful to you for allowing me a short while to rest." Margaret rose from her chair. "I will be back to stay the night."

"How is he?" John asked.

"You could always ask me." Mark's voice sounded soft and strained, but John smiled down at him.

"I'm sorry," he said. "I thought you were asleep, and I didn't want to disturb you. How are you?"

Margaret took her leave, leaving John alone with Mark. Darkness had closed in, and the candles cast shadows that danced along the walls of Mark's bedchamber.

"I've been better," Mark said. "Mother makes me eat honey and tells me it's good for me, but I long for actual food if I could only keep it down."

"Is there anything I can get you?"

"No, Mother takes care of everything. What book do you bring?"

"It's my favourite – Henry V and Agincourt, and I know you like it too."

"Indeed. Please read it to me."

John read for several minutes until Mark lurched forward and vomited in a pot Margaret had ready for him. John felt helpless watching him painfully vomit before he fell backwards in a heap, completely spent.

"Is there anything I can do? Both Sarah and I are worried about you."

"Keep that honey away from me." Mark spoke in a barely audible whisper.

"The what? The honey? Wouldn't that help to soothe your throat and mouth?"

"Be careful, Jo—" the door opened, and Margaret rushed back in again. "Thank you. John. Now if you will leave us, I will tend to his needs."

John gave a slight bow and looked at Mark's face as he left. *The poor boy is delirious. He doesn't know what he's saying.*

Over the next few nights, John continued reading to Mark, and he stayed longer and longer as darkness fell. Margaret seemed to trust him more and more.

As Margaret left the room, John followed her out, closing the door behind him so Mark couldn't hear them.

"What is ailing him?" he asked. "He seems to be getting worse, not better. Whatever you are giving him, it isn't working."

"I know." Margaret's face fell and John actually felt sorry for her for the first time in his life. "I don't know what else to do for him. The doctors try, but they don't know what ails him. I believe you reading to him is helping him some. He looks forward to your visits each evening."

"I'm happy to help, Lady Margaret. I just hope he gets better. Sarah has read a little to him as well, and he seems to like that too."

Margaret smiled. "Don't leave him alone too long. I need to make sure he is well cared for."

"Of course not. I was merely enquiring as to his health." John went back into the room.

"How are you this evening?" John asked.

"Better," came the hoarse reply. "I feel like talking this evening, rather than listening if that's alright."

"Of course," John said. "What do you want to talk about?"

Mark shrugged his shoulders. "You decide."

John pondered for a moment. "Who is Henry Colte?"

Mark jerked a little and looked at John with a quizzical look. "He's my uncle. What made you bring that up?"

"I just thought of it. You said to think of a subject."

"He's the Earl of Farnborough and is – was – my father's older brother. He was the true owner of Saddleworth Manor, where we lived until father died. I never saw much of him because he spent most of his time in London."

"Why wasn't he invited to the wedding?"

"He and Mother don't get along. Come to think of it, Mother doesn't get along with many people. Uncle Henry was glad to see the back of us, and I doubt he will ever rush to see us again."

"Why is that?"

"I was very young, but I remember Uncle Henry shouting at Mother and blaming her for Father's death. Mother spoke to him in the manner she speaks to you, and Uncle Henry didn't appreciate it, so after Father died he gave us a small home in Warwickshire and sent us away. I've never seen him since."

"Why would he think she was responsible for your father's death? Didn't he die of the sweating sickness?"

"Yes, which is why it's preposterous. I've honestly never given it a second thought until you mentioned it just now."

"I was merely wondering why he wasn't at the wedding." John shrugged his shoulders. "How about some more of Henry the Fifth's exploits? They were much more exciting than anything we can talk about."

On the fifth day, a weary Robert Howard returned to

Broxley, surprising everyone when he strode into the grand house late in the evening.

"Father, what are you doing here?" Sarah leapt up and ran to him. "We thought you would be in London for the rest of the year."

"The king was vexed because I may have been in contact with the sweating sickness, so he sent me away until we cleared it up. How is Mark?"

"He is still sick, Father," John said. "I read with him every night, and if anything he is getting worse."

"Strange," his father said. "Where is Lady Margaret?"

"She's with Mark in his chamber," Sarah said. "Shall I get her?"

"No need." Robert rang the bell to summon the servants, and one was dispatched to tell Margaret of his arrival.

Four days later, Mark took a terrible turn for the worse. A priest arrived, as well as a doctor. Once the doctor emerged from Mark's chamber, the priest went in and read a prayer over his bedchamber.

"What is going on with my son?" Margaret demanded of the doctor, who looked terrified at the tone of her voice.

"Lady Margaret, I am not the first doctor to have seen Mark, and like the others, I cannot tell you what ails your son. It could be the sickness, but you are all well, so I am not sure what it is."

"What do you suggest?" Robert asked.

"I suggest you all stay away from anyone else in case you are carrying the sickness and leave Mark's fate in God's gracious hands. I have bled him again, but at this stage, the priest can do as much good as I can."

"Very well," Margaret said. "That is what we shall do then."

"May I read to him this evening?" John asked as

evening fell. "We are getting to the great battle itself now, and we are both excited to find out what happens."

"That's kind of you, John, but I'll take care of him from now on. I am worried he may not recover if I don't pray harder over his body."

"We shall all pray for him," Robert said.

Margaret left to sit with Mark, leaving Robert, John and Sarah playing a card game by candlelight.

Around an hour later, Margaret barged through the door, her eyes as wild as any animal John had ever seen.

"John Howard, what is the meaning of this?" she demanded.

Before John could say anything, she threw down the book he'd been reading to Mark on the table, scattering the cards everywhere.

"It's the book on Agincourt I have been reading to Mark," John said, leaning backwards in surprise. "It's been in Mark's room since I started reading to him."

Margaret's eyes looked like red demons in the flickering candlelight. "What about the book inside it?" She asked, her voice now barely above a whisper.

"What book? What are you talking about?" John threw his hands into the air. "I have no idea what you are talking about."

"This!"

Margaret picked up the book and shook it. A smaller book fell from inside the pages.

"Pick it up and read what it says," Margaret hissed, staring at John as though he was the devil himself.

Sarah picked up the book and flipped it over so she could read the title.

"It's old, whatever it is," she said. "I can tell by the cover."

The words were in Latin, but no one in the room had a problem reading it:

Planta Venenosas, 1357

Poisonous Plants, 1357

"I found this in the drawer beside the book." Margaret threw a bag at Robert. "It contains plants and herbs. The same plants and herbs that are in this book."

Robert looked at the book and then the bag of herbs and plants. "What is the meaning of this?" he asked.

"What is the meaning of this?" Margaret repeated the question, staring straight through John.

"This is the reason Mark is dying. John Howard is poisoning my son."

Poisoning

A stunned silence filled the room before everyone started speaking all at once. John sat rigidly still, paralysed from head to foot. The voices seemed far away and distant, his ears refusing to hear what was being said.

Slowly, he returned to reality as the sound of Margaret's screaming accusations invaded his mind, forcing him to listen and respond.

"Can't you see?" Margaret fell to the floor, sobbing at Robert's feet. "This is why Mark is so sick. He's being poisoned. He's killing my son." Margaret sobbed uncontrollably on the floor.

"John Howard is a murderer!"

John leapt up from his chair. "I am nothing of the sort. I have never seen this book before, and I don't know anything about poisons. These are false allegations, Father."

"She's lying," Sarah shouted. "John would never do such a thing. If anyone is poisoning Mark, it surely isn't John." Sarah curled her lips into a snarl and pointed at Margaret.

"If anyone is poisoning him, it's you."

Margaret sobbed and wailed on the floor.

"This is pathetic." John stood over Margaret, his muscles now quivering with anger. "Sarah is right. If anyone is poisoning Mark, it's her, not me. Why don't you ask her to tell you about the honey she feeds him that he is so afraid of? I swear, Father, I had nothing to do with it."

Margaret's jaw dropped momentarily, and the familiar look of hatred surfaced again. "What mother would ever poison her own son?" she yelled in a high-pitched voice. "No mother would ever do that. What a wicked thing you accuse me of, but you won't get away with this, John Howard. I will not allow it."

Robert, who had sat in stony silence so far, suddenly burst into life.

"Enough," he said. "You are confined to your rooms until we sort this out. If someone has poisoned Mark, then it is a very serious matter. You all remember what the king did to that poor cook a few years ago. We don't want that to happen to us."

"I swear I am innocent, Father, and you know it. I'm not even capable of considering such a crime. Margaret has hated me from the moment she arrived at Broxley."

Robert stood up. "We must keep this to ourselves until we find out what happened. You two, go to your rooms. Do not come out until I tell you. The connecting door will remain locked until further notice."

Robert strode out of the room.

John's face was pale. He was floored. This had completely taken him off guard.

"Why are you doing this to me, Margaret?" he asked. "I thought we were getting along much better. You know I didn't do this."

"All I know is that you are a wicked boy and deserve

severe punishment. If my son dies, you will pay a hefty price. I shall tell the whole of England what you did. You will not get away with this, John Howard."

"Why don't you tell us about the honey you gave him?" John snapped. "Why is he so wary of it? Why don't you eat some yourself right now in front of all of us?"

"You have no idea what you are talking about." Margaret's eyes glowered in the glow of the candles. "The honey is to soothe his throat and nothing more. I shall gladly eat it myself in front of Robert and the doctors. You will swing for this."

"What happened to the cook?" Sarah asked after Margaret left the room.

"A few years ago, in 1531, he died a horrible death if I remember it right." John closed his eyes as he tried to remember where he had read the story of the cook.

"They accused him of treason and poisoning a bishop. The king was so outraged, he ordered him to die by public boiling. It was so terrible the people who watched it were sick at the sight. It was a horrible way to die."

Sarah shuddered. "Surely the king won't do that to you. He loves our father."

"He can't do that to me," John said. "I didn't do anything. I will fight this to my dying breath. Margaret is setting me up."

John ran to his room and lay on his bed. He knew he was in deep trouble. Margaret must have planned this from the very beginning. If she would poison her own son, then she would do anything to get him out of the way.

He wouldn't get much sleep that night.

Banishment

John spent the next day pacing around his bedchamber. His eyes stung from the lack of sleep and from the tears he had cried. Minutes seemed like hours, and nothing could distract him from the heavy clouds that hung over him like a wet blanket, smothering him, and forcing him to gasp for air.

He couldn't take this much longer. The open window brought scant relief, but he looked outside at the calmness of a perfect spring day in the countryside, saddened by the contrast to what was happening inside the four walls of his virtual prison.

He sat on the floor and pulled his knees to his chest. Whatever happens from here, it would never be the same again.

His nostrils flared, and he felt the blood rushing to his head. *It's all her fault. If Father hadn't brought that mad woman to our home, none of this would have happened. How can any mother do this to her own...?*

"Psst. John, over here, but be quiet."

John pulled himself from his thoughts and moved

towards the friendly voice of his sister, who had cracked open their dividing doors slightly.

"Sarah, what news do you bring? I'm going insane just waiting in here."

"I'm sorry," Sarah said. "Father summoned the doctors who had seen Mark, and along with Margaret, they are locked inside his study. I can hear their voices, which are sometimes raised, but I can't hear what they are saying."

"Surely Father won't believe that evil witch? He must know I didn't commit such a terrible crime."

Sarah shook her head. "I'm sure he won't. He's probably arranging for her to be arrested as we speak."

"How is Mark?" John asked.

"He's still sick. Margaret won't let anyone near him, not even the doctors."

"He has suffered much at the hands of his mother," John said. "I wouldn't be surprised if she was responsible for his illness when he was young."

"Was that why Uncle Thomas and Rochford didn't like her?" Sarah asked. "Do they know what happened to Mark and his father?"

"She has to go before she tears apart our entire family," John said. "I wish Mother was here. I've never needed her as much in my life as I do today."

"Me too," Sarah agreed. "I miss her terribly."

Sarah stiffened. "Someone's coming. I have to go."

She swiftly closed the door. Moments later, John heard footsteps thumping their way down the narrow hallway towards his room.

His heart leapt into his mouth, and he shivered as needlelike sensations ripped through his body.

A key turned in the lock to his bedchamber, and two of his father's guards entered his room. "Your father has summoned you, Master John. You are to accompany us to his study."

John took in a full breath and stood up. "Am I to be finally rid of that evil witch?"

The guards said nothing. Flanked either side by guards carrying their halberds, John could feel the tension as they made their way down the narrow corridors towards his destiny.

"How is Mark?" John asked, trying to steady his shaking voice. He looked around the room to see who was present, but he was alone with his father.

Robert Howard sat behind his large desk, looking stern and unhappy. John felt sorry for him.

"Sit down," he said. The tone of his voice was flat and hard. John took a deep breath. He was hoping he would be friendly and assure him of his innocence.

"Tell me what happened," his father said after a lengthy pause.

"There's nothing to tell. The first I knew of this was when Margaret threw the book at me and accused me of poisoning Mark. You sent me to my bedchamber, and I've been there ever since."

"You didn't poison Mark?"

John stared at his father. "Of course I didn't. You know I'm not capable of such a terrible deed."

His father's head sank to his chest.

"Lady Margaret has been up all night reading that book to see what might be wrong with Mark, who I will say was close to death."

"And?" John asked. "How is he?"

His father gave John a long, hard look. "One potion in the book described Mark's symptoms exactly. With Margaret's care and attention, he will make a good recovery."

"This proves what Sarah and I have been saying – that she poisoned him. I assure you, Father, I did not do this. You know I didn't."

"All I know is that someone poisoned Mark, which is probably the most serious offence in England. I also know that no mother would ever subject her own son to such an ordeal. So unless you are accusing either Sarah or one of the servants, that leaves just you."

The blood drained from John's face. "Surely you don't believe her?" he asked. "You know she has never liked me. She wants me out of the way so Arthur will inherit your estate. It is Margaret who is guilty, not me."

His father slammed his hand onto his desk. "I refuse to accept that any mother would poison her own child. It pains me to say it, but I believe you to be guilty of this heinous act of treachery and treason. I know you have never liked Margaret, but I never thought you would go to such extreme lengths to get her to leave. To say I am disappointed with you is an understatement. I expected so much more from my son."

John leapt to his feet, his entire world collapsing around him. "Father, I didn't do this. I swear on my life."

"You might lose that life for this act."

Robert looked like he hadn't slept in days.

"Sit down, John."

"I didn't do it," John said. "You know I didn't."

"You really believe that I committed this evil act?" John's temper flared. "You really believe that I am capable of such a thing? It is Margaret who is guilty, not me, and you know it."

"Do not raise your voice to me, boy." His father spat out the words. "I will not tolerate it."

"And I, sir, will not tolerate being accused of something I didn't do, especially something as hideous as this. I will go to my grave if necessary, but I am innocent. Why don't you ask Uncle Thomas or George Boleyn what they think of Margaret? You married a monster."

His father slammed his fist into his desk once more. "I will not listen to your insolence, John. If you listen to me, I am trying to save your life."

"How so?" John shouted back. He was not backing down. "How are you saving my life by believing her over me?"

"Margaret wants to go public with this. She wants the king himself to know what happened and he would execute you in the most terrible way. I calmed her down so she would accept my compromise."

"Which is?"

Robert Howard lowered his head again. He refused eye contact with his son.

"The only way I can save your life is to banish you from Broxley forever. You are to be sent to a distant cousin in France where you will live out the remainder of your life. I will disinherit you from my estates. As much as this pains me, you are hereby disowned by the Howard family and ordered never to step foot on English soil again. If you disobey this order, I cannot save you, and you will be executed. It's the best I can do, John. You brought this on yourself."

John sat completely still, his mouth gaping at the words he had just heard.

"Father, I didn't do this, I swear. Who will take over the inheritance? Arthur? Don't you see what Margaret is doing?"

"Enough," his father ordered. "Even though these thoughts haunt me, I can find no conclusion other than your guilt. It's your own fault, son."

"I will not accept this," John said, jumping to his feet.

"I will fight this to my dying day." He turned to leave the room. When he opened the door to the study, he jumped back in amazement. Two guards blocked his path.

John turned to his father. "What is this? Am I a prisoner now?"

"It will take several weeks to arrange things in France. Until then, you are to be held under guard in the basement." His father looked away again. "You will have no further contact with this family."

"What about Sarah," John yelled, tears streaming down his face. "Can I not even say goodbye to my sister?"

"You are no longer a part of the Howard family. You are not to speak to Sarah ever again. Take him away, guards, but ensure he is well treated." Robert Howard paused. "I'm so sorry, John. You know I always loved you."

The guards grabbed John by his arms and led him out of his father's study. They took him down the servants' stairway and into the basement then pushed him into a room that had bars on the windows and straw on the floor. There was no bed and nothing to remind him of his home comforts.

John Howard sank onto the floor and sobbed.

Plans to Escape

John watched his shadow dancing on the wall in the fading light. Grabbing a loose stone, he scratched a third mark on the wall.

Three days! Three days and nothing!

His father refused his request for a candle, but at least the clear night skies illuminated the room enough for him to see his way around.

The only comfort Robert allowed his son was a piece of folded parchment and a quill pen. In the fading light, John unfolded the parchment and grabbed the quill. If he could get a note to Sarah, maybe she could reply with news of what was happening.

There was just about enough light left for John to see some words at the top of the parchment in his father's handwriting.

Confess, and I shall be lenient. Refuse, and I cannot guarantee your safety even in exile.

John threw the parchment across the floor.

As night settled and the house went quiet for the night, John heard a noise through the bars of his basement prison. He could hear horses and the wheels of a carriage, and he could just about make out the shapes in the clear night sky.

Who could this be at this time of night? Have they come for me?

John shuffled back to his corner and awaited his inevitable fate.

Margaret had won.

The sound of a key in the door turned John's blood to ice. *Have they come for me already?*

He stood up as the heavy door swung open, fully expecting to see his father and a gloating Margaret. John readied himself for what was to come.

What was to come? I wish I knew.

Sarah stood at the doorway, holding a candle in front of her. In normal circumstances, John would have laughed at the way her face looked in the dim light, but these weren't normal circumstances, and the last thing John wanted to do right now was laugh.

He rubbed his eyes to make sure he wasn't dreaming.

"Sarah? What are you doing here?"

"I had to see you, John. I've been frantic trying to find out what Father is going to do with you and I'm so sorry you are down here all alone."

"How did you get down here? Surely Father doesn't know you are here?"

Sarah shook her head. "Of course not. He would be furious if he knew. Willis believes in you just as much as I do."

John looked at the friendly guard stood behind Sarah. Willis had been with the family for as long as he could remember. He was as loyal as anyone could ask for, and John was grateful to him now.

"Thank you, Willis. I am indebted to you for believing in me and allowing my sister to visit."

"I am at your service as long as I am guarding you, Master John. If I may speak out of place, I don't trust the Lady Margaret any more than you do. I've heard her in some fierce arguments with Master Mark since she arrived here. I don't think you're guilty at all, sir."

"Thank you," was all John could think of to say, although he knew it wasn't anywhere near enough.

"What news do you bring?" He turned to Sarah. Willis went out the door and closed it behind him.

"A messenger arrived earlier this evening. He and Father talked for a long time in his study before they retired to their chambers. I don't know what they said because guards blocked the hallway to his study. It must have been important because even Margaret wasn't allowed in there."

"It must be about my exile in France." John sighed. "I'll most likely be gone tomorrow, and I can never see you again."

Sarah's eyes filled with tears, and she grabbed John's arm. "I won't allow it. Margaret can't get away with this."

"How's Mark?" John asked.

"Margaret says he is improving rapidly. The doctors are very pleased with his progress, although I am not allowed to see him. Father says he will be back to full health in no time."

"I'm happy for him," John said. "He doesn't deserve what he's been through."

"I have to go," Sarah said. "If I'm found here, we'll both be sent to France. I'll be back as soon as I can."

John hugged his sister and sank back into the straw scattered across the floor. It was going to be another long night.

Before dawn the next morning, Robert summoned

John to his study. His eyes were red, and he looked like he'd been up all night.

"Well? Did you sign the confession?"

"You know I didn't, Father. I will not admit to something I never did."

His father shook his head and wagged his finger at John. "That was your only chance of redemption. If you confess, I can keep you in England – perhaps even with Thomas, who I know is your favourite uncle."

"Bribery won't work, Father. Why don't you ask Margaret to confess?"

"Enough of this," Robert said. "I don't have the time for your games. There's been a change of plan."

John said nothing.

"I must leave immediately to attend urgent matters in London. I'm sworn to secrecy, so all I can tell you is that you will now leave from London. You will travel alone and leave from the Thames."

"What's so important that you must leave right now?" John demanded. "What can possibly be more important than the fate of your son and heir?"

Robert shot John a dark look. "You are no longer my son and heir. Documents are being prepared for Arthur to be my successor."

"So Margaret wins," John said. "Why am I summoned here this morn?"

"I wanted to give you one more chance before leaving for London. The next time I see you will be the last."

John didn't look back at his father before being led back to his cell.

After a hurried early morning goodbye with Margaret, Robert left for London. Nobody knew it at the time, but this would lead to one of the most notorious and infamous days in English history.

The next night, Sarah visited John's basement cell again. "Willis volunteered to guard you during the night so I can see you," she told John. "Once you are earl, you need to reward him for his loyalty."

"When I am earl?" John scoffed. "You do know Father has disowned me and declared Arthur the heir, don't you?"

"Yes, but once Margaret is found guilty, you will be reinstated."

"I love your optimism, sister, but I don't expect that to happen. Margaret has won. What news do you bring?"

"Something big is happening," Sarah spoke in a hurried voice. "Father left with the visitor at dawn, and Margaret is making preparations for us all to go to London."

"Why? Are you all going to wave me off from the banks of the Thames?"

"I don't know although, from the way Father looked before he left, it's important."

"It's always important with Father," John reminded her. "He's probably arranging for a ship to take me to France."

"I hope not." Sarah gave her brother a hug before leaving John alone in the darkness.

Within days of Robert leaving, everyone except John knew what was going on. Royal guards arrested Anne Boleyn on May 2, 1536. She stood accused of treason, incest and adultery, and was being held at the Tower of London. If found guilty, she faced the death penalty.

For the first time in England's long history, a queen was facing execution. The country was awash with gossip, and many people began making their way to London to witness this historic event.

"What news do you bring? When am I leaving for London? How's Mark?" John was impatient and wanted answers. "I sit in this cell day after day and nobody can tell me anything."

"Mark's doing remarkably well," Sarah told him. "He's weak, but he's out of bed and walking around. He'll be back to full strength in a few more days."

"When are we going to London? When am I going to France?"

"There's been a big change of plans. We're all going to London. You won't believe what is happening down there. They arrested the queen and accused her of treason. She will have a trial, and if they find her guilty, they will execute her."

"Wow, they arrested Queen Anne?" John said. "The coronation was such a spectacular event, too. What is she supposed to have done?"

"They arrested George Boleyn too," Willis chimed in. "Her Majesty is accused of adultery, incest, and high treason." He was at the door, making sure nobody came to surprise them. He would be in serious trouble if Margaret found out he allowed Sarah to visit her brother.

"What?" John said. "I bet she's about as guilty of her crimes as I am of mine."

"I'm sure you're right," the guard said. "Nobody believes any of it for a second. Mark my words though, they will find her guilty."

"Just like I was, with no evidence. I'll wager they framed her, just as Margaret framed me."

"You are to travel to London in a separate carriage from us," Sarah said. "Father has arranged for you to travel from the Thames to France after the trial or execution. He wants us all to be there to show we are a happy family."

"He wants to show us as a happy family? How is he going to explain why I'm being exiled to France?"

"He has told everyone you are going there to further your education," Sarah said.

John shook his head. "So I get to spend one more day with the lying Lady Margaret and I'm supposed to act like everything is fine? Father told me I was going to leave from London, but he never mentioned any of this. I won't do it. I can't."

Sarah held his hand. "I'm sorry, John. Is there anything I can do?"

John shook his head. "Are you all right, Sarah? You look a little pale."

"I'm fine," Sarah said. "I'm just worried about you."

"You'd better leave before Margaret finds you. If she does, you'll find yourself on that boat with me." He smiled at Sarah. "How is Arthur doing? She didn't poison him too, did she?"

"No," Sarah replied. "Arthur is way too young. She would have killed him."

They said their goodbyes, and John found himself alone in the darkness once more.

A plan was forming in his mind.

Argument

Sarah crept silently up the stairs in the darkness on the way back to her bedchamber. She stepped lightly past the darkened rooms where the servants slept, being careful not to let anyone know where she had been.

A faint light shone through the half-open door of Margaret's sitting room on the ground floor, and raised voices came from inside. She crept as close as she dared so she could listen to what was being said.

"I know it was you." Mark was screaming at his mother. "It was the same as the last time you poisoned me when I was young. It wasn't John and we both know it – it was you. You poisoned me then, and you did it again now."

"Nonsense," Margaret replied. "What mother would poison her own son? You're being ridiculous. Perhaps you are still suffering from the effects of the poison John gave you."

"It was you, Mother. Stop lying to me." Mark shouted even louder. "I like John, and I trust him. He is kind, unlike you, and he wouldn't do anything like this. But I know you would because you already have. You destroy anyone who gets in your way."

"This is ridiculous, Mark. Go back to your room and be thankful that I caught the evil boy in time before he killed you."

"You won't get away with this. I'm going to tell Robert what you did to me when I was young. And I'll tell him what you did to me now. I'll make sure you hang for this. You're evil and I am ashamed you are my mother. You never loved me, how could you when you keep poisoning me?"

Sarah could hear Mark sobbing, and she felt pity for him. If Margaret hadn't been there, she would have run to him and comforted him.

"Enough, I said," Margaret bellowed. "Go to your room at once. I shall hear no more of this nonsense. Perhaps I should summon the doctor for you because you are clearly not making any sense."

"I will tell Robert as soon as he gets back and clear John's name. You're finished, Mother. I can't allow you to ruin anyone else's life. You deserve to hang for your crimes."

"Listen, you stupid boy. Do you really think I wanted to kill you?" The sudden change in Margaret's tone took Sarah aback. "If I wanted to kill you, you'd be dead already. You and Arthur will one day inherit all of this and then you will thank me."

"You've already caused so much misery and suffering to this family, just like you did to my father's."

"Stop!" Margaret shouted. "I know people in places you would fear to be seen, and they would be more than willing to break in here one cold, dark night and drive a blade through your weak, pitiful heart. Don't think I won't do it because I will. Furthermore, if you think you are brave enough to stand up to me, then remember the only reason that wretched girl is still alive is because you have a soft spot for her. You blush every time she looks at you. It's sickening. You're weak and useless, but remember, her life is in your hands. If one word of this ever leaks out, I have people ready to kill Sarah slowly and painfully. So the choice is yours, Mark."

"You're bluffing."

"Try me, I dare you."

"I hate you," Mark screamed as loud as he could. "I hate you."

He ran from the room, slamming the door behind him. He was sobbing so hard he didn't notice the shadow hiding in the doorway. Sarah watched him run up the stairs and out of sight.

She hid in the room next door before Margaret came out and locked the door behind her. She watched as Margaret made her way up the stairs to her bedchamber.

Anger and resentment welling up inside, Sarah resisted the urge to confront her. Instead, she waited for almost an hour before silently making her way up the stairs.

The next morning Mark was pale, sullen, and quiet. His eyes were swollen and red, and Sarah could tell he had been up all night. She felt sorry for him.

"Good morning," Margaret announced as she walked past. "You look lovely today, Lady Sarah."

"Thank you." Sarah almost choked on her words.

She followed Mark up to his room. He tried closing the door behind him, but Sarah stopped him.

"I heard you arguing with your mother last night," she said.

Mark looked stunned. "I... I.." he stammered. "I don't know what you're talking about."

"I heard everything, Mark. If you will go with me to

Father, we can stop all this and clear John's name before they send him away. Your mother needs to pay for her crimes."

"You don't understand," Mark said. "You shouldn't have been there. I don't know what you thought you heard, but it wasn't what you think. My mother is a gentle lady who is only trying to protect me."

"Mark, you said—"

"No, I didn't. Now get out." Mark yelled. "If you don't, I'll get my mother and tell her what you said. Believe me, you don't want that to happen."

Mark pushed Sarah out of his room and slammed the door.

Sarah tried talking to him several times over the following days, but he refused. He was his usual distant and sullen self again.

The next time she sneaked into the basement, she told John what she had overheard.

"What shall I do?" she asked. "Everyone knows Margaret is guilty except Father. I need to make him understand before he banishes you."

"It's no big surprise," John said, holding his sister's hand. "Mark is no doubt terrified of her and is probably trying to protect you in his own way. Father won't listen, even if you and Mark go together and tell him. Margaret has him under her spell."

"I can't allow her to get away with this," Sarah said.

"Let it go for now," John said. "There is nothing we can do. I need you to promise me you won't do or say anything. You need to stay here and keep an eye on her, for both our sakes. Keep out of her way and don't give her any reason to go after you, please promise me that."

"I can't—"

"Yes, you can. Please, Sarah, for me if not for yourself,

please promise me you will never go after her, at least not until we are older and much better prepared."

Sarah sighed. "John, I—"

"Please, Sarah. For me."

"Okay, you win. I promise I won't do or say anything. But I will watch her like a hawk for the rest of my life."

"Thank you." John shook his head. "We don't need both of us exiled from here. One day we will get our revenge, but for now, let it go. Someone has to look out for Arthur."

"I promise, but only for you." Sarah bit her lip in frustration.

Last Meeting

By May 15, the Howard family had settled into their house on the Stronde. As before, Robert banished John to the basement. He had not seen Sarah on his way to London, and he was desperate to find out the latest news.

That night Sarah visited him with Willis by her side.

"What news do you bring?" John asked.

"The Archbishop of Canterbury, Thomas Cranmer, declared Anne's marriage to the king null and void yesterday," Willis said. "They found Anne Boleyn guilty of all the charges at her trial, and they will execute her in four days time at the Tower."

"Why am I not surprised?" John shook his head. "I guess we are all going to it?"

Sarah nodded. "It's supposed to be a private execution at the Tower, but the gates will be open so the public can walk in."

"When did you say this was happening?" John asked.

"Four days from now, Master John," Willis said.

"Thank you."

John settled into his straw bed in the darkness, deep in

thought. The plan he'd come up with during his trip to London might just work! There would be vast crowds of people watching the gruesome execution, and there would be chaos everywhere. With everyone engrossed in witnessing Anne Boleyn die, he would back away and melt into the crowds and learn how to live on the stretes of London. He would be free once and for all of Margaret Colte and her evil ways. It would be difficult, but it was better than living as a traitor in France.

The next night, he waited for Sarah and Willis to visit him. He trusted them both with his life.

"I need your help," he said as soon as he saw them.

"What do you need me to do?" Sarah asked.

"I need both of you to help me. But first, you must swear that what I am about to tell you will remain between us."

John looked at both their faces in the dim light of the candles they were carrying. Willis nodded. "I am loyal to you, Master John," he said.

John looked at Sarah. She looked worried, but she nodded and clasped his hand. "You have my word. What are you going to do?"

"Sarah, I need you to stock as much food, water, and coin as possible in the treehouse and bring my sword and longbow. Just make sure nobody sees you."

John looked at his sister.

"I'm not going to France. I will never admit to a crime I didn't commit, especially one as vile as this. Margaret needs to pay for her crimes, and one day she will, but right now my only concern is to get away from both her and our father, who is under her spell."

"What would you have me do?" the guard asked.

"Anne Boleyn's execution will transfix everyone, so I will use that time to lose myself in the crowds. I plan to run away and live here in London. I need you to allow me to vanish without being seen."

Willis nodded, but Sarah looked worried.

"That's too risky, John," she exclaimed. "London is a dangerous place."

"I will learn. It's far better than living as a criminal for the rest of my life in exile. That's why I want you to stock the treehouse for me. At least I will have food and shelter while I learn to adapt."

Sarah gave John a hug. "I'm worried for you, and I fear for your safety."

"Do you think I will be any safer in France? Do you think Margaret will leave me alone when I'm gone? Once I am out of the way, she will send someone to kill me. I'm safer here in London. At the very least I will know who my enemies are."

Sarah nodded. "You're right, but I still worry about you."

"If I don't see you again until the execution, always visit the treehouse whenever you can. Try to bring me food, supplies and news. I will be there as often as I can. I will always be your brother, no matter what my lowly status becomes."

Tears ran down Sarah's cheeks.

"At least this way I will get to see you," she sobbed. "If you went to France, I would never see you again."

Sarah hugged her brother one more time and then left him alone in the darkness. He sat in the corner and finalised his plans.

A guard escorted John to his father's study before dawn on Friday, 19 May 1536. Robert Howard was waiting for him behind his desk. John saw sadness in his eyes as he addressed his son for the last time.

"I'm sorry it has come to this, John. I will give you one

more opportunity to confess your crimes. If you do, I might convince Lady Margaret even at this late hour to show some mercy and allow you to remain in England."

John stared into his father's eyes.

"Father, you know me better than any man alive. I am incapable of committing the crimes Margaret accused me of. I am innocent and I didn't do it. Deep down, I know you believe me. Margaret framed me and poisoned her own son so she could remove me from my heritage. Why don't you ask Mark what really happened? I will never admit to a crime I didn't commit."

Robert Howard sighed. "I hoped after all this time you would realise the error of your ways. I stand by my opinion that no mother would ever poison her own child. Margaret is a caring lady, not the monster you make her out to be. You are fortunate Mark has made a full recovery."

John said nothing. He stared at his father, his mouth so dry that his tongue stuck to his palate. He clenched his jaw and his fists, even as the tears stung his eyes. How could he live, cast out from his family?

"You aren't aware of what is happening, so I will bring you up to date," his father said.

"It appears 1536 is quite the year. Our queen, Anne Boleyn, has been found guilty of committing high treason, adultery and incest with her own brother. The others involved, including George who was at our wedding not so long ago, have already been executed and Anne's will follow this very morn. We have the privilege of watching the first queen ever to face execution in England."

"The privilege?" John blurted out. "She is no doubt as innocent as I am, and I doubt she is guilty of anything. It is certainly no privilege to watch the queen have her head removed."

"Regardless of your feelings, this is a rare moment in

history. They will talk about the execution of Anne Boleyn for centuries to come, and by his good grace, the king has allowed us to witness it."

John shook his head. "It's barbaric. What has happened to your morals, Father? Mother would never have allowed you to behave like this."

Robert slammed his fist into his desk. "I will not tolerate your insolence any longer. You are to attend the execution and act like we are a family. Everybody will be there, so it's in your best interests to act accordingly. If word ever gets out that you have poisoned Mark, it will be you up on that scaffold with Anne."

John scowled once again. "I would rather die than admit to a crime I didn't commit. It is Margaret who should be up there today, not Anne Boleyn or myself. And perhaps even you for allowing her to get away with it."

Robert leant over his desk and slapped John hard across his face. "Enough," he roared.

John rubbed his face, shocked at his father's actions. He had never struck him before in his entire life.

"What has that woman done to you? I would rather live in exile than here with the man you have become."

John backed away, out of reach of his father's hands.

"As soon as the execution is over, my guards will escort you to the Thames, where a boat is waiting to take you to France. You will never see us again. From now on John Howard is dead. You are nothing to me anymore."

John stared at his father. He didn't know this man. He wasn't the same father he grew up with.

"Get him out of here," Robert yelled to the guard.

Backing away, John realised his father was right on at least one thing: From today onwards, John Howard was dead.

Execution

As dawn broke, the Howard family made their way to the Tower by barge. People packed the narrow stretes, making them impassable. It would have been folly to travel by road.

John sat at the back of the barge by himself. Sarah waved and gave him the thumbs up, telling him she had done as he asked regarding the treehouse.

Margaret and his father sat in stony silence, facing the opposite way from John. This was the first time he had seen Margaret since that fateful night, and he could sense the hatred she had for him.

Mark looked like he was back to full health again. Sitting away from everyone else, he acted like he always did – sullen and dour. He never once looked towards John, who took pity on him. He had a monster for a mother who would stop at nothing to fulfil her twisted ambitions.

There was no sign of Arthur. *He must be with the governess.*

John was glad when the barge docked at the Tower. He was happy to get away from the oppressive atmosphere.

They entered the Tower from the Henry III Watergate. Even though they were early, there were already vast crowds there. It was supposed to be a private execution, but the gates to the stretes were open, so the public flocked in to bear witness to the grizzly execution.

John cringed at his father, smiling and greeting other dignitaries. He was making it look like a celebration, and it made John's stomach heave. Robert shook hands with Eustace Chapuys, the Spanish Ambassador, who looked more than happy to be here. It was no secret how much he despised Anne Boleyn.

He looked at the scaffolding where the queen was about to breathe her last gasps of air. It was about four feet high and draped in black. John shivered, wondering how Anne would react when she saw what awaited her.

The crowds got bigger and bigger, and the tension mounted as the big moment arrived. Willis whispered in his ear.

"Master John, stamp on my foot when you are ready to leave. I will make sure no one follows you."

As they spoke, the guard pressed a bag of coins into his hands. "This is from Lady Sarah. She said you will need it to survive."

"Thank you," John said.

"We will miss you," Willis said. "Take care of yourself out there. London is a dangerous place for an inexperienced boy."

John nodded and shook the big man's hand, his skin tingling. He didn't know if it was excitement, fear, or a combination of both. All he knew was that he was ready to get this over with and get away from his father and stepmother.

Sarah hugged him one last time. "I did as you asked," she whispered in his ear. "Please take care, brother. I will see you when I am in London. Don't worry, I shall tell no one what happened to you."

John wiped the tears from her eyes. "Don't be sad for me. I will be free of the monster that Father has become, and I will see you when you are in London. You be careful around them," he nodded towards his father and Margaret. "They're becoming evil."

The tension rose to fever pitch as a group of people approached the scaffolding from the direction of Cold Harbour Gate. It was time.

Anne Boleyn walked onto the scaffold and moved forward to address the enormous crowd. John felt a large swell of empathy inside him. She was acting like a queen, even in the last moments of her life.

He listened as she spoke.

"Good Christian people, I have not come here to preach a sermon; I have come here to die."

"For according to the law and by the law, I am judged to die, and therefore I will speak nothing against it. I am come hither to accuse no man, nor to speak of that whereof I am accused and condemned to die, but I pray God save the King and send him long to reign over you, for a gentler nor a more merciful prince was there never, and to me, he was ever a good, a gentle, and sovereign lord. And if any person will meddle of my cause, I require them to judge the best. And thus I take my leave of the world and of you all, and I heartily desire you all to pray for me."

Tears ran down John's face. How could she be so forgiving and regal, even in her final moments? He felt inadequate when he thought back to earlier when he had faced his father for the last time. He was unworthy.

Anne gave a brief farewell to her servants, who were weeping openly. She gave one last request that people pray for her, and then she knelt, ready to die.

The crowd fell silent as the executioner stood over

Anne's body, his sword poised to strike. Anne was talking the whole time, asking God to take pity on her soul. The tension was so high, John could almost touch it.

It was time. Everyone's attention was transfixed on Anne Boleyn. He stood on the guard's foot and waited. Willis nodded gently and released his hold on John's arm.

John slowly stepped back into the crowds. His last sight of Anne was of her head being severed from the blow by her executioner. He saw her ladies-in-waiting cover her lifeless body and collect her head.

With one last glance at his family, John backed away. He squeezed through the crowds and made his way over the moat at Baynard Tower. He was free!

Early Struggles

John's stomach played havoc as he fought his way through the enormous crowd gathered on the narrow walkway over the moat. He kept looking behind him, expecting to see his father and his guards chasing him down, but all he saw was masses of people chattering excitedly about what they had just witnessed.

It took him a long time to reach the gate at Towerstrete, and he sighed in relief when he got there. He turned one more time to make sure he wasn't being followed and then began making his way along the busy road.

As he looked behind him, he accidentally walked straight into a man standing on the strete corner. The man, concealed by a cloak, staggered backwards. As he stumbled, several loaves of bread fell from beneath his cloak.

The man dived to the ground, frantically trying to retrieve them before the crowds saw them, but he was too late. He gathered a few of the loaves, but hungry hands quickly devoured the rest. Fights broke out as men, women and children grabbed the meagre offerings.

The man stood back from the fracas and hid the bread he'd saved under his cloak.

"I'm sorry, I wasn't looking where I was going," John said. "I didn't mean to cause you to lose your bread."

The man gave John a hard look before answering.

"It's okay, laddie. I saved some of them." The man spoke in a faint Scottish accent. His hood had fallen off during the scramble, so John got a good look at him.

He was tall, somewhere around six feet, and broad shouldered. He looked muscular and physically capable. John was glad he didn't appear to be angry at him.

His long brown hair was unkempt and hung loosely over his shoulders. What struck John the most was his bright green eyes. John saw kindness in them, mixed with a lot of experience of life.

The man pulled a loaf of bread from under his cloak and offered it to John.

"Thank you," John said in surprise. He hadn't been expecting that to happen.

"You sound posh, laddie. Don't get caught out on the stretes by yourself with that accent. The people will tear you apart."

John nodded. He hadn't thought about that.

"Thank you," was all he could say.

"My name is Andrew," the man said, offering John his hand.

"John," came the reply.

"Take care of yourself, laddie. Don't get caught wandering around the city after curfew or the watch will get yea."

"Who's the watch?"

"Men you don't want seeing yea after curfew. This city is a dangerous place after dark."

"Thank you."

The man strode off, and John hoped they would meet again. He seemed safe somehow, and John knew that was something he needed more than ever now he was alone.

He wandered from narrow strete to narrow strete with no clue where he was going. The houses almost touched each other from across the stretes, blocking the light and making it difficult to see what he was stepping in.

The stench! In the name of God, the stench!

Piss from the chamber pots emptied from the upper stories of the cramped houses mixed with the previous day's rain on the cobbled, filthy stretes sent John's senses into the abyss.

Several times he stopped to bend over and vomit as the grotesque smells overwhelmed him, making it almost impossible to breathe in the heavy, putrid London air.

The only part of London he was familiar with was the Stronde, and that wasn't close. He hadn't thought of this when planning his escape. All he'd thought about was getting away from Margaret, and now reality was setting in. He hoped he hadn't bitten off more than he could chew.

Still, I'm better off on my own than living as a criminal in France. Even if I die here, at least I will die sticking to my principles. My principles are all I have left.

John found himself in the busy markets along Cheppes Syed. He felt like a small insect crawling around with millions of other insects as people barged into him and walked around him from all directions.

His hands were shaking, and he noticed he kept wiping his hands across his face, trying to wipe away the grotesque stench that attacked him relentlessly, like an unseen enemy assaulting every sense he possessed.

John had never seen this side of life before, and he'd never realised how much privilege he had enjoyed until today. He was completely unprepared for life as a poor homeless boy. He had to adapt at record speed or he wouldn't survive. That much was obvious, even at this early stage of his journey.

The markets were vibrant and full of life and energy. John tried to cast aside the tingling in his chest and arms that besieged him the moment he'd walked out of the Tower, but he knew it was hopeless. The intense weight bearing down on him was crushing his senses, and as much as he tried to enjoy watching people barter for fruit, fish, and bread, he barely heard a word because of the ringing in his ears.

Snap out of it, or my freedom won't even last a day.

Every glance from a stranger made his heart leap into his chest. He saw everyone as a guard or a spy, and every hand that reached in his direction was a hand that was going to detain him and hand him over to Margaret. He jumped back from one pair of hands that reached out for some vegetables, and clattered into a disgruntled old lady behind him, knocking the goods from her arms.

"Watch where yer goin', boy," she exclaimed, before diving to the ground to save her food before other hands grabbed them.

"I'm sorry," John said. "If you like, I'll…"

He stopped, the words of the stranger ringing in his ears: *"You sound posh, laddie. Don't get caught out on the stretes by yourself with that accent. The people will tear you apart."*

He hurried on, pushing his way through the crowded marketplace.

The next place he found himself at was the Shambles. This was where he found the slaughterhouses and meat markets. Like the markets on Cheppes Syed, the Shambles were buzzing with life and activity. Like before, he felt everyone was watching him, waiting for him to be discovered at any moment.

He forced his way down a narrow lane that led to Grey Friars Church and its surrounding gardens. He slumped to the ground behind the church, glad of the respite from the throngs of people and the smells of the busy stretes.

It suddenly struck him why so many people stared at him with suspicion and disdain. Everyone around him wore terrible-looking old clothes that didn't seem fit for cleaning the privies at Broxley.

John was walking around looking every bit an entitled aristocrat, and he could see immediately that he would be quickly discovered if he continued looking the way he did. He shivered at the thought of wearing such disgusting clothing, and his stomach retched at the thought of the grotesque smells that hung on them being near his body. But he knew he had no choice if he was to survive out here for any length of time.

The late afternoon shadows had appeared by the time he found himself on the Fleet Bridge that crossed the River Fleet. The first thing that struck him was the obnoxious stench coming from the filthy river.

Everything in this city stank worse than the farm animals at Broxley, which was something he'd better get used to quickly. The stench of London was far better than living in exile in France waiting for Margaret's assassins to arrive to end his life.

Fleet Prison was off to his right, and John wondered what unsavoury characters were being held there. He shuddered at the thought of being imprisoned before making his way down Fletestrete.

He found his bearings when he reached the Fleet Bridge and knew his way to the Stronde from there.

The light was fading by the time he reached Temple

Bar. This was where Fletestrete ended and split off in two different directions: Halywell Strete and the Stronde.

John moved swiftly down the Stronde before coming to a sharp halt. He realised he couldn't just walk down the strete and wander into the back gardens of his house. His father's guards would surely see and capture him. He was an outlaw now, and he had to remember to live like one. He no longer belonged to the aristocratic, privileged world from whence he came.

He darted down the side of the Bishop of Exeter's Inn and trudged through the muddy gardens towards Milford Lane. Fresh vegetables grew there, reminding him of the many times he and Sarah had gorged themselves in happier times.

He climbed the small wall onto Milford Lane and crossed the strete, using the evening shadows to hide his presence. Jumping over the wall, he avoided the stables and followed the wall away from the house to a line of trees separating the garden plots, then found the largest tree of them all and climbed high into the branches, safely out of sight of the house and its occupants.

He entered the large treehouse, wishing Sarah was with him. Darkness had fallen, and he'd never felt more alone than he did right now.

It began raining outside, which was normal for England. It rained all the time, so he was grateful for the shelter the treehouse provided.

He rummaged through the sacks Sarah left for him and grasped some candles, although he didn't dare light them in case they were seen from the house. He would save them for when the house was empty.

After a small meal to conserve his food, John lay down to rest. His mind wandered, and he was cold and restless. He couldn't stop fretting about the situation he had got himself into, and he worried he wouldn't be able to adapt to his new life. He didn't know the first thing about strete life in London, and he was quickly realising he hadn't given this a single thought when he was planning his escape. Now reality hit him.

He wasn't ready.

Alone

After the sun rose, John berated himself for being so weak the day before. He had to grow up and accept his new situation. A new era had dawned for John Howard, and from this day forward he would be grateful for the advantages he had over other homeless children, and he would be strong and brave.

Except he wasn't. He knew his false bravado wouldn't last long. As soon as he left the familiar confines of his treehouse, he would be just as nervous and on edge as he had been the day before.

He felt like a fish out of water.

The supplies Sarah had given him lay scattered all over the floor when he froze. Someone was climbing up the tree!

"John," Sarah whispered hoarsely in the early morning breeze. "John, are you there?"

Her head appeared in the treehouse and John had never been happier to see his sister's face. She struggled to pull a large sack behind her, so John grabbed her arm and helped her into his new home.

"I'm so glad you're safe. I worried about you last night."

John hugged his sister. "What happened after I left?" he asked.

"Father and Margaret were furious that you got away, Margaret especially. Poor Willis is in serious trouble. Margaret demanded Father have him tied to a whipping post and taught a harsh lesson."

"Now I feel even worse," John said. "Is there anything you can do?"

"No, I tried. I pleaded with Father to show mercy, but he wouldn't listen."

"Please tell him I'm sorry," John said, knowing full well that he could never repay the guard's kindness. "What else did they do?"

"Father has business with the king, so he never came home last night. Margaret ordered Harris to ready her horse, and she left at first light in a furious mood. She questioned me at length last night, accusing me of helping you escape. I told her I knew nothing about it and had no clue where you went, although I'm sure she didn't believe me."

"Where did she go this morning?"

"She warned me last night that you won't be free for long. Father and Margaret are putting up a large reward, and she said the worst people in London will search for you. She said you'll be sorry when they find you. I'm worried, John."

John sighed. "It's nothing less than we expected. I don't know who she means, but I can imagine everyone in London will look for me when they hear of the reward. How much am I worth?"

"Five pounds." Sarah could barely look at her brother.

"Five pounds?" John repeated. "That's a year's wage for most people. I need to be vigilant."

"Please stay here," Sarah pleaded. "At least until it dies down a bit. I fear she means to kill you. She's already spread word of why you're wanted."

"So everyone thinks I'm a poisoning knave? I don't have much chance, do I?"

"Get out of London. Go north to Scotland, or go to France on your own terms. Go anywhere but here."

John shook his head. "I wouldn't last five minutes if I tried that. They'll make sure every road and river out of London is watched closely. I could steal a ride hidden on a boat, but then what? Without your help, I'd starve to death within a week. At least here I can hide in the large gatherings that seem to be everywhere."

"They have tripled the guards on duty here at the house and Father has dozens more searching London for you."

John shook his head. "I figured he'd react that way. He hates being challenged. I need to be incredibly careful."

"I brought you some more supplies. There are blankets, warm clothing, food and water."

"Thank you," John said. "Did they say when you are leaving London?"

"Father thinks I'm helping you, so we're leaving today. I won't be able to help you after I leave."

"You have helped me enough, Sarah," John said. "Don't get yourself into trouble for me. God alone knows what Margaret would do to you."

"Is Father leaving too, or is he staying here?"

"He said he had to stay behind with all the turmoil in the Royal Court, but he will stay at Whitehall to be near the king. He has posted guards here to catch you if you try to break into the house."

Sarah handed John another small pouch of coins. "It's

all I have, but I want you to take it. I don't know when I will see you again, but I hope it will be soon."

"I'll be here," John said. "If I cannot, I will leave a note telling you I'm safe. Don't worry, dear sister, we will meet again soon. I cannot thank you enough for all you have done for me."

After one last hug, Sarah climbed down from the treehouse. He was alone.

John shook himself back to reality and set about organising his food and supplies. He found his weapons and placed them near the exit, in case he needed to make a fast escape. He laid his food out and rationed it to last as long as possible, and he laid out the blankets so he wouldn't be as cold as he'd been the previous night.

Sarah had given him her life's savings, so John told her where he hid his in Broxley. He counted it out, and he had over three sovereigns, which was enough to last him until spring if he was careful. He took a few coins and hid the rest until he needed them.

He watched as Sarah, Mark, and Margaret climbed onto their barge to leave London in the early afternoon and considered using his longbow to kill Margaret there and then, but his father would hunt him relentlessly if he did that. In any case, he wasn't a murderer. He was better than that.

Once they had gone, the guards patrolled the grounds of the house. He counted four, and he watched what they did so he could work out their routines. If he could predict their movements, he had a better chance of evading them. He would have to be very cautious from now on.

Steelyard

As dawn broke, John slid down the tree and made his way to the banks of the Thames, staying behind the banking until he reached White Friars, where he moved through the gardens until he got to the Cock and Key Inn. He found himself on Fletestrete, and from there he went through the walled city gates at Ludgate and walked by the magnificent St Paul's Cathedral. He wanted to pray, but guards walked around it. They might be on the lookout for him, so he huddled underneath the hood of the long cape Sarah had given him and carried on along Carter Lane.

At the end of Carter Lane, he turned and walked along the side of the great cathedral. He saw more guards, so he hurried down Watelyng Strete before turning up the narrow and foreboding Bred Strete. The hustle and bustle of the markets were heard long before they came into sight.

The strete was narrow, crowded, and dark. The eaves closed in from above, blocking out the light and trapping John inside his worst nightmare. Once again, the putrid smells of city life invaded his nostrils, forcing his chest to heave and add the contents of his stomach to the already filthy stretes.

The doorway was open to one of the many tightly squeezed houses, and John got his first glimpse of how the poor lived in this grimy, unclean city. Straw covered the small floor, and chickens ran around loose inside, making noises that would drive John crazy. A small fire ring circled the middle of the room, and John felt his eyes burning from the strete outside.

What took his interest was the sight of a boy around his size running outside to relieve himself in the strete. As much as this made him want to gag, the boy was barely half dressed, and John noticed his clothes neatly folded on the floor near the doorway. John darted into the house and grabbed the clothes, leaving a pile of coins that he was sure would cover their cost several times over. He ran off before the boy turned away from the wall and saw him.

John ran up Bred Strete and darted into a small churchyard at Gerard's Hall. He hid behind the building and quickly changed into the dirty clothing that fit him almost perfectly. He shivered at the thought of the nasty clothes on his skin, that felt so rough he was sure they would cut him to pieces by the time he returned to his treehouse later.

He bundled up his fine, upper-class clothing and hid them under a stone, making a mental note of where they were so he could retrieve them later. The only evidence of his aristocracy was his cloak, and he wasn't going to let that go for anything. It was the only thing that comforted him from the cold and the oppressive smells of the walled city.

Walking around the markets, John felt emboldened in his new attire. He hung around and listened to the many conversations going on around him, concentrating on the accents and promising himself he would practise when he was alone in his sanctuary. His cultured accent had to go.

"Did you hear they captured one of them Underlings last week?" John listened to several young boys deep in conversation.

"Yea," another replied. "That'll be a good 'un to watch when they kill him."

"Do you really believe they killed that rich duke like they say they did?"

"I dunno. It was a duke's brother they killed, or so they say. They've bin tryin' to catch them for ages."

John took a sharp breath. His father had talked about this over dinner several times at Broxley. Every aristocratic family knew of the vile murder of the Duke of Berkshire's brother.

"Did they catch their leader?" one of them asked. "I hope not. He sounds like a hero to me. All he was doin' was tryin' to take care of his family."

"No, it wasn't him, it was one of his followers. I'd love to be an Underling. Sounds exciting if you ask me."

"I dunno. I'd be scared if they were after me all the time. I hope they don't catch him, though. He's a bit like that Robin Hood fella that me mum used to tell me about."

"Never mind the Underlings," another of them said, who'd remained quiet until this point. "Did you 'ere about the reward for that rich kid that's runnin' around London? He poisoned his brother, so I 'ere. Reward's five pounds, so everyone's goin' to be lookin' for him."

"Yea, I heard about that. His name's John Howard, from what the cryer shouted earlier. They must want him badly for that much coin. Just shows their big houses and all that coin doesn't mean they're good people. They're just as bad as us."

John shrank back into his cloak at the mention of his name. Margaret had got the word out quickly. He doubled down on his promise to himself to learn how to speak like the locals as fast as he could.

"I wouldn't want to be him when Walden's strete gang get hold of him." The boy laughed. "He'll be lucky if he's not in pieces by the time he hands him over."

"Me neither," another one agreed. "I'd rather be hung, drawn and quartered than be caught by Walden and his gang."

John shivered deep inside his cloak. This Walden – whoever he was, must have been who Margaret rode off to see before she left London. How does she know these people? There was a lot his family didn't know about Margaret Colte.

He hurried away before he was noticed. More than ever, all he wanted was to be in the safety of his treehouse. He trembled at how vulnerable he truly was. It seemed everybody in London was looking at him. At least he found some irony in the fact he wasn't alone. Whoever these Underlings were, they appeared to be in the same boat as he was.

Except he was alone. He shivered again and hurried away.

Another conversation caught his attention, so he stopped and pretended to look at the apples the trader was selling. The trader was arguing with an older man with a deep German accent about a place by the Thames called the Steelyard. He complained that all the good produce was being taken by them, and all the traders got was the cast-offs they didn't want.

John closed in to listen further. The German defended the Steelyard, telling the trader that it wasn't their fault the traders didn't get to the docks early enough to meet the ships as they docked. John smiled as the German called the trader lazy and berated him for complaining when he should get up earlier instead.

He shadowed the man through the busy stretes, hoping he was heading towards the Steelyard. From what he'd overheard during the argument, it could be a perfect place for him to hide in safety.

The Steelyard was a German-run walled community that was exempt from city taxes. Local traders called it a 'city within a city' and John couldn't wait to find it. The two arguing men had said it was near London Bridge on the banks of the Thames, close to the shipping docks, which the trader argued gave them an advantage over everyone else in London.

He hoped his German was good enough to get him access, and he quietly thanked Mark for helping him with his studies when all he had wanted to do was practise his longbow.

Their tutor was from Cologne, and from what he'd gathered from the man at the markets, the Steelyard was full of people from that area. He wanted to see if he could stay there instead of the treehouse. If it was a separate, walled area of London, he reasoned he would be safer there than anywhere else.

The man disappeared into a tavern on Thames Strete, so John wandered alone for what seemed an age. Once again, he avoided eye contact and buried his neck inside his cloak to avoid the stares that everyone seemed to be giving him.

Eventually, more by good luck than anything else, he saw the walled area that surrounded the Steelyard. He was about to go inside when a guard at the gate stopped him.

"What business do you have here?" the guard asked him in German.

John stopped. This was the first time he had ever used his language skills outside of his tutoring, and his stomach knotted up, hoping he was good enough.

"I have family in Cologne that I was hoping someone here could help me locate," he said. It wasn't true, but he didn't know any other way of being allowed past the guards.

"Who are you?"

"My name is John Broxley." He thought of the first name that entered his head. Anything other than Howard would do. The guard gave him a long stare before allowing him in.

Once inside, John's legs suddenly gave way, and he collapsed to the floor. His hands trembled, and he let out a huge sigh. It took him a few minutes to regain his senses, and when he did, he looked around to see where he was.

The gates and the walls that surrounded him reminded him of the caring arms his mother used to wrap around him when he was a small boy. His eyes moistened when he thought of his gentle mother, and how angry and disappointed she would be with his father for allowing Margaret to destroy his life.

He quickly regained control of himself. The last thing he wanted was for the German people inside the walls to see him wailing.

He knew even Margaret wouldn't be able to get her guards or strete gangs inside the Steelyard, and this made him feel much safer. For the first time since he'd run away, he relaxed and enjoyed himself. The traders were correct; this was a separate city. It had everything the Hanseatic traders could ever need to be self-sufficient: Shops, halls, wine cellars and residential homes. He spent some of his coin buying German food, which was a pleasant change from the fare he was used to.

Now that he knew where it was, John planned on visiting as often as possible. The feelings of dread and fear that accompanied him constantly on the stretes of London vanished, and he knew he would be safe if he could find a way of being accepted inside the Steelyard.

First Beating

John filled his sack and headed for the gates. The afternoon sun was beginning its descent, and he wanted to get back to the treehouse before dark. In summer, the church bells rang at nine pm, signalling the curfew that meant everyone had to be indoors by this time. London had such a terrible reputation after dark that nobody in their right mind dared to venture out after curfew. The old Roman gates were closed, sealing the city off from the outside world.

A group of five boys came out of nowhere and tried surrounding him as he walked past the New Inn on the corner of Pawles Wharfe Hill.

John silently cursed himself for allowing his guard to drop. He ran up Pawles Wharfe Hill and pivoted down the side of Derby House. They caught him before he could reach Peter Lane.

"What's in the bag?" one of the young rascals asked.

"Why did you run away?" another asked.

"He looks like he's the one we're after," yet another said.

"Boss's gonna be happy if we've got him."

"Looks like it's him."

"What's yer name, boy?" The one who seemed to be the leader stepped forward.

John shuddered and stepped backwards. The boy was taller than John, but what stood out was the long scar running down the right side of his face. He was the most frightening person John had ever seen.

John froze, rooted to the spot. They had him, and there wasn't anything he could do about it.

"What's in the bag?" the leader asked again.

"Nothing," John said. His legs trembled beneath him.

"Nothing?" the boy repeated. "So why's it full then?"

"It's just food for my family," John said.

"It's just food for my family," another boy mimicked John's posh accent. "Not from round here, are ya, rich boy?"

"What's yer name?" Scarface glared at John, moving ever closer with each step. John was trapped.

"John Broxley." John tried sounding like the local boys, but he knew he was failing badly.

"I'm just trying to go home."

"We've got him, Stephen," one of the other boys said. "This has to be him. We're goin' to be rich."

"I bet that sack is full of rich boys' food too."

John turned the sack over and emptied the contents onto the ground. "It's all I have. It's yours if you let me go." He backed away, hoping the boys would take the sack and leave him be.

One boy stood behind John, blocking his path. "Not so fast, rich boy," he said. "We think you're the scum who poisoned his brother. We think you're John Howard."

"I don't know who you're talking about," John said, almost pleading. "My name is John Broxley."

The leader gestured at the others, and they closed in. John stopped shaking. He was remarkably calm, given the circumstances, clenching his fists and waiting for the inevitable beating that was coming his way.

Four boys, all older and stronger, jumped on him. Scarface stood back, watching the proceedings. They kicked and beat him with their fists until he fell to the ground under the weight of the blows. Hands tugged at his cloak, and before he knew it, they had stripped him of almost everything he possessed. They even took his shoes, but at least they left the tattered rags he was wearing alone.

"We hate liars, especially rich liars." Scarface pushed his face into John's, his rancid breath invading John's nostrils. "The lady will be pleased when the boss tells her we've got him."

John's frozen mind sprang to life at the mention of the lady. Did they mean Margaret? Anger coursed through him, and he tried rising from the ground. A hard kick in the head sent him crashing back down again, his thoughts of Margaret and escape receding backwards in the fog of his mind.

Scar man, or Stephen as his friends called him, counted the coins he had taken from John. "There's enough 'ere to last us for weeks, boys," he said triumphantly. "And I've got a new cloak and shoes so I'll look good."

"Pick him up and let's take him to Ren."

The other boys lifted John from the ground and started dragging him after their leader. Just before they turned into the main strete, John heard a commotion from somewhere off to his side. A vaguely familiar voice sounded out in the wilderness of his semi-conscious state.

"Let him go."

John felt himself drop to the floor and vaguely saw

several boys armed with sticks and knives pushing back the rascals who'd attacked him.

"This is the one everyone's after," Stephen said. John glimpsed his scar through his swollen eyes and shuddered. "He's worth a lot of coin."

"Is he worth your life?" John recognised the voice from somewhere, but his foggy mind couldn't place where he knew it from.

"Let him go and we'll let you live, but your master isn't getting his hands on this boy today."

"No way – he's worth a lot more than you think." Stephen moved closer towards the familiar voice.

"Let him go, Stephen. You know what'll happen to him if you hand him over."

"He poisoned his own brother. He deserves what's coming."

"You don't know what he did. You don't even know who this boy is. All anyone knows is what the cryer tells us, and we all know how truthful he is. He's only allowed to tell us what they want us to hear. We know that as much as anyone."

John's senses were returning, and he surveyed the scene before him through his bruised and battered eyes. The man with the familiar voice had his arm wrapped around the neck of one of the rascals and had a knife pressed into his neck.

Two other boys dragged John away from the rascals, while the big man stepped slowly backwards towards Thames Strete, pulling the strete rascal along with him with the knife sticking into his neck. Droplets of blood trickled down the rascal's neck as the blade held the pressure against him.

"Ren will kill us all if we let him go," another of the gang said.

"We'll kill you if you don't."

The big man and his friends dragged both John and the gang member to Thames Strete, where a large crowd watched as they emerged into the road.

Stephen scowled and backed into the shadows of Peter Lane with his companions close behind. The friendly saviour waited a few minutes and then roughly shoved the gang member towards his friends.

"I won't forget this," Stephen shouted. "You're all dead men walking."

John stood up gingerly and tested himself for broken bones. His eyes were badly swollen and he couldn't see too well, but at least he was safe for now.

But was he?

The big man took everyone away from the crowded strete and up a side road before stopping and turning towards John.

John stared straight into the eyes of the friendly Scotsman who he'd bumped into outside the Tower of London during his escape.

"You again. Who are you?"

"We just happened to be in the area when we saw them chase you down the lane," the Scotsman said. "We knew what they'd do to you, and we can't stand by and watch that happen. Ren Walden and his gang are bad people that you don't want chasing you."

"It didn't seem to bother you," John said. "I'm grateful to you for saving me, but why risk yourselves for a stranger like me?"

"Laddie, you don't know us, but we don't stand idly by and watch people get captured by Ren Walden. If we see it, we stop it if we can."

A heavier set boy around John's age chimed in. "It's him, isn't it? He's the one everyone's talking about."

"Aye, this is John Howard alright." The Scotsman held out his hand. "We know who you are, laddie, and we know what you're accused of. Like I told you outside the Tower, London isn't safe for you, especially now. Ren's gang will search for you everywhere, just as Asheborne's and Howard's guards are. You're a wanted man."

John lowered his head. "Are you going to hand me over?"

"No. We're wanted just as much as you are."

"Who are you?"

"I already told you before. My name is Andrew. Andrew Cullane. We're the Underlings if you've ever heard of us."

John's bruised eyes widened. "I've heard of you. You're wanted for murdering the Duke of Berkshire's brother. I've heard of you before. You're the most wanted man in London."

"Not anymore I'm not," the big Scotsman said. "It seems you are now."

"I didn't do it," John said quietly, before getting louder. "I didn't poison anyone."

"Aye, I'm not surprised. You'll be surprised to know that we didn't kill the aristocrat either. It seems we're kindred spirits. Walden set us up and blamed us when it was his boys that were guilty all along."

The heavyset boy who'd spoken earlier held out his hand. "I'm Isaac, and this here is Abraham." He pointed to a man of similar age to Andrew, probably in his early twenties. Like Andrew, he was muscular and looked like he could handle himself well.

"You won't make it out here on your own," Andrew said. "We all do better together. We don't accept many into our small group, but we think you'd do well to join us if you want to."

Blood ran down John's face and neck as he stood in silence, trying to take in what had just happened. After a long pause, he shook his head.

"I appreciate you saving me, but I don't think it's a good idea. Everyone is after me, and if they're after you as well, we'll all be hunted relentlessly. Now the gang knows what I look like I'm a danger to everyone who's with me."

"That's why we stick together, so we have a fighting chance of making it out alive."

"Thank you, but I'm better off alone." John backed away slowly. He didn't know who to trust anymore. For all he knew, this could have been a setup to make him go with them and walk straight into Margaret's trap.

"It's your choice, laddie. Be careful out there. We won't always be there to save you."

"Thank you again," John said. "I am truly grateful for your help today."

Isaac gave John a longer stare than normal, and then they were gone. John slumped to the ground, the agonies of his injuries jumping to the fore now he was alone. He lay there for a long time, hurting all over. Eventually, he got to his feet and tested himself one more time to see if anything was broken.

Every step was agony. He'd lain there so long the sun was sinking over the horizon. The church bells would soon ring, and he would find himself trapped inside the city. That was the last thing he needed right now. He moved as fast as his pain-wracked body allowed and forced himself towards Ludgate and the way out of the city.

The church bells rang out as he approached the gate.

"Please, sir, I am late home. My father will worry if I am not allowed through the gates."

The guard looked at the forlorn figure standing in front of him. He never spoke, but he must have felt sorry for him because he stopped long enough to allow the injured boy through the gates.

Relieved, John slowly made his way home, keeping away from the stretes in fear of another attack. Instead, he cut through the gardens of White Friars and New Temple Gardens, staggering through the mud with each painful step.

Eventually, he reached Milford Lane. He tried climbing over the wall, but the pain was unbearable, so he followed it down to the banks of the river and crawled around it that way. The climb up the tree sent streaks of pain through his body, making him wince in agony with each slight movement. It took an age to reach the sanctuary of his shelter, and when he did, he collapsed onto his makeshift bed and fell into a pain-filled sleep.

The sun was high in the sky when he stirred. The pain hit him like a hammer blow, forcing him to lie back down again. He barely moved for the rest of the day, such was the pain he felt.

Finally, after several days' rest, he recovered enough to move around, albeit with painful reminders of his beating. He would have to be more careful from now on. He was lucky they hadn't killed him. His body was a mass of black and blue, and he was sure his face was the same. He struggled to eat and drink because his jaw hurt so much and he vowed he would lose the aristocratic accent as soon as he could talk without discomfort.

Thoughts of the Underlings filled his mind.

Was I right to turn them down? Were they really saving me, or were they setting a trap for Margaret?

If they had been, they'd let him go too easily. John realised he had made a mistake. In his haste to get away, he had turned away the only people that could help him survive the dangerous stretes of London.

No. I want to go to the Steelyard. That's where I'll be the safest.

He kept telling himself that every time a doubt popped into his mind, which was every few seconds.

After a few more days' recovery, John found himself in the Shambles buying meat. He'd thanked himself a million times for only taking a few coins each time he went out. If he hadn't, he would be in serious trouble. Luckily for him, Sarah had given him several changes of clothing, including a few different cloaks. He hid his battered face deep into the hood as he shopped.

He made a point of listening to how the local boys spoke, and he practised hard to sound like them. The biggest single danger to his safety right now was the way he talked, and John was determined to do something about it.

Back at the treehouse, he was practising his accent when he heard a sound beneath the tree. Kicking himself once again for not paying attention, he peered over the edge. He froze when he saw his father and two guards. They were talking and pointing to the gardens around the tree.

Do they know I'm here? Have I left footprints giving away my hideout?

His heart beat loud in his chest and he held his breath, waiting for his father to find him and send him to gaol.

To his great relief, his father started turning over the soil and pointing to the vegetables. John let out a silent sigh. He certainly had to pay more attention to his surroundings or it would all end badly for him.

He vowed to be better from this moment on.

Steelyard Slams Shut

John got into a routine of spending his mornings at the Steelyard, getting to know the inhabitants and spreading his story about his family in Cologne, and his afternoons at the treehouse practising his strete accent. After a week or so, he was confident enough to try it out for real. To him at least, he sounded just like any other boy out there, and he felt much safer because of it.

Even though he had enough coin to last until the spring, he worried about it. *What if Sarah couldn't see him again? What would he do then?* He subsidised his purchases by stealing vegetables from the many gardens around London, although he took them from places farther away from his hiding place so as not to draw attention to himself.

On the way back from the Steelyard, he stopped off at the Shambles to buy himself some meat. As he waited in line, he saw a group of strete boys gathering around an older man with a big flowing beard. He gawped as the man passed out bread and pieces of meat to the hungry boys then left the line and joined the melee.

Eventually, the old man's eyes locked onto John's, and he beckoned him forward.

"You're new here. I haven't seen you before. What's your name, boy, and where are you from?"

John hesitated before answering in his best strete voice.

"My name is John, and I'm from outside London."

The man stared for several uncomfortable minutes before holding out his hand. "I'm Gamaliell Pye. Everybody knows me around here because I give food to the poor every month."

"I've heard some of the boys talking about you," John said, taking his hand. "You are very generous helping the poor the way you do."

Pye smiled. "You need to work on your accent if you want to pass as a strete boy. You sound way too educated for the stretes of London."

The blood drained from John's face.

Is he going to turn me in?

"Don't worry, son. I'm not going to say anything. But if you are who I think you are, you'd better be careful. Robert Howard has his guards looking everywhere for you and his wife has the strete gang on the prowl. Believe me, you don't want to get caught by them."

John stood rooted to the spot. For once he didn't know whether to run or whether he could trust this strange man who handed out food to the poor.

"I... I.."

"It's okay, son. You have no need to fear me. You're not the only wanted man in London I've helped. I have no love for Walden and his gang any more than you do."

"What shall I do?" John's legs were shaking, and his heart was hammering in his chest.

"You've done fine so far," Gamaliell said in a softer voice. "They haven't found you yet."

"They almost got me a week or two back. If it wasn't for a man named Andrew, a man with a horrible scar they called Stephen would have caught me."

"I heard about that," Pye said. "Like I said, you're not the only wanted man I know in London. Andrew asked me to watch out for you and tell you his offer still stands."

John felt the blood circulating again and he relaxed a little. "Thank you. You have no idea how much I needed to hear a friendly voice."

"Are you staying warm at night?" Pye asked.

John shook his head. "I should, as it's still summer, but I do get cold."

Gamaliell Pye wandered away and returned holding a thick woollen blanket. "Use this. It'll keep you warm." He also handed him a package of bread and meat that would keep him going for several days.

"Stay safe out there, John from outside London. If you need to contact Andrew, you know where to find me."

John thanked him and ran back to his hideout, humming and whistling to himself.

Not everyone in this filthy city was bad after all.

He still thought his best chance of success was to move into the Steelyard so he didn't follow up on Andrew's offer, but he felt better knowing there was a way to contact him if he needed to. He didn't yet have the trust of the Germans in the Steelyard, and until he got that he wasn't able to move there full time.

One afternoon on the way back to his treehouse, he stopped off at the West Fish Market. As he wandered around the traders, someone started shouting.

"That's him." John looked up and saw one of the strete boys pointing at him. Two guards in Lord Asheborne's colours stared straight at him.

He ran, pulling the hood of his cloak over his head to

hide his face. Even though he was running in the afternoon sunshine, the cold tentacles of fear swarmed all over his body.

He ran for the only safe place he knew – the Steelyard.

The narrow stretes closed in on him, and the inhabitants sat against the walls, staring as he bounded past them. At any minute, a foot would trip him, or a hand would come out of nowhere and grab him. Five pounds was a fortune to these people.

One guard was fast and almost caught up to him.

"Stop," he commanded breathlessly. "We know who you are."

John ran even faster. He reached the Steelyard just as the guard was reaching out for him. Luckily for John, he knew the guards on the gate well enough by now, and they allowed him to run right past. The chasing guards weren't so lucky. They were stopped and turned away.

John spent the rest of the afternoon hiding in his German town. A young man he'd befriended called Hans went to the gates to see if the coast was clear. When he returned, he shook his head at John. "At least a dozen guards are waiting for you outside the gates. You cannot leave that way."

John's heart sank when he looked for himself. Aside from the guards, he saw the unmistakable Scarface that was Stephen prowling around with several other gang members.

Powerless to prevent his capture, John sensed the end had come.

Margaret has won.

He couldn't remain in the Steelyard, but how could he escape before the curfew? He didn't want to be inside the city after dark. That was asking for trouble.

"Wait here," Hans said. He reappeared with an older, senior looking man that John hadn't seen before.

"Come with me," the man ordered, turning on his heels and striding off.

John looked at Hans and followed. The man led him into a large office that reminded him of his father's study in Broxley. The man sat behind his desk and spoke in broken English.

"The guards waiting for you outside the gates tell me you are wanted for high treason by Lord Howard."

John's shoulders dropped, and he looked at the floor. He sighed before looking up at the man's face. "I have done nothing wrong," he said in his normal, aristocratic accent, taking the man by surprise.

"They accused me of a terrible crime I did not commit and now I am paying the price by living like a thief on the stretes of London. This is the only place I'm safe because they can't get me in here."

"Yes, they can," the man said flatly. "Someone as powerful as Lord Howard can cause us no end of problems. I cannot risk the safety of my men for you. I'm sorry, but you can no longer come here."

John nodded. "I understand. My father has the ear of the king. You do not want to get on the wrong side of King Henry."

The man let out a low whistle. "So it is true. The son of Lord Howard is loose on the stretes of London. You are a wanted man and it isn't safe for you here."

Hopelessness washed over him as he realised his time was done. He stood to his full height and faced the man as any proud aristocrat would – with pride, courage, and dignity.

"I'll walk out and give myself up," he said. "I do not wish to bring any harm to your community."

He'd already decided to hand himself over to the guards. Whatever fate awaited him – and he was sure it would be painful, it was better than what the strete gang would do to him.

At least he would die on his own terms.

John turned to walk out of the door when the man bellowed at him.

"Stop."

John stopped and turned around. "Everyone knows why you're wanted, although very few of us here believe you to be guilty."

"I'm not," John said. "And one day I'll prove it."

The man nodded. "Personally, I do not believe a word that woman says, so I will give you the benefit of the doubt. If they catch you, John Howard, it will not be because of us."

This was the first time anyone had used his full name in a while, and it sounded strange. It almost didn't feel like him anymore.

"It isn't safe for you to leave via the gates. Hans will take you by barge to a destination of your choice along the Thames."

"Thank you," John said. "I didn't mean to bring trouble to the Steelyard."

"You are not to come here any longer. It is not safe for either of us."

John nodded. He had outlived his welcome.

"Give me your cloak," the man ordered.

John's eyes furrowed.

"I will exchange it for you. One of my boys who resembles you will walk out in your place. The guards will stop him but then he will be released. I will spread the word at the highest levels that they were mistaken. We have never seen John Howard."

John let out a sigh of relief. "That is too kind of you, sir," he said. "How can I thank you?"

"Just stay safe," the man said. "That is enough. And stay away from here."

Fortunately, the tide was in John's favour, so it didn't take long for the barge to sail the short distance to Bridewell Palace, which was under construction. It was just past the River Fleet on the other side of the walled city, which was perfect.

After exchanging goodbyes, John made his way along the banks of the river to his treehouse.

He had lost his safety net.

Calm Before the Storm

With enough provisions for a few days, and his longbow hidden under his cloak, John slipped out of the walled city at Mooregate. He wanted to get away from everything – the cramped stretes, the terrible smells, the crowded markets – but most of all the intense anxiety he felt every time he ventured out from his hideout high in the trees.

He walked for hours along rocky lanes and muddy fields until he couldn't walk any farther and finding a stream running alongside a cluster of trees, he laid out his meagre belongings.

At least I will be safe here.

Lying in the late afternoon sun, John felt the fatigue of the last few weeks drain away from his body. He sighed and drifted into a peaceful state that he hadn't experienced for a long time.

His eyes watered, and from out of nowhere they stung from the salt in his tears. He missed Sarah, and as his thoughts drifted to his comfy bed chamber in Broxley Hall, he missed his mother.

She would know what to do. She would save me from this nightmare.

His heart yearned to hear Sarah's voice above the breeze, and he concentrated on the image of her in his mind.

Has Margaret turned on her now? Is she safe in Broxley Hall with Father away in London all the time?

Did Margaret discover she helped him escape?

What about Willis?

An uncomfortable sensation surged through him as he thought of poor Willis being whipped for allowing him to escape.

And finally, what of Mark? Is he now fully recovered? Will he come forward and turn his mother in, and in so doing, prove John's innocence?

Judging by the word on the stretes, the hunt for John Howard was very much the main topic of conversation, so Mark couldn't have said anything yet.

The answer hit him like an arrow in the heart.

I need to find Mark and show him what his mother has done to me. I must make him see what he is doing by remaining silent. I must force him to come to his senses and tell the truth about what happened. That is the only way I will ever be free of this woman.

As darkness fell, John lay beside the gurgling stream, making plans to leave London and make his way back to Warwickshire. He would sneak into Broxley Hall during the night and confront Mark, forcing him to break his silence and tell the truth about John's innocence.

He would worry about getting out of there safely after he had Mark's signed confession.

I will bring Sarah with me to London to confront my father. Perhaps even Mark too, if his life is in danger for telling the truth. I wouldn't put anything past Margaret, not even the murder of her own son.

The longbow had always been John's favourite weapon and he enjoyed a few days by the river in his idyllic setting, practising his skills and making his plans to prove his innocence.

It was only when he was running out of food and the skies turned an ugly shade of dark grey that he packed up his belongings and headed back towards London.

Margaret's day of reckoning was coming.

He entered the city through Bishopgate and made his way through the crowded stretes with a spring in his step. His spirits didn't even drop when it started to rain. Lightly at first, before the heavens opened up and the dark clouds spilt their contents onto the drenched city below.

He turned down a narrow lane, not quite sure where he was. He still didn't know London that well, and he was in a part of it he hadn't seen before. If he kept moving south, he would either reach a strete he knew, or he'd hit the Thames. Either way, he would find his way home from there.

Movement in front of him caught his eye, and he stopped to see what it was. Two boys, both bigger than him, ran towards him, cutting off his path to the wider strete ahead. He ran past a tavern called The George Inn to a churchyard nearby but by now, two other boys had joined the chase, and John was left in no doubt as to who they were.

"He looks like it could be him," one of them shouted.

"Yea, the boss will be pleased if it's him," another agreed.

"Let's get him," the biggest of them yelled, urging them forward.

John hid behind a tombstone, glad of the dark clouds and heavy rain that obscured their view. The boys spread out and began closing in on him.

"He's in here somewhere. He hasn't run off, so we've got him."

"Come out and we'll take pity on yer," the big one shouted. "If you make us find you, we'll give you a good kicking for making us work so hard in the pouring rain."

John silently took his longbow from under his cloak and readied himself to use it. He felt remarkably calm, considering he'd never killed anything other than a deer before. Whatever happened, he wasn't going to be taken by these strete rascals.

The circle started closing in on him, and he saw no way past them. He picked up a large stone and waited until they came into full view.

One by one they appeared, walking slowly towards him, although they still couldn't have seen him, or they'd have charged by now.

John hurled the rock at the biggest boy, striking him straight between the eyes. Even through the pouring rain, John could see the blood flowing down his head before he collapsed to the ground.

The others stopped momentarily, so John took the opportunity to aim his longbow at one of the boy's legs. He struck him in the thigh, and he heard him slump to the ground, screaming in agony.

The two remaining gang members charged. They were too close for the longbow, so John grabbed the arrow like a knife and jumped out in front of them.

They stopped.

"I don't know why you're chasing me," John said in his best strete accent. "I'm not him, so leave me alone and I won't hurt you."

He disguised the trembling in his voice well, because even in all his bravado, he didn't rate his chances against the two older, larger boys.

The one in front lunged, so John sidestepped him and stabbed him in the shoulder with his arrow. He was about to step backwards when he felt a dull thud before losing his senses.

He dropped to the muddy ground, clutching his head, scrambling to get his bearings, realising he'd been hit in the head with a stone before feet and fists pummelled him from all directions.

Blood, mud and heavy rain marred his view, and his brain didn't want to respond in its fuzzy state, but somehow his hand wrapped around the stone that hit him, and he rolled over and over, trying to get away from the crazed strete rascal hellbent on killing him.

As his senses started to unscramble, he heard the boy screaming at him as he kicked and hit him.

"I don't care who you are. You hurt my boys, you're going to die for it."

Another venomous kick hit John in the jaw, loosening his teeth and forcing him to spit blood as he gasped for air. He managed to roll behind a gravestone, and as the boy ran after him, John lunged forward with his foot, kicking him in the groin. The boy bent in half and stepped backwards, giving John the chance to get to his feet and swing as hard as he could with the rock in his hand. He hit the boy in the temple, and his eyes closed the moment they connected.

The gang member with the wounded shoulder staggered forward, but he was hurt and moved slowly. John ran as fast as he could, losing his pursuer in the half-light and heavy rain, slipping in the dark mud as he ran.

After what seemed like an age, he stopped and hid behind a house wall, watching to see if he'd been followed. Satisfied that he hadn't, he began trying to find his sense of direction and his way home.

From out of nowhere, another stone crashed into his head.

John collapsed in a heap, his head bursting into a thousand pieces as he fell.

They're still out there!

Gathering what was left of his senses, he dragged himself to his feet and staggered down the muddy, rain-swept stretes, clinging to the walls for balance. Somehow, he found himself on Cheppes Syed, and from there he knew where he was.

He heard shouts behind him on the almost deserted stretes. Nobody wanted to be out in such foul weather. Shaking his head and trying to gather himself, John ran for his life knowing what would happen if they caught him.

The next thing he knew, he was in the Shambles. Without thinking, he ran to the large house near the Old Baker's Hall and staggered around to the rear and hopefully out of sight of the screaming frenzy chasing him.

He banged on the door with all the strength he had left. Leaning against the large wooden door, he fell forward onto the stone floor as it slowly opened. Gamaliell Pye stood to the side, his eyes wide open as John hit the ground unconscious.

Underlings

It was daylight when John opened his eyes and tried to move. Searing pain coursed through his body, and his head felt like it had been run over by a charging stag.

Daylight streamed through open windows, and although his eyes were swollen and badly bruised, he could see enough to make out shadows standing over him.

He moaned as panic set in and he opened his mouth to speak. The moment he did, white-hot embers of pain ripped through his jaw. He threw his hands to his face and shuddered at the overwhelming agony that invaded his every sense.

He struggled as hands reached down to touch him, peering through swollen eyes to look for the scar that would confirm his worst nightmare.

"It's okay, laddie. You're safe."

The familiar voice of the Scotsman was somehow soothing, and he let go of the tension that was wracking his battered body.

"You took a fierce beating." Another voice John recognised.

What was his name? Isaac? Yes, that's it. Isaac.

"You're lucky you got away. From what we heard, you messed those strete rascals up pretty bad," Isaac continued. "They'll be after you even more now."

"Aye," Andrew said. "If they'd caught you, you'd be wishing you were dead by now."

John tried answering, but the pain was unbearable.

"Don't try speaking," Andrew said. "Just rest for a while. From what the doctor said, you've nothing broken. You'll be up and about in no time."

John moaned again before drifting back to a happy place where nothing hurt.

A short while later – it could have been a week for all John knew – he opened his eyes once again and tensed himself for the inevitable agony that would follow.

He didn't have to wait long.

"He's awake." A female voice John didn't recognise spoke up.

Footsteps approached and hands raised him so he could sit up. John's eyes were matted and swollen, but he could make out enough to see where he was.

He was lying on the ground on a bed of straw in an otherwise empty room. The window shutters were open, allowing daylight to stream in, the warm sun soothing his aching body.

Several people stood over him. Andrew and Isaac held him up, while the girl he had heard speaking held ale to his mouth and urged him to drink.

John pushed it away.

"How long?" he croaked. It still hurt to speak, but not as much as the last time.

"You need to drink," the girl insisted, forcing the ale to his lips. John suddenly realised his throat burned and he opened his mouth just enough to allow the liquid to pass through. Although it hurt, the ale felt good, and it revived him enough to gather his senses a little more.

John made out the shapes of two more people, both boys as far as he could tell, although one of them was much bigger – about the same size as Andrew.

"Where am I?" John croaked again.

"You've taken a nasty beating and you need to rest," Andrew said. "But you need to drink as well. You've been out for almost a week off and on. We managed to get some ale down you, but not much. You've been out cold."

"A week?" John didn't recognise his own voice it was so croaky and damaged.

"You were half dead when we picked you up," the other big man said. "We didn't know if you'd make it at one point. Ren's gang did a job on you."

"From what we heard, you did a good job on them as well," Isaac said, smiling. "I always like it when they get some of their own back."

"What happened?" John asked.

"We'll explain everything once you get your strength back," Andrew said. "For now, you need a bit more rest. Don't worry, John. You're safe with us."

John looked at Andrew and opened his mouth to speak, but the young boy who'd remained silent until now spoke over him.

"We know who you are. The way you speak gives you away. You're the one they're all after, John Howard. You should be glad we found you before anyone else did or you'd be dead by now."

"That's enough, David," Andrew said sharply. "Whatever your name is, you're safe with us."

John felt himself being lowered to the floor again, and although he fought it, he fell into a deep, unconscious sleep.

Stephen stood over him, so close John could smell his rancid breath. His long scar glistened in the afternoon sun, enhanced by the maniacal sneer etched on his face.

Stephen raised his axe above John's head and held it there. "You're worth the same dead or alive. I'm going to send them your head. That'll be enough, won't it, boys?"

Laughter echoed around the room, and John shivered and tensed his aching muscles in anticipation of what was coming next.

"This will teach you not to mess with us."

"I'll show Sarah your head. She will be delighted to see you again." More laughter roared.

Margaret! Margaret is here as well?

Stephen swung the axe.

"John! John! Wake up!"

Isaac's voice burst through the mist, and John jumped up with a start.

"You were yelling and screaming in your sleep," Isaac said, still shaking John vigorously.

John shook him off, his heart pounding like a cannonball exploding inside his chest.

"I was dreaming? It felt so real."

He slumped back down and felt his neck, relieved that it was still attached to his body.

"You need to get up and walk about." It was Andrew who spoke this time.

John's mouth still hurt, but not as much as it had before. "I need to go."

He tried getting up, but dizziness clouded his mind once more. He stumbled and fell to the ground.

"Take it steady, laddie," Andrew said. "You've taken quite a beating. Get up slowly and we'll help you."

Hands grabbed him and helped him slowly to his feet. Waves of nausea rolled over him, and John wobbled from side to side as he fought to control his feet.

"Where am I? What happened?"

The young boy John didn't know passed him some ale, and John gratefully gulped it down. He then passed him some vegetables, and John fell back in pain when he bit down on them.

Andrew sat in front of John to tell him what he wanted to know.

"You were in a bad way when Pye told us he had you. He couldn't keep you there because Walden's boys had seen you run to his house. He had to get you out of there before they found you. Even a man like Pye doesn't want to get on the bad side of Ren Walden."

"Gamaliell Pye told you I was there? How does he know you?"

"It's a long story, laddie, but Pye has been good to us for a long time. He knew we'd help you, so he hid you that night and took care of you. Walden himself showed up at his door, demanding to see if you were there. Anyone who hurts his chiefs is hunted until they're found and killed. Not many dare stand up to Walden and his gang."

"Is he alright?" John asked. "I didn't mean for any harm to come to him. I just didn't know what else to do, and I knew where his house was. He'd been kind to me before and I was desperate."

"Relax, he's fine. Gamaliell Pye is a powerful man in his own right. He has friends in high places who would come down hard on Walden if he dared do anything to him. Men like Pye are out of bounds, even for a man like Ren Walden."

John sighed.

"I can call you John, can't I?"

John looked up at five knowing faces. He nodded. There wasn't any point in lying. They knew exactly who he was.

"You need to get rid of the way you talk," the other boy John still didn't know said. "As soon as you open your mouth, it's obvious who you are."

"You mean like this?" John spoke in his new 'stretespeak' as he called it.

"Yes, like that."

"So what happened next?" John asked.

"Once Pye told us what happened, we smuggled you out on a covered cart and got you out of the city. We brought you here and you've been recovering ever since."

"Are they looking for me?"

"Are you kidding?" Isaac yelled. "Every strete rascal in the city is after you. Walden has eyes and ears everywhere, and all of them are looking for you."

"So why are you helping me? If everyone's looking for me, surely this puts you in danger too?"

"We're used to it," Andrew said. "But not normally this much it has to be said. They've been after us for years and they'll never stop."

"But surely all I will do is make it worse?"

"For sure," Andrew said. "But more than anyone else, we know what you are going through. We can help you stay alive, and that's all we want to do. We've lost people, and we've seen innocent people die in our name. We stay together and we stay alive."

"Surely no innocent people are dying in my name?" John rubbed the back of his neck. "They're looking for me, right? Not anybody else."

"You really don't know?" The girl in the group spoke up. "You really don't know what all the guards and Walden's gang are doing?"

John shook his head. "All I know is that my father's guards are searching for me, and now for some reason, Lord Asheborne's guards are as well. I know Walden's after me, and I believe my stepmother paid him to find me. They've come close a few times, but so far I've managed to evade them. It seems I owe both you and Mr Pye a debt of gratitude."

"He really doesn't know." The girl looked around the room.

"I really don't know what? What are you not telling me?"

Andrew placed his hand on John's arm. "They're rounding up anyone that looks like you. If the guards catch them, they're taken to a heavily guarded house where we heard they wait for someone who's a family member to come and identify them. Once they know they have the wrong person, they toss them some coin and send them on their way."

"What about the one's Walden catches?" John felt eyes burning into him, and he shivered. He almost didn't want to hear the answer, because deep inside he already knew.

"Walden takes them to his stronghold south of the river. Everyone knows where it is, but nobody dares go near it. We're sure they're beaten and tortured before someone tells them if it's you or not. All those captured so far have either never been seen again or turned up dead. Either way, they don't get out alive."

John's head sank. "How many?"

Andrew sighed and spoke quietly. "At least thirty so far that we've heard of."

John took a deep breath, convulsing with pain. "All of this because of me? I can't allow it. I must turn myself in immediately."

He stood up on shaky legs before being forced down again by Andrew.

"That's not a good idea, laddie. Yes, you might save lives if you turn yourself in, but you say you're innocent, and yet many lives have already been lost. Walden enjoys killing. If you hand yourself in, they'll kill you and get away with the murder of all those innocent people."

"I have to stop this," John said.

"No." Andrew looked him straight in the eyes. "You need to prove your innocence and make these evil people pay for their crimes. This affects more than just you. We're hunted for crimes we didn't commit, just like you. We need to bring this to an end together."

"How?" John asked. "What can I do against all of them? I barely got away from them with my life last time."

"We prove your innocence at the same time we prove ours," Andrew said. "That is how we get justice for those killed in your name."

"I don't know," John said. "I have to stop this before anyone else is killed in my name."

"Do you think Walden will stop killing innocent people if you just hand yourself in?" The other older man said. "He enjoys killing. He'll never stop until he's dead. Giving yourself in won't change a thing. He'll take the reward and just keep on killing like nothing ever happened."

John looked at Isaac, his eyes wide in bewilderment at how anyone could be so callous and cruel.

"It's true," Isaac said. "We need to stop him."

"How?"

"That's the big question. First, we need to prove your innocence and then make them admit to their crimes, which proves our innocence as well." Andrew said. "It won't be easy, but we can do it if we stay alive long enough."

"I need to think about it," John said. "This is the first I've heard of this and I need to consider my actions."

"Fair enough," Andrew said. "You need those bruises to heal anyway. You can't go out looking like that.

Everyone knows what happened, and it'll be obvious it was you as soon as they see you."

"Where are we, anyway?" John asked. "If I'm staying here, I need to know where I am."

"We're at our home," Andrew said.

"Which is where, exactly?"

"We call it the Old Mill," Isaac said. "It's outside the city walls, right by the river in case we ever need to get away fast."

"Where is it?" John asked.

"We're in the grounds of White Friars at an Old Mill that isn't used anymore," Andrew said. "We've been here for a while, and it fits our needs perfectly. We're safe here."

John lay down, his head buzzing with all he'd heard that day. The only thing he knew was where he was. Unbeknown to the Underlings, his treehouse was less than half a mile from the Old Mill. It was his escape route if he needed it.

He closed his eyes and considered his options. Giving himself up was probably the right thing to do, but the Underlings were correct. If innocent people were being killed in his name, they would get away with it and no doubt carry on with their criminal activities.

If he somehow managed to prove his innocence, not only would Walden and his gang swing for their crimes, but so would Margaret Colte.

Watching Margaret pay for her crimes was something worth living for.

Life as an Underling

"So," John said when his mouth felt loose enough to speak freely without it hurting too much. "Who exactly are the Underlings, and what am I joining?"

"You already know me and Isaac," Andrew said. "The big man is my best friend, Abraham. We've been friends since we were young boys. These two are David and Helena."

They all nodded at each other.

"How old are you all?"

"Abraham is as old as me, which is old enough." Andrew winked at John when he said it. "And the rest are around your age."

"I'm sixteen," John said.

"So am I, I think," Isaac said. "Truth be told, I'm not really sure. I had a bad home and ran away when I was young. I've lived on the streets ever since. Andrew found me in a rough state, and I've been with him ever since."

"How long?"

"I dunno. Years."

John looked at Helena. "What about you?"

"Andrew found me hiding from Walden before he could send me to the brothels about half a year ago after my father died. I'm sixteen. My mother died having me, so I never knew her."

John shook his head. "Walden would do that to you?"

Andrew laughed. "You have no idea who you are up against, do you? Walden is the worst man I've ever known, and I've known a few in my time."

John looked at David.

"I was a runner for Walden for years until I ran away and Andrew saved me. I don't know how old I am, but Andrew thinks I'm around thirteen, so I'm thirteen."

"What's a runner?"

David looked at Andrew, who nodded for him to continue.

"Walden's got lots of young boys who run for him. Carrying stuff from the docks to traders who buy it from him. We never took any coin, he had his chief's for that. We ran stuff back and forwards, including messages when the boss writes them down."

"What messages?" John was interested.

"I dunno. I can't read. None of us can. That's why he used us, because we can't tell on him."

"Who does he send his notes to?"

"Rich folks normally. We'd go in their big houses at the back and give 'em to someone who was waiting for us."

"Did you ever go to any big houses along the Stronde?" John was fascinated now. This was probably how Walden communicated with Margaret.

David's eyes glazed for a few seconds before he answered. "Nah, not that I can remember. I've been with Andrew for over two years though, and there were loads of us."

John nodded. "That's probably how my stepmother

communicates with Walden. I'd love to find out which ones are running for him. Where do the boys live?"

"All over the place. We'd go to the docks every morning and we do as we're told from there."

John grinned. "We have a starting point at least. So what do the Underlings do? You still haven't told me."

"We break into rich houses when they're away and take whatever we can find to sell for food," Andrew answered. "We work when we can and steal when we can't. Mostly though, we keep out of the way so they don't hang us."

The bruises were almost healed by the time John ventured out again. He made sure to cover his head with his cloak's hood, and for a while at least, he never went out alone.

The first place he went to was to the Shambles to see Gamaliell Pye. Isaac, who was fast becoming a good friend, went with him. They found Pye at his meat market, ordering his workers around.

"Mr Pye," John hissed through his cloak.

Pye grabbed them by the arms and dragged them off to the side. "I hope you weren't followed," he said, looking around. "I've had them here every day since it happened."

"We were very careful," Isaac said. "We weren't followed."

"Good. What can I do for you?"

"I came to thank you for saving my life and to find out what happened after you found me," John said.

"After I found you?" Gamaliell Pye laughed. "You literally fell through my door onto the floor. I couldn't help but find you."

"I am very grateful, Mr Pye."

"Stop calling me Mr Pye. I have a name and I'd be glad if you used it. After you fell into my home, I cleaned you up as best I could and hid you in a place I keep for such purposes. I saw Walden's boy watching you at the door, so I knew he'd send someone along to pay me a visit. I wasn't expecting to see Walden himself though."

"What did you tell him?" John asked. "I'm sorry if I caused you any misery. I didn't know what else to do."

"No need to say sorry, boy. I've no love for Walden. You were in a terrible state, that I can tell you. Walden was mad. He threatened me to hand you over, but his threats don't frighten me. I have friends too, and he backed off when I reminded him who they were."

"What did you tell him?" John asked.

"I told him his boys had the wrong one. I told him the one they'd beaten half to death was a local I'd known for years called Thomas. When he demanded to know where he lived, I told him I'd never known that. I told him I'd patched him up and sent him on his way."

"Did he believe you?"

Pye shrugged his shoulders. "Who knows? All that mattered is that he didn't find you. I knew he'd be watching me closely, so at first light, I found Andrew and arranged for a cart to get you out. You're much safer with him than you are with me."

"Thank you for your help, Mr Pye."

"Gamaliell."

"Sorry. Thank you for your help, Gamaliell."

"Is there anything else I can help you with?" Pye asked.

"Not right now," John said. "I just wanted to thank you for saving me."

"Be careful out there," Pye said to them both. "Walden has eyes and ears everywhere. Both Howard and Asheborne have guards posted all over the city looking for you. You'd best lie low until all this blows over."

"I need to prove my innocence, but I thank you for your concern," John said.

"If I hear anything I'll let you know," Pye said, pressing his hand into John's. When he looked down, there was a bagful of coins in his hands.

"You'll need that," Pye said, turning away and striding back to his workers, shouting at them all the way.

On the way back to the Old Mill, they stopped at the West Fish Market to buy some fish for the Underlings from the money Pye had given them. On the way down Old Fysshestrete, Isaac suddenly froze.

"Behind us," he said. "Six of them. They've been following us ever since we got the fish."

John looked behind him at the boys following them and kicked himself for not noticing earlier. They quickened their pace and made a right up Do Little Lane. The boys behind started running.

"Quick," John said. "We've got to get out of here."

"Hey, you. Stop." The yell came from behind them as they ran around the side of St Paul's and down Mayden Lane, hoping the crowds would hide them. John looked behind and saw them gaining ground.

Taking a sharp right down Bred Strete, Isaac pulled John into a large building on his left side. John knew it was Gerard's Hall, but he hadn't been inside it before. They raced inside, slammed the door shut, and then hid behind the window frames and watched as the six rascals searched for them.

One of them tried the door to Gerard's Hall.

"Quick," Isaac hissed.

They ran into a room at the rear of the hall, and John closed the door behind him. The gang members were now inside, shouting and screaming. Isaac opened the window and motioned for John to follow him through it to the grounds of Holy Trinity the Less churchyard.

Isaac silently closed the window behind them as John

led the way and they hid behind one of the bigger tombs at the rear of the graveyard.

The six gang members burst out from the rear of Gerard's Hall. John cast a worried glance at Isaac, knowing they were in serious trouble.

"Get away, Isaac. It's me they're after," John whispered to his friend.

"No way," Isaac replied. "We've got to get out of here."

John looked at the name of the tomb they were hiding behind.

Whittington.

How stupid of me. How's this going to help?

Frantically, he pushed on the top of the large stone slab while they were still out of sight of the gang. It moved slowly at first, and then faster as John pushed for all he was worth. He looked down into a large, uninviting black hole.

His eyes adjusted, and he saw a set of rough-hewn steps leading down into the abyss. He nudged Isaac, who was watching for the boys, and gestured down into the tomb. Without a moment's hesitation, Isaac leapt inside and made his way down the steps and John followed, closing the heavy slab behind him. Now it was completely dark.

"They've got to be 'ere somewhere." John could hear them talking and crashing around the graveyard.

"Where are they?" one of them yelled. John could hear the anger and frustration in his voice.

"They must 'ave sneaked off down Garlyk Hill," another of them said. "They didn't go the other way, or we'd 'ave seen 'em."

"Let's go," another one said. "He's not getting away this time."

"We don't even know if it was him or not."

"We will when we catch him."

John and Isaac waited inside the tomb for a long time without moving or speaking. They had to be sure the gang wasn't waiting for them.

"I'm still not sure they're gone," John whispered. "What's down there, I wonder?"

"I don't really want to find out," Isaac replied. "At least not without a candle."

"Me neither, but it might lead somewhere. It's better than walking straight back into them."

John pushed past Isaac on the narrow staircase. "Let's see if it goes somewhere," he said.

He led the way in the pitch darkness, taking care to step slowly so as not to fall. Isaac clung to his cloak behind him. They walked, hands against the sides of the narrow tunnel, for what seemed like an eternity until John's feet hit something hard. He fell forward, reaching out with his hands to break his fall. He groped around in the dark, his hands feeling the rough edges of whatever had stopped his fall.

"Steps," he whispered to Isaac. "We've reached the end."

One by one, they climbed the steps until they got to the top and John's fingers touched a cold slab of stone over his head.

"It's a tombstone, just like the other one."

It was heavy, so Isaac helped him. Once it began moving, light streamed down into the darkness, blinding the two boys. Once they readjusted, John opened the gap wide enough for them to climb out into the open air.

"Look," Isaac said, pointing to a large building across the strete facing them. "That's the Star Inn. We're on Watelyng Strete. This must be St Mary Aldermary church."

John realised he was right as he found his bearings.

"That was amazing," he said. "There must be secret tunnels everywhere. I wish we knew more of them."

"That's one to remember," Isaac said. "It just saved our lives."

"Let's get out of here," John said. "I've had enough excitement for one day. I don't want to see those rascals waiting for us somewhere."

"It's getting late," Isaac said. "See?" He pointed to the pale setting sun casting shadows as it sank behind the buildings. "I hope we can get through the gates in time. I don't fancy staying inside the walls tonight after they call curfew, especially after what happened today."

Darkness fell as they approached Ludgate, their gate of choice to exit the city. The sounding of the curfew bell pierced the fading light, signalling that the gates were about to close and they hurried through just in time.

Secret Tunnels

"I have to go back to Warwickshire and show Mark what his mother's actions have done to me." John laid out his plans to the Underlings. "If I can convince him to help me, I can prove my innocence and put an end to all of this."

"You'd never get away with it," Andrew said. "Surely your stepmother would have the house under heavy guard?"

"The last place she would ever expect me to break into would be Broxley Hall. She probably thinks I'm cowering in a dark cave somewhere in London. It's risky, but it's my only chance of ever getting out of this."

"What will you do once you get there?" Isaac asked. "If Mark was going to tell the truth, surely he'd have done it by now?"

"I have to show him what Margaret has done to us. Not only what she's done to me, but also to him and Sarah. She's poisoned him twice now – and that's from his own account, not mine. Who knows how many other lives she's ruined besides ours? If I have to drag him out of there, I will. He must tell the truth."

"Where will you take him? Is anywhere safe from the Howard family?" Abraham spoke for the first time. "With all due respect, John, your family is one of the most powerful in England. Your father and stepmother will crush anyone who gets in their way."

"True," John replied. "But for some reason my uncle Thomas doesn't like Margaret. If I can get Mark to Norfolk, he will guarantee his safety and do what's right for our family, even if it means bringing down my father."

"Norfolk?" Andrew almost shouted. "The Duke of Norfolk is your uncle? I don't know whether we should bow to you or throw you out. We've never seen anyone as important as you, never mind lived with them as an equal."

John pondered for a moment. He'd never thought of common people as his equals before, not even after his recent change in status. It felt alien to him.

He forced his feelings aside.

"Please," he said. "You saved my life. Not once, but twice now. Once I regain my former status, I shall not forsake you. I will get to the bottom of the Duke of Berkshire's murder and prove your innocence. Then I shall reward you handsomely for helping me. Your kindness will not be forgotten."

"How will you prove we didn't kill the duke's brother?" Helena asked. "Everyone thinks we did it, and every aristocrat in England wants us dead. It's our word against Walden's and he has the ear of aristocrats like your stepmother."

"Not every aristocrat." John corrected her. "I believe you, and I shall make my uncle believe you as well. He will petition the king himself if he has to but you shall be pardoned."

"If we're going all the way to Warwickshire, we need

provisions," Andrew said. "Let's go to the markets tomorrow and get whatever we can. John, do you have enough coin to get us to Broxley? We'll need coin for barges and carriages if we're to get there before we're old and grey."

John stared at Andrew for a long time before shifting his gaze around the other Underlings.

"I didn't mean for you to come with me," he said. "I was merely laying out my plans and explaining why I can't stay with you. It's far too dangerous for you to travel to Broxley. If you're captured, I won't be able to help you. If my father captures you, I guarantee that you will be hung, drawn and quartered. I can't allow that to happen. I must go alone."

"What say you?" Andrew looked around at his fellow Underlings. "Do we risk everything by helping John, and by so doing, help ourselves? I say that if we don't, we'll be forced to live like this for the rest of our miserable lives."

"Aye," Isaac said. "Even if we weren't hunted like vermin, I'd be going anyway. That's what friends are for."

John squeezed his friend's arm. He had never known kinship like this, and Isaac was the best friend he'd ever had. It was strange how he felt closer to the common people than he did to his own kind.

"I'm going," David said. "After what Walden's done to us, I'd love to watch him swing at Tyburn."

Helena nodded. "Don't think for a minute you're leaving me out. I want Walden dead just as much as anyone. If saving John gets that, then I'm in."

Abraham was the last to speak. He watched John intently as he spoke. "Are you sure you can break into your house and get to Mark and your sister? What happens if you're caught?"

"Then we all die," John said firmly, returning the

intense stare. "I know many secret ways in and out of Broxley. What happens once I'm inside, God himself only knows. But if I don't try, Margaret and Walden will win and we'll never prove our innocence. I can't allow anyone else to die because of me. If I fail, at least Margaret will stop Walden from killing boys whose only crime is that they look like me."

"It's settled then." Andrew stood up. "We leave in three days."

At dawn the next morning, John hung back when the rest of them were ready to leave.

"What's wrong?" Isaac asked.

"I have to go and get the coin I've hidden. It's in a special place at my old house on the Stronde."

"Are you ready?" Andrew asked, oblivious to the conversation going on out of earshot.

"John has to get the coin he's hidden at his old house," Isaac said.

"How much do you have?" Helena asked.

"Enough to get us to Broxley and then to Norfolk," John replied.

David shook his head. "I hate rich people."

"But I like you," he quickly added.

John smiled. "I'll meet you in the Shambles. I shouldn't be long."

"I'll come with you," Isaac said, looking at Andrew for confirmation. "It isn't safe for you to be out alone."

Andrew nodded. "Okay, be quick and we'll see you in the Shambles."

"So where is this place?" Isaac asked as he and John trudged through the muddy grounds of the New Temple Gardens.

"Not far," John said.

They rounded the wall at the end of Milford Lane,

where it joined the banks of the River Thames, and John gestured for them to lie down and survey the scene. The sun hadn't yet risen fully, but there was enough light to see where they were going.

Making sure the coast was clear, John led Isaac along the wall until he was level with the row of trees that hid his safe house.

"See that big tree over there?" He pointed to the tallest tree. "That's where my stuff is hidden. If we ever get separated, climb that tree and wait for me up there. Be careful though, because my father has guards patrolling all over here."

Isaac nodded. "That's a great hiding place. I wish we had something like that."

"We do now, although it won't hold all of us. Stay here and keep a lookout. If you see anything, jump over the wall and stay hidden. I'll be right back."

John quickly climbed his tree and gathered what was left of his coin. With one last look around his safe place, he hoped he was doing the right thing.

I can't keep living like this. Whatever happens, it can't be any worse than this.

With one last sigh, John slid back down the tree and made his way back to Isaac, who was waiting on the other side of Milford Lane.

"I saw some of your father's guards, so I jumped over the wall. John, your home is enormous!"

"This is just our London home. Wait until you see Broxley."

"I can't imagine," Isaac said. "Oh, to be so lucky to be born into aristocracy."

"It didn't work out too well for me, did it?" John said. "Come on, let's go."

Isaac followed John past the Old Mill and through

White Friars towards Fletestrete. Once there, they walked along the road to cross the River Fleet at the Fleet Bridge but there were too many guards on the bridge, so they turned up Showe Lane and went to the much busier Holbourne Strete, where they crossed the river with no issues.

From there, they entered the city at Newgate and walked past the gaol. John always shuddered when he went this way. He tried to imagine what it would be like if the guards caught him and held him there until Margaret had him hanged.

The Shambles were close by, and John and Isaac rejoined the rest of the group at Gamaliell Pye's meat stalls where they found Pye busy talking to Andrew and he beckoned for John to join them.

"There'll be a covered carriage waiting for you outside Cripplegate at dawn the day after tomorrow. That will take you as far as Cambridge. When you get there, Andrew has a letter from me that will guarantee your passage to Coventry. From there you are on your own. It's a long way around, but it's the best I can do on such short notice."

"Once again, you have come to my rescue. How can I ever repay you, Gamaliell Pye?"

"You will repay me if you rid the stretes of Walden and his gang," Pye said. "That's enough for me."

"Thank you. I shall not forget your kindness."

"Now go, before you are seen and we're all sent to the Tower."

They always took different routes back home in case they were followed, and this time they went down the narrow Lambert's Hill. John shuddered as they entered the foreboding, stinking strete. It was as if the sunlight itself was afraid to enter these tightly packed stretes.

Visions of the last time he was in a strete just like this

made John lengthen his stride, eager to reach the sunlight again on the bigger, more open stretes ahead.

Ludgate was swarming with Robert Howard's guards, who were looking closely at everyone entering or leaving the city, so once again they changed direction and tried Newgate.

As the Underlings shuffled through one by one, John and Isaac were the only ones left to cross. John was almost through when a shout went up.

"Hey, you! Stop!"

John looked at who was shouting and his heart almost stopped. It was one of his father's closest guards. He'd been with his family for years and knew John very well.

"Have a good look at him." The guard jumped off the wooden rail he was sitting on and moved towards John.

"Run!" John shouted at Isaac, and they bolted back inside the walled city. Andrew and the other Underlings could do nothing other than watch them and hope they got away.

The guards chased John and Isaac down to St Paul's, shouting at them the whole way. Hands reached out to grab them, but swerving and diving allowed the boys to evade them.

They finally made it to Black Friars with the huge area of land surrounding the church and the cluster of buildings where John and Isaac hid in the gardens behind the library, watching the guards and those who joined in hunting for them.

It was only a matter of time before they were caught.

John looked over at Isaac. His eyes had a dull glaze to them, and he looked like he'd given up.

"They haven't got us yet," John whispered. "Come on, there's a covered bridge over the Fleet near the smithy. We might be able to sneak over that."

"No chance," Isaac whispered back. "The bridge may be covered, but it's got guards all over it. We've tried before, but we could never get over it."

"Well, we can't stay here," John said. "If we're going to get caught, at least let's get caught trying to get away."

Before he moved, Isaac grabbed John's arm. "Promise me something, John. I mean it."

"What? We don't have time for this right now."

"I mean it. Promise me that you'll do as I say."

"Tell me what you want first." John looked impatiently at Isaac. "Come on, we've got to get out of here."

"If they catch us, you've got to promise me you won't give yourself up, no matter what they do to me or anyone else. Do you hear? You're the only hope any of us have of ever living free again."

"I can't promise you that."

"In that case, I'm not going with you. I'm giving myself up now and I'll tell them I'm John Howard."

Isaac started to stand up, but John grabbed him. "Don't be stupid. You know what they'll do to you."

"Promise me then."

"I can't."

"Then I'm going."

Isaac moved more forcefully this time.

"Okay, I promise." John's eyes darkened. "But for the love of God, let's not get caught."

They ran to the covered bridge, but the guards were not far behind them. They would be spotted at any moment.

Guards patrolled the entrance to the bridge, so that was a nonstarter. John looked for a way to escape, but their pursuers were closing in.

They shrank back towards the old Roman wall and

squeezed inside a big old bush that must have been there for decades.

"We can wait here until after dark," John said. "At least they can't see us in here."

John stumbled and fell backwards as they forced their way into the middle of the bush. Reaching for the thick branches, he was shocked when he fell onto rocks.

He was right up against the wall of the city itself and as he looked around in the half-light he noticed a gaping black hole behind him.

"Isaac." He prodded Isaac, who was concentrating on the approaching guards. "Isaac, look. There's some kind of hole in the wall."

Isaac shuffled back towards John, and they both peered into a dark opening in the wall big enough for one person at a time to enter.

Without uttering a word, John stepped into the hole and stepped right inside the old Roman wall surrounding the city of London. Grabbing the walls, he groped around for a foothold. He reached a small wooden platform and slid into a small crawlspace. Above him, he could hear the footsteps of the guards walking along the bridge.

We're under the covered bridge!

On the other side, another wooden platform, and then small amounts of daylight as he emerged into the middle of another bush.

The passage they had just crawled through was a tunnel inside the Roman wall itself, leading to a secret escape route under the covered bridge!

John was speechless.

He prised open the bush and saw that he was in the construction site of what would one day be Bridewell Palace. From there it was an easy walk to the Old Mill and the safety of their home.

Isaac looked at John in disbelief. "This is a game changer. We'll never be trapped inside the city ever again."

"The monks must have built it as an escape route when Henry started sacking the monasteries," John said. "This must have been their way out."

"I can't wait to tell the others," Isaac said. "Come on, let's get out of here."

Plans

"Thank the good Lord you made it," Andrew said when John and Isaac walked into the Old Mill. "We thought they'd got yea."

"They almost did," John said. "If it wasn't—"

"You won't believe what we found!" Isaac shouted over John's voice.

Everyone looked quizzically at Isaac.

"The guards were right on us, and we thought that was it. We hid in a bush near the old Roman wall. I still can't believe it. We found a secret passage through the wall! We never have to use the city gates again. That's how we escaped."

"You found a way through the wall?" Abraham exclaimed. "I've heard stories of secret passages through the wall all my life, but I've never found one."

"We have now," Isaac said. He was bouncing from foot to foot, so John nudged him.

"Calm down, Isaac," John said. "We were lucky because the guards were closing in. The one that shouted for me to stop knows me. He's worked for my father for as long as I can remember. Now that he's seen me, my father will double and triple the guards on the city gates and bridges. It's a good thing we found the secret passage when we did."

"Where is it?" David asked.

"It goes through the wall and under the covered bridge at Black Friars," Isaac said. He was still bouncing around the room.

"This might give us an advantage," John said, thinking out loud.

"What do you mean?" Helena asked. "How can being seen by someone who knows you be an advantage? Your father will flood the stretes with guards now that he knows for sure you're here."

"Not to mention Walden is still out there as well," David added.

"Yes," John said. "But they'll all be looking for me in London. We'll be far away in Warwickshire, which is the last place they'll expect me to be."

Andrew wagged his finger at John. "The boy's got a good point. They'll all be searching for him – and us – here. We'll be safer up there than we are here."

"And we can come and go in and out of the city without being seen. The gates and bridges always made me shiver." Helena clapped her hands. "This crazy idea might just work."

"Okay, here's the plan," Andrew said. "We'll leave here before dawn and use the secret passage you just found to get into the city. Once we're inside the wall, we'll break up into smaller groups like we often do. I'll go with Helena, Abraham will go with David, and you two stay together. We'll meet outside the Almshouses near Cripplegate."

"Can't we just stay outside the walls and meet outside

Cripplegate?" David asked. "That way we wouldn't have to go through the city at all. It'd be safer."

"Not unless you want to swim across the Fleet," Andrew replied. "I know I don't want to be anywhere near that nasty water. Who knows what terrible disease we'd die of if we swam through that."

"I never thought of that," David said. "I'd rather be caught by Walden."

"What do we do when we get to Coventry?" Andrew turned his attentions to John. "Once we get there, you'll be in charge."

"We'll have to get some horses, but I have the coin for that," John said. "Once we get to Broxley, we'll wait in the woods until it's dark. I'll go alone because I know where I'm going and it'll be safer."

"What about Mark?" Andrew asked.

"I'll either get him to come with us to Norwich under promise of protection from Uncle Thomas, or I'll force him to write a letter explaining what happened. If he comes with us, I'll bring Sarah as well because it won't be safe for her to be alone with Margaret."

"What if he writes the letter?"

"Then I'll still bring her because it won't be safe for her when Margaret finds out what I've done."

"What next?" Abraham asked.

"We go to Norfolk and hand over the evidence to Uncle Thomas. He'll know what to do."

"Are you sure we'll be safe with your uncle?" Isaac asked. "How do you know he'll protect us? We're not rich like you and he might hand us over to Asheborne."

"No, he won't." John shook his head. "We're going to stop Walden as well as Margaret. Once everyone hears what he's done to those poor boys that look like me, the gang will be arrested and hanged. One of them will tell the truth about you in exchange for their lives. Just not Walden or the Scar faced one they call Stephen. They have to die."

Andrew shrugged his shoulders. "Maybe Stephen will be the one who comes clean about us to spare his own life. If he does, he'll be allowed to live."

"We'll worry about that when the time comes," John said. "There's a lot that can go wrong between now and then. Is everyone clear about what we're going to do?"

Nods and grunts confirmed they were.

"Good. Let's hope the good Lord favours us in our quest for innocence." John clasped his hands together and prayed.

Hard.

Capture

John pushed back the bushes pressing against the old Roman wall on the city side of the River Fleet. Even from this distance, the stench from the rancid water made him want to vomit.

He squinted in the pre-dawn shadows, listening for any signs of human activity. Satisfied they were alone, he pushed his way out into the open to make way for the rest of the Underlings to follow.

"Right," Andrew said. "It'll be light soon enough, so let's split up and meet where we agreed. In the case one of the group doesn't make it, we call it off and try again another day. Good luck to you all, and I wish you a safe journey."

John and Isaac waited until everyone else had gone before making their way out of Black Friars towards St Paul's. It was daylight by the time they reached it, and John jumped back in surprise when the bells suddenly rang out, signalling the end of curfew.

As they headed towards Cheppes Syed, a large group

of people were already starting to gather around St Paul's Cross where the town cryer normally gave his speeches.

"Let's listen to what he's got to say," Isaac said.

"We don't have time." John shook his head. "In any case, if everyone is coming here, it gives us more chance to get away without being seen."

"True," Isaac said. But he slowed down and cocked his head just the same.

"Oh yeah, oh yeah, oh yeah," the cryer began, but John couldn't hear what he was shouting because he was too far away. He was sure he heard the name John Howard being yelled out, and it forced him further into his hooded cloak.

Margaret never gives up, does she?

They hurried away from the gathering towards the meeting place at the Almshouses close to Cripplegate. Although John had got used to the stink that accompanied his every footstep in the city of London, every now and then a smell so vile would come out of nowhere and invade his senses, almost knocking him out with the overwhelming feeling of nausea.

This was one such time, and John fell to his knees, struggling for breath. He didn't know what it was, but it made his stomach relieve itself of last evening's dinner, and his head was swimming like a drunken man staggering home after a heavy night's drinking.

When he came to, Isaac was stood over him, pulling at his cloak.

"Come on, John. We can't stay here."

John followed his gaze and saw a group of at least seven or eight boys walking towards them, staring at them as they approached.

"Are they Walden's rascals?" he asked, jumping back to his feet.

"I think so. Let's get out of here."

"Damn. We're almost there as well." John could see the Almshouses from where they stood.

The narrow stretes were now bustling with people going about their daily lives, and this made it difficult to run with any speed. The only consolation was their pursuers were having the same problems.

They turned onto a wider lane that wasn't as busy and started running faster. The short lane branched off in several directions at the end, and John was hoping they'd lose them in the confusion.

To his horror, some of the boys were standing at the well where the stretes branched off. They were staring right at John and Isaac.

"They must have split up and run over the fields to cut us off," John panted, trying to catch his breath. "Come on."

He led the way through the field and crossed Aldermanbury trying to get to the Guildhall, which was said to have been built on the old Roman Amphitheatre. The church of St Lawrence was next to it, and if they could get in there, the boys wouldn't dare to approach them inside. Even the Strete Masters didn't violate the sacred churches.

If they could make it in time.

The boys from the well cut them off again and John and Isaac had no choice other than to run for Bassett's Inn and hope the drunken rabble inside would take pity on them.

They never reached it.

Isaac stumbled on a tree root and fell to the ground and John could hear him hyperventilating on his knees.

John squeezed his eyes shut, trying to stop his heart from bouncing out of his chest.

"Run, John. Get out of here," Isaac yelled.

But John would never leave his friend. He stopped to

face their pursuers, shuddering when he saw the scar glistening on the side of Stephen's face. He clenched and unclenched his fists, trying to stop his body from shaking.

"What do you want?"

Some of them started laughing as John took a fighting stance against them.

"Got ya," Stephen said. "Ren's gonna be happy."

"What do you want with us?"

Stephen smiled. "We know who you are. Get 'em, lads."

John counted eight, which was far too many to either outrun or outfight and caught Isaac's worried glance as he looked for something he could use as a weapon.

The gang members whooped and hollered like they were in some kind of bard's play and John's stomach heaved, but he wouldn't allow his adversaries to see his fear. The boys walked towards them slowly, which John knew was a fear tactic, but he held his ground.

He bent down and picked up a palm-sized rock. As the boys advanced, he threw it at Stephen, catching him on the side of the head. The boy fell to the ground in a heap, blood spurting out of the large wound on his face.

The rest of them charged and piled upon him. Unseen, a man who had been watching approached the fight scene. Isaac was at the rear of all the action, although he was picking up rocks to join the fight.

The man grabbed Isaac from behind and yanked him away, picking him up with remarkable speed and strength before dragging him back towards the inn. Isaac kicked and fought, but he was too strong. The man dragged him behind Bassett Inn, out of sight of the boys with Isaac still fighting as hard as he could.

"Calm down, Isaac. It's me, Andrew."

That was the last John heard or saw of Isaac. He fell

under the weight of the heavy blows being rained down upon him. Fists and feet crashed into him, turning his world dark and hazy. Mud and horse turd filled his mouth, and he tried turning his head sideways to stop from choking to death.

Angry voices screamed at him, and another heavy blow thudded into his head. Blood flowed down his face, and he was in serious trouble. The last thing he remembered before passing out was hoping Andrew had dragged Isaac to safety. They could live to fight another day and somehow come to his rescue.

He felt himself being dragged and carried and tried seeing where he was, but all he saw were legs and arms. People on the stretes watched them dragging him, but not one of them tried to intervene and save him.

He opened his mouth to shout for help, but gargled noises replaced his words. His mouth was so swollen he could barely breathe, and he choked on the blood running down the back of his throat.

He noticed the great river on either side of him and it took his scrambled senses a few seconds to realise what was going on. He was being carried over the London Bridge!

Oh no.

If that rock allowed Isaac to escape, I will accept any punishment, even if it means my death.

Will I ever see Sarah again?

He doubted it. Very few ventured to the south side, especially after dark. Unless you lived there, only drunkards, gamblers, and desperate people ventured over to the south side of the river.

St Mary Overy Priory and a few churches dotted the landscape, along with St Thomas's hospital. The monks of the priory operated the hospital, and it offered free health care to those souls brave enough to cross the river.

I might need their help if I can ever escape.

John saw the signs for Winchester Palace, which was the home of the Bishop of Winchester then made out a sign for Maiden Lane before being dragged into one of the brewhouses. He knew from gossip that this area was notorious for brothels and illegal activities of all kinds. It was, as one person described to him, 'a den of iniquity'.

After what seemed like hours, the boys dumped him onto the floor. His eyes would barely open, such was the beating he'd received. He tried looking around, but couldn't see anything.

"Boss, this kid bashed Stephen's face in with a stone. We 'ad to rough 'im up a bit so we could get 'im 'ere."

"Kid, meet your new master, Ren Walden. He's the greatest Strete Master who ever lived. He'll whip you into shape in no time."

Laughter broke out when whoever was speaking said the words 'whipped into shape'. Like everyone else in the room, he knew exactly what they meant.

"Have we got a name?" The voice sounded harsh. This must be the one they called Ren, the most feared Strete Master in London. He shivered on the floor.

"Not that we know of, boss. We didn't have time to ask him after he hit us wiv rocks."

John felt rough hands grab his jaw. The pain seared through him like a hot knife, but he didn't make a sound. He would not give them the satisfaction of knowing he was in pain.

The man yanked his face up and John could smell his rancid breath as he put his face close to his.

"I know who you are, boy. We've been looking for you ever since you ran away from your father. If you tell me your name, I'll treat you nice. But if you lie to me…"

John heard several sharp intakes of breath before a collective "ooh, you don't wanna do that."

"If you lie to me," the man continued, "you will regret the day you were born. And that's a promise."

John felt the threat and shivered again. He tried to see what Ren looked like, but his eyes wouldn't open far enough and he lowered his head in pain and submission.

"My name is Ren Walden. You can call me boss. From now on I am your king, your lord and your master. I have complete control over your miserable life."

The man kicked John in the ribs, sending shards of white-hot pain through his already battered body.

"Take him away," the man said in German. "Don't hurt him anymore. He needs time to recover."

John felt himself being dragged down some stairs before being thrown to the ground. He heard a door slam shut and a key turning in a lock.

He was alone.

Walden

John had a restless, painful night on the icy floor of his new prison. He tried moving, but sharp pains coursed through his body every time he tried. He wanted to see where he was, but his swollen and matted eyes wouldn't open. Every tiny movement sent red-hot flashes of pain in every direction, so he just lay there, trying to control the agony.

How many more beatings can I take? Every time I try to do something, I end up like this. I'm going to die before they even find out who I am.

He thought of the best things in his life, like Sarah and the treehouse, and he remembered how his mother used to comfort him whenever he hurt himself. How he wished she was with him now in this cold, empty cell.

Then he thought of Margaret and what she'd done to him and his family. Anger welled above the pain.

She has to pay for what she's done. I have to survive this.

He sighed, and the movement in his chest made him convulse and curl up in a ball.

Isaac! Where's Isaac?

Then he remembered vaguely seeing Andrew from the

corner of his eye, grabbing Isaac and dragging him away. Everything had happened so fast, and after all he'd been through, he wasn't sure what was real and what was a nightmare anymore.

But he was sure Isaac getting away was real and knew the others would try to rescue him once they got back to the Old Mill and had a chance to work out what to do.

His thoughts turned inward to his own predicament. *What will Walden do to me? What will he say to me? Does he know it was me who battered his boys a few weeks ago?*

He struggled to control the shaking in his legs, feeling cold and clammy from the sweat that was building inside his shabby clothing. He knew he was in for a whole world of hurt.

Is Margaret already here, ready to identify me? What then?

He already knew he wouldn't survive once Margaret saw him. Walden would kill him and make his body disappear.

I can't let that happen. Whatever I face, I will escape this evil, nasty man. This will not be my ultimate destiny.

This silent vow gave John renewed inner courage and strength. He decided there and then, broken and beaten on the icy floor, that Ren Walden would not defeat him.

The key turning in the lock brought him back to earth. He tried opening his eyes to see who it was, but all he saw were hazy shadows dancing in the pale light of the room.

"Here's some food and water," a boy's voice he didn't recognise said. "You've got to get better so the lady can tell us if you're him or not."

The boy left the room and locked the door behind him. John forced a painful smile at the ridiculousness of locking the door. He wasn't even able to open his eyes, let alone run out the door.

He was thirsty, so tried grabbing the water jug. The

pain was unbearable as he sat up far enough to take in the much-needed fluid. His jaw and mouth burst into a million agonies when he tried opening his mouth to drink, but he persevered. The rancid water stank, but he needed it inside him. He was in enough trouble without adding dehydration to his long list of ailments.

Most of the water ran down his chin and onto the floor, but at least he got some inside him, which made him feel better straight away. Fatigue washed over him again, and he slumped back to the floor in a pain-induced sleep. His last thoughts were that sleep takes away the pain, albeit for only a short while.

He lay on the cold floor, glad of the solitude. His eyes were still swollen, but at least he could see out of them somewhat. The sound of a key turning brought him back to his senses.

It was time.

Hands roughly dragged him up the stairs and dropped him onto the floor of what looked like a brewhouse. A man sat at a table opposite him, gazing at him like a lion looks upon its prey. He took an immediate dislike to this man, whoever he was.

Brown hair flowed down past his collar, and he had a full beard and moustache. Cruel slate-grey eyes, that looked to John like the eyes of a mythical monster, dominated his thin features and long nose. They displayed no emotion at all, and he looked like a man who got what he wanted.

He was staring into the face of Ren Walden.

"How are we feeling today?" the man asked, clearly enjoying seeing a helpless young boy squirm in pain and discomfort.

"I've felt better," John said, making sure he spoke in his best strete accent.

"So he speaks," the man said. "You were a little bruised the last time we met, so you might not recognise me. I'm your new lord, Ren Walden. You can call me boss."

John was silent. One of the boys who'd dragged him up the stairs kicked him hard in the stomach, sending him into spasms of agony as his already bruised body quivered in pain.

"He said you can call him boss." He spoke with a heavy German accent.

John nodded. "Sorry, boss," he gasped. "I didn't understand you."

Ren laughed. "You'll learn quickly enough. So, boy, what's your name?"

"My name is Isaac." He'd thought better of using John.

"Isaac what?"

"Isaac Conway." He thought of a strete name he'd seen somewhere.

Another hard kick in the chest sent John spinning towards the edge of insanity.

"He said you can call him boss." The German sneered.

"Sorry, boss. My name is Isaac Conway."

"Where you from?"

"I don't know," John lied before quickly adding "boss," at the end. "My parents died when I was young, and I drifted from uncle to friend before finally living on the stretes. I've been in London for as long as I can remember."

"Who was the other boy you were with?"

"He was just someone I knew from the markets, boss. We met up sometimes, but we weren't friends."

"I know who you are." Walden leant forward, his face almost touching John's. His rancid breath made John want to back away, but he knew better. He held his ground and looked down, hoping the show of submission would spare him another kicking.

It didn't.

"The boss said he knows who you are." The German lashed out again. John didn't know how much more his battered and bruised body could take.

"I'm sorry, boss. I don't know what you mean. I already told you who I am. My name's Isaac Conway."

"You're lying," Walden said. "You're John Howard, the aristocratic lowlife who poisoned his own brother."

"I've heard of him, boss," John said. "We all have. I've never seen him, and I'm not him."

"Not to worry. The lady will be here soon, and she'll recognise you."

John shuddered. If Margaret saw him, it was all over. He'd be dead by the end of the day.

"Was it you who attacked my boys recently?"

"Me? No, boss. I don't know what you're talking about. I didn't attack anyone."

"Rolf, come and 'ave a look." Walden beckoned the German forward. "Is this the one who did it?"

Rolf yanked John's head up by the hair and glared at him for several painful moments.

"I dunno, boss. I can't tell for sure. It was raining hard, and it was dark and muddy. I didn't see his face at all. It might be him though."

John's heart sank.

Rolf's fist smashed into John's battered face, fresh blood joining the congealed blood that was already there. John fell to the floor, convinced he was about to die. He couldn't take any more.

"Hmm. Where did you live before I rescued you?" The boys sniggered again at Ren's comments. "Maybe they know where this John Howard is?"

"I lived in a warehouse near Queenhithe, boss, but I had to get away fast when they started dying of the plague."

"The plague?" Ren jumped up and backed away. "When was this?"

"A couple of days before you caught me, boss," John said. He hoped he would take fright at the mention of the plague and throw him out.

"Get him out of here," Ren ordered in German. "Lock him up by himself next to the others at The Bear and watch him for the next week. Tell me if he gets the plague."

"Yes, boss," Rolf answered in his native German.

"Make sure he's on his own." Walden repeated his order.

Once again, John noticed the use of German when they didn't want him to know what they were saying.

Is this how they communicate when they don't want anyone to know what they're saying? After all, they usually dealt with the poor strete kids, not educated aristocrats or traders. Most of them couldn't read, let alone speak another language.

Hands grabbed him, but this time John took comfort in their reluctance to touch him. At least they might leave him alone for a few days so he could recover a little more.

They dragged him out of the brewhouse and down a strete by the banks of the river. He thought about pulling away and jumping into the Thames, but he knew he wouldn't make it. His body was too weak, and the river would sweep him to his death. He would not die today for these strete rascals.

He saw a sign over the door of the brewhouse they were entering. It said, "The Bear".

At the rear of the building he saw some cages, and what he saw inside made his stomach heave. There were several bears in the cages, some with signs of obvious distress. They used them for bear fighting, and people would drink ale while betting on the outcome of the fights. John turned away. Even in all his discomfort, he couldn't stand to see such cruelty.

One cage held some boys; John couldn't make out how many but they all looked around his age. They threw him into another one next to them.

"Watch out," one of Walden's rascals shouted as he opened the door to the cage. "This one's been around the plague. Hopefully, you'll all catch it and die to save us from killing you."

Even though they were in separate cages, the boys retreated as far away from John as they could. It was obvious none of them wanted anything to do with him. For now, it was his best form of defence and as long as people thought he might carry the plague, nobody would dare go near him.

It struck him that all the boys in the cage were similar in appearance and age to himself. He counted twelve of them. Then reality dawned on him. These are the boys the Underlings were talking about! These poor souls were about to die because of him.

John turned away, tears stinging his swollen face. He gripped the bars tightly and screamed out loud.

It was the worst feeling he had ever experienced.

He remembered the promise he'd made to Isaac before they'd found the secret passage through the Roman wall. Oh, how he regretted making that promise now.

"Screaming won't help you," one boy shouted at him. He looked younger than John by a year or two. "We're all waiting here until some lady tells them we're not this John Howard. Then they'll let us go."

John squeezed his eyes tightly, trying – and failing – to stop the flow of tears from his eyes.

"Are you him?" the boy asked. John noticed his two front teeth were missing, and he felt sorry for him. He did look a lot like him though. From a distance, John imagined they would be difficult to tell apart.

He shook his head. "I was about to ask all of you the same thing. Which one of you is John Howard? The sooner they find him, the sooner we can all go home."

"Is it true you've got the plague?" another boy asked.

At the mention of the plague, everyone shrank back even farther.

"I don't know," John said. "I saw some people with it, but I ran away and didn't touch them."

"We might not even get out of this cage alive," someone else chimed in. "If I ever find this John Howard, I'll kill him myself for being a coward and making all of us suffer because he's too scared to come forward."

John choked back more tears and stayed quiet while a loud conversation erupted around him.

Crowds began to gather in the courtyard outside. As more people joined, the bears became more aggressive and restless. They roared and shook their cages, making John shiver at their aggression and enormous size.

What's happening? Is it a bear fight, or is Margaret here to identify me?

"Friends, welcome to today's activities." Ren Walden stood on an elevated box in the middle of the yard.

John Two

The drunken crowd raised their ale glasses and roared back at the Strete Master.

"Today is an important day," Ren continued. "It is a day of judgement for those who dare betray Ren Walden."

John stared at him in wonderment. *What was he going to do? Make the boys in the cage fight the bears?*

A group of Walden's rascals led by Stephen dragged a middle-aged man into the middle of the yard, dropping him in front of Ren's platform. John couldn't see his face, but he could hear him pleading with Walden.

The crowd bellowed. They wanted blood.

"This man stole bread from my bakery. Three whole loaves. What do you have to say for yourself, thief?"

The man looked up at Ren. "Boss, you didn't pay me, and my daughter was starving. I was trying to feed her so she wouldn't die."

He bowed his head. "I ask for mercy, boss."

Ren laughed as the crowd roared. "I gave this man a job at my bakery. Instead of showing me gratitude, he stole from me. And now he wants my mercy." Walden waved his arms, playing up to the crowd. He reminded John of an old mediaeval lord, punishing the villagers for daring to want to live.

Walden pulled his sword from his side. "I will show this man my mercy," he yelled, raising his sword high in the air, whipping the crowd into a frenzy. "No man steals from Ren Walden and lives to tell the tale. Here is my mercy, thief."

He brought his sword down in a violent, swift movement, striking the poor man on the shoulders. He fell to the ground, screaming in agony, blood spurting from his wounds.

Ren struck him again. And again. His sword action was crude and violent. It took him several blows before he finally bent over, and covered in the man's blood, lifted his head high in the air in triumph.

John grimaced and curled into a ball, trying not to look. This was the most gruesome thing he'd ever seen. Some of the other boys in the cage next to him threw up through the bars.

If Walden was trying to make a point, John heard it loud and clear.

The crowd bellowed in response, oblivious to the man's suffering.

"The king may have the finest swordsmen from France to do his beheading, but my justice is the best kind," Ren roared at the crowd, enjoying the adulation he was receiving.

"Let it be known throughout London and beyond that no man crosses Ren Walden and gets away with it. This man's whore daughter will work in my brothels."

He turned from side to side, displaying the severed head to everyone before throwing it to the ground.

The crowd thinned as Ren jumped down from his

pedestal and turned towards Stephen, who was scowling at the boys in the cages. Once again, he spoke in German.

"Take the boys to the lady at the usual place. She's waiting for you. Not this one, though." He pointed at John. "He's been near the plague. She's staying in London until we find him, so he can go later if he's still alive."

"Yes, boss." Stephen beckoned to Rolf and two others and dragged the boys out of the cage one by one. The boy with no front teeth smiled at John on his way out, but John could tell he was putting on a brave face. He was as pale as a full moon, and John felt sorry for him.

John stared at his hands, tears once more staining his bruised cheeks.

All these poor boys are suffering for me.

He considered giving himself up, but then he remembered his promise to Isaac. He sighed and made a silent vow to avenge the boys who were unknowingly walking to their deaths at this very moment.

Later that afternoon, loud noises woke John from a fitful sleep. Rolf and two others he didn't know were kicking the life out of some poor boy for no apparent reason.

"Serves you right for wasting our time." Rolf spat the words out as he beat the boy senseless.

When they finished and stepped back, John shouted out in anguish. It was the toothless boy who'd taken the time to speak to him before they'd taken him to see Margaret.

Now he was blood soaked and barely conscious.

"Throw him in there with him." Stephen snarled. "If he's got the plague, they can both die together."

John gently laid the boy's head in his lap and used the filthy rag he called a shirt to wipe the blood from the boy's face. It was the least he could do.

"What happened?" John asked when he finally opened his eyes.

"What are you doing?" The boy tried getting up, but he staggered and fell into the bars, sending the bears into another angry frenzy.

"I was trying to clean the blood from your wounds," John replied. "I was trying to help."

"You've got the plague!" he yelled. "Get away from me."

"No, I don't," John said quietly. "I just told them that so they'd leave me alone."

The boy looked closely at John. "Really?"

John nodded. "They'd beaten me half to death, and I said the first thing I could think of to make them leave me alone."

"You're smart. I wish I'd thought of that."

The boy sat down. "I'm sorry. I don't trust anyone anymore. These people are murderers!" he shouted as loud as he could.

Luckily for him, there was nobody there to hear him.

"What happened?" John repeated.

"They took us to a big house in the city. A blonde-haired aristocratic woman walked in and looked at us. She told them she wanted to look closer at me, but the rest of the boys were taken out nearly as fast as they went in. I'm guessing Walden let them go once they knew they weren't Howard."

John winced at the mention of his name and the mention of Margaret.

"Are you sure they let them go? Did you see them?"

"No, how could I? Rolf took them out, and I never saw him or them again. Stephen made me wash my face and stand in front of her. The lady looked me up and down and then got mad. She yelled at Stephen and told him he was an incompetent fool. She told him Walden would be replaced if they didn't find Howard soon. Walden's boys were so mad they wouldn't let me go. They beat me all the way back here."

"What's your name?" the boy asked.

Without thinking, John answered. "John."

He instantly regretted it.

The boy broke out into a bruised, toothless smile. "I'm called John, too."

John smiled back. "Hello, John Two. Nice to meet you."

Outwardly he smiled. But inside he cried. What had he done to this poor young boy who looked just like him? What had happened to the others that were with him?

He huddled into the corner of his cage and sobbed quietly.

Murder

The bears threw themselves at their cages as the crowds taunted them in the courtyard. Stephen and Rolf threw open John's cage doors armed with big sticks and prodded John Two.

"Get out here," Rolf shouted above the commotion. "You're going home."

John Two's eyes lit up, and he smiled at John. "My turn," he said. "Take care, John. I hope they let you go soon."

John winced when he said his name. Luckily, neither Stephen nor Rolf seemed to hear him because they never gave him a second glance.

"Stay away from us," Rolf prodded him with the big stick. "You've been around the plague."

Ren Walden appeared and took his place on his raised boxes. The drunken men cheered his name and waited impatiently for the day's gruesome events.

John opened his mouth to shout to John Two, but no words came out. He froze when he realised what was happening. He shook the bars of his cage as hard as he could, but all he managed to do was to rile the bears even more.

"Come here, boy." Walden beckoned for John Two to step forward.

John Two stepped forward, smiling at Walden. "See, boss, I told you I wasn't him. Can I go home now?"

Walden's face turned purple. "I've served this city well. Even now, I'm doing my duty to the lords by searching everywhere for that runaway son of an earl who poisoned his own brother. Can you imagine anyone doing such a terrible thing? Let alone an aristocrat, who's supposed to be better than us?"

John Two remained quiet and shot a look of confusion at John. The crowd stayed quiet as well.

John tightened his grip on the bars of his cage.

"I finally caught him – or at least I thought I did. I go to all the trouble of taking care of him and making sure he was unharmed. Then, when I took him to the lady, she got angry and threatened to replace me because it wasn't him. I had the wrong John."

A few groans came from the crowd, but John Two remained frozen to the spot. Another glance at John told him that John Two had finally cottoned on to what was happening.

"I've been generous with the boys I've taken to her. As soon as she's told me they weren't Howard, I gave them all coin for their trouble and sent them on their way. But none of them caused me the grief this one did."

He moved to the edge of his pedestal to get closer to John Two.

John watched, transfixed in horror.

"What am I to do?" Walden's raised voice caused a stir in the crowd, that was now beginning to bay for more blood.

"I can't let him go home and tell his friends and family that I was ridiculed, can I?"

The crowd got louder, and John started pulling violently on the bars. The bears were going crazy at the heightened tension.

John Two made a run for it. He made it no more than twenty feet when a large fist crashed into his face from one of Walden's strete rascals. John Two fell to the muddy ground in a heap.

"Leave him alone," John shouted, but nobody heard him.

John Two lay on the ground sobbing. Rolf kicked him hard in the ribs.

"Shut your mouth," he hissed.

"I've earned my name in this town, and nobody is going to take it away from me!" Walden shouted. He knew how to whip up a crowd, that much was obvious to John.

Walden looked around in triumph at the adulation being bestowed on him by the crowd and his rascals.

"Let this be a warning to anyone who thinks I am weak. I am kind and generous, but if anyone threatens me, I will show no mercy."

The crowd roared as Walden jumped down from his pedestal. Stephen yanked John Two to his feet.

"Rolf here is going to show what happens when I'm threatened. Let this be a warning to you all."

Stephen stepped back and gave John a long stare. John held his gaze and was taken aback when he saw not anger, but almost pity in Stephen's eyes. He shook his head.

I must be mistaken. He's as big a monster as his boss.

Two chiefs pulled John Two forward, towards the pedestal. They pulled both his arms over the platform and held him there. In one swift movement, Rolf severed his right arm above the elbow.

John Two screamed.

John Howard screamed.

Then he sobbed.

This can't be happening.

Another blow severed his other arm, and John Two screamed again, weaker this time. Blood spurted everywhere.

John threw up in his cage. He tried not to look, but he couldn't peel his eyes away from John Two's writhing body being held up by two blood-soaked, evil men.

Rolf turned around and smiled at John, waving his sword in twisted triumph. John wished the bears would tear the doors off their cages and attack Walden and his gang.

Walden grabbed John Two by the rear of his cloak. His screams had died down to a whimper, but he was still writhing in agony. He dragged him to the water's edge.

Ren Walden stood John Two up one more time, smiled, and shoved him as hard as he could into the unforgiving waters of the River Thames.

Even the crowd went silent at the brutality and anger on display. John stood rooted to the spot, unable to move or think.

Walden gathered all his chiefs outside John's cage and spoke again in German. John listened intently.

"He's not got the plague. Even if he has, the bitch deserves it after what she said about me. Rolf, take him to her in the morn. If it isn't him, kill him and leave him to rot with the rest of them. Stephen, you're in charge here. The rest of you, get out there and find me the real John Howard. When I find him, she won't need to kill him. I'll happily do it myself."

"Yes, boss."

Rolf looked at John and leaned towards the cage, sneering at him.

"I'm sorry about your friend," he said in broken English.

John dived at the cage bars, but Rolf had already backed away.

Escape

During the night, John was wakened from his nightmares by the sound of someone gently shaking the bars of his cage. He looked up in the half moonlight and had to look twice to make sure his eyes weren't deceiving him.

Stephen's scar was glistening in the moonlight.

"What do—"

"Shhh." Stephen held his finger to his lips. "You don't want to disturb the bears or everyone will come running."

"What do you want?" John said. "Why did you have to—"

"Shut up and listen. Rolf is coming for you tomorrow, and you don't want to go where he's taking you."

Stephen tossed something wrapped in cloth towards John.

"What is this?" John asked.

"I know who you are."

Stephen turned and vanished into the night.

John sat in stunned silence for several minutes.

What just happened? Stephen is almost as evil as Ren Walden, so why is he helping me? Or is he setting me up?

For what? They already have me.

What did he mean when he said he knows who I am? If he knows I'm John Howard, then why didn't he just say so and spare John Two's life? Not to mention all the other boys they killed yesterday in my name.

He reached over and grabbed the object Stephen had thrown into his cage. He knew what it was before he'd finished unwrapping it:

It was a large knife! It was sharp too because John cut his finger on it when he was unwrapping it.

What was Stephen up to? Was the look he gave him before John Two's execution for real? John had put that down to his imagination, but now he wasn't so sure.

Is Stephen somehow a saviour that is trying to save my life? How? Why?

John's mind raced with the possibilities, but he kept going back to the same thing; the Stephen he knew was cruel, hard, and evil.

Now he didn't know what to think.

He rolled the knife in his hands and tried to understand what had just happened. His heart hurt every time he thought of John Two, and his anger boiled at Walden and Rolf for being so cruel. He'd included Stephen in this as well, but now he wasn't so sure.

Salty tears flooded down his face once more, and he thumped the ground, splashing mud up into his face.

John Two's death will not go unpunished.

He was still sitting in the same position when he heard footsteps approaching his cage in the early morning fog. He couldn't see very far, but he didn't need to. Ren Walden's chiefs didn't know how to be quiet.

"As soon as I leave with this dirty knave, get out there and find as many more as you can." Rolf's broken English was unmistakable. "The lady's patience is wearing thin, and the boss isn't happy. It won't be good for us if the boss gets angry."

John bristled at being called a dirty knave.

"Where's Stephen?" someone asked.

"He gets to stay here and act like he's in charge again." John detected jealousy in Rolf's tone. "He thinks he's next in line to the boss."

The sniggers got louder as they approached the cage.

"Where is the boss, anyway?" The language changed to German, so John couldn't understand what was being said.

Except he could.

"He's getting the bread thief's whore daughter ready for the Unicorn tomorrow morning. She needs cleaning up so she looks good."

More sniggers as they reached the cage.

"Get up, you filthy knave." Rolf changed back into English. "You're going to meet the lady. If you're Howard, then we're rich and you're dead."

More laughter behind him.

John stood up to his full height, his aching body protesting for all it was worth. But he ignored it.

Today was the day everything would change. Either he died, or John Howard and the Underlings started fighting back. There was no going back after this.

He walked out of the cage with his head held high, right into the heavy fists of Rolf the German.

"Don't try anything stupid, boy," he snarled. "Any foolish moves and I'll snap yer neck. The lady wants you alive, but I don't care."

John's shoulders sank so as not to antagonise him any further. For now, he'd be compliant.

The cold steel of the knife pressed against the inside of his thigh, hidden beneath his torn, filthy clothes.

They remained silent as Rolf pushed John over London Bridge and past the Steelyard. He thought about making a run for it, but shivered and forced himself to carry on. The guards wouldn't allow him to pass in any case.

They turned right up a dark, narrow strete that made John shudder. He should have been used to it by now, but he wasn't. His clothes stank as bad as the stretes and he stifled the urge to vomit.

"Where are you taking me?" John broke the silence. He wanted to know where Margaret was waiting for them.

Rolf responded by slapping him hard around the back of the head.

"Speak when yer spoken to."

Rolf stopped outside a bakery on Walbrooke Strete and pushed John roughly around the back, where the waste grounds hid them from view from the rest of the city.

John's stomach churned, and he rubbed his sweaty palms together.

Is this it? Is Margaret in there?

"I need a piss. Wait there." Rolf shoved John aside and turned away from him.

John's hands trembled, and he closed his eyes momentarily.

This is it.

He grabbed the knife from under his clothes and stepped forward. Visions of John Two pleading for his life sent his heart racing.

"Hey, Rolf. Do you know who I am?" John spoke in his normal aristocratic accent. He wasn't going to stab him in the back.

Rolf spun around, his mouth wide open. John lunged forward and plunged the knife deep into his chest.

Rolf made a gurgling sound and slid down the wall, his eyes transfixed on John. The only expression John saw was pure hatred mixed with shock.

"Mein name ist John Howard, und ich spreche sehr gut Deutsch."

Rolf's head jerked backwards as John forced the knife in even further.

"You had me all along, and you were too stupid to know it. This is for John Two and every other boy you've murdered in my name. I hope you rot in hell."

John pulled the knife out and staggered backwards. Rolf's lifeless eyes stared at him, taunting him, mocking him.

He turned away, bent over, and threw his guts up.

He sat with his back to Rolf for an age, not able to look at him or acknowledge what he'd just done. His entire body quivered, and every time he thought about it, he threw up again.

And yet the spirits of John Two and countless others seemed to reach down from the heavens to tell him that it was okay and that what he'd done was both necessary and good.

Images of Margaret's furious face made him feel slightly better, and after sitting there for way too long, he knew he had to move. He couldn't just leave Rolf's body where it was, so he forced himself to face what he'd done and drag it into the middle of a nearby bush. He covered him over as best he could and knelt in prayer for his soul.

Then he left before the constable could find the body and start searching for the culprit. He headed for the safety of the Old Mill and a reunion with the Underlings.

He stopped inside the darkness of the Roman wall, his legs trembling as they gave way, and he grabbed for the walls as he fell. His body convulsed, and he lost control of himself.

Is this what I've become? A strete beggar who has to murder to stay alive?

What about John Two and all those other poor souls who have died because of me? What about the Underlings that are relying on me to prove their innocence? Am I up to all of this?

And what about Stephen? Who is he?

It was the thoughts of Stephen that broke him out of his trance.

What was it Rolf had said that morning? John strained to remember what he'd heard.

"He's getting the bread thief's whore daughter ready for the Unicorn tomorrow morning. She needs cleaning up so she looks good."

John didn't know where the Unicorn was, but it didn't matter. This meant that Walden would be alone with the girl. It gave John the chance he needed.

He decided this was something he had to do alone. Taking on the most ruthless Strete Master in living memory was no small undertaking, and if he was to fail, he would fail alone. He wasn't going to endanger the Underlings any more than he already had.

He shook himself to regain control of his body, stood up, and headed back into the city. He would hide across the river and follow Walden the next morning.

It was up to God to decide what happened next.

The Unicorn

John reversed direction once again and went back to his treehouse. There was plenty of daylight left, so he had time to make the excursion.

Even though his beloved longbow was at the Old Mill with the Underlings, he wanted the safety of a hooded cloak, and Sarah had left several of them in his safe house. He wished he had his longbow with him now; it was bad enough taking on Walden with that, but armed with just a knife, he knew his odds of success were almost zero.

But he had to try. He owed it to John Two and all the others.

He grabbed his cloak and headed back into the city.

The stretes of London were crowded, which was a blessing. He would be hard to spot with this many people roaming around. Twice he glimpsed someone he knew, but with so many people on the stretes, he knew he was safe though he was glad of the extra protection his cloak provided.

Walden's chiefs wouldn't be looking for him in any

case, but they certainly wouldn't be looking for a boy in a cloak headed back into the lion's den.

London Bridge was so full of people that John thought it might sink. He saw one of the chiefs at Drawbridge Tower, but it was so busy that he slipped by without being seen.

Drunken people spilt out of the many brewhouses on the south side of the river. One man was so drunk, he staggered out of the Swan with Two Necks and sidestepped like a crab into the grounds of St Thomas Hospital. John shook his head and hoped he never ended up like these poor souls.

He entered the church inside St Mary Overy Priory, knowing he was safe inside. Even Ren didn't cause violence in a place of God. He found a great hiding place in a storeroom at the rear corner and wedged the door so nobody could open it from the outside.

Then he waited.

And shivered.

The souls of the dead weighed heavily on his shoulders, and he felt the warm breath of John Two against his neck, whispering to him, urging him to get revenge for his death.

He was glad when the late afternoon shadows fell so he could get out of there and move around.

Yes, keep moving.

At dusk, he made his way out of the church. He knew Ren and the chiefs would have searched for him and the German by now, and he reasoned the last place they'd look was right on their own doorstep on the south side of the river.

Keeping to the grasslands and trees of Winchester Park, John followed Maiden Lane past the brewhouses and brothels. He was looking for the Unicorn, hoping it was somewhere on this side of the river.

The Bull was the furthest point John had seen on Maiden Lane, so he was relieved when he found the Unicorn just a few hundred yards further down. It was the biggest of all the brewhouses and brothels in the area.

As daylight faded, he found an excellent hiding place in the middle of a large bush in Winchester Park that was between a stream and Maiden Lane, opposite Ren's stronghold at the Vine brewhouse. He could see most of Maiden Lane, and all the buildings between it and the Thames. Whichever way Ren took the girl the next morning, he would see them.

Suddenly, he stiffened. Ren Walden appeared to his right near the grounds of the Vine. He was alone and in a perfect line of sight.

If only I had my longbow. I could kill him right now and get it over with.

He quickly realised he'd never get away with it. Besides the two boys on permanent guard around the gang's compound, London Bridge was closed after dark. Everyone would pile after him before it opened again.

No. He would have to suffer and wait.

What about the girl?

John hadn't given a single thought about the girl until this point. Rescuing her from a life in the brothels went some way to making up for the suffering his escape had unleashed on London's strete boys, but what about after he'd rescued her?

If he rescued her.

John dragged himself away from his dark thoughts.

Rescuing the girl would be a happy accident. The main objective was the end of the evil Strete Master's reign of terror.

Ren Walden had to die.

The night was long and cold, and John shivered as drunkards came and went from the brewhouses and brothels. He forced himself to keep his mind on anything other than the haunting visions of John Two, and instead concentrated on working out how he was going to kill the much bigger and more powerful Strete Master.

However he sliced and diced it, he couldn't see any way of defeating him other than sneaking up behind him and stabbing him in the back. It was the coward's way of doing it, but he saw no other option.

A man staggered out of the Boar's Head, which was next door to the Unicorn. It was dark, but the sky was clear and the moonlight was strong. All things being equal, John could see surprisingly well.

He watched the man stagger up the lane, past his hideout. John could just about make out the shape of a longbow strapped over his shoulder. He must have been hunting before stopping off at the brothel. If he could somehow get hold of that, he would have a much better chance of defeating Ren when daylight came.

He followed in the shadows, watching where he was going, trailed him past the priory towards the houses on the other side of St Thomas's Hospital, and watched him wobble down Tooley Strete and stumble into the doorway of one of the houses near Tenter Alley.

John saw his chance and, taking a deep breath, he ran up behind the man and crashed his head into the door, knocking him to the ground. John dropped his knees hard onto the man's chest.

"I don't 'ave nuthin'," the man said in a high-pitched tone, the whites of his eyes clearly visible in the moonlight. Assaults of this nature often happened on the south side. It was, after all, London's den of iniquity.

The man's breath reeked of alcohol. John spoke in as deep a voice as he could muster. "The longbow," he said.

The man moved his shoulders so John could remove it.

"Arrows," John said, pushing into the man's throat with his knees.

The man pointed to his side and John removed about a half quiver, which was four arrows. He released the pressure on the man's chest and stood up in one quick motion.

"Are you goin' to kill me?" the man asked, his voice shaking.

"Not today. Just go home and sleep it off."

The man barged through his door and slammed it behind him. He didn't need a second invitation.

John made his way back to his hiding place, feeling mightily relieved. He'd stressed all day about how he would tackle Ren without his favourite weapon. He knew Walden was older, stronger, and much more stretewise than he ever would be. In a fair fight, Ren would win every time, but John doubted Ren had ever taken part in a fair fight in his life.

Now the odds were on his side.

The rest of the night was freezing cold and John huddled deeper and deeper inside his cloak, glad of its warmth. The clouds rolled in and strangled the moonlight, making it impossible to see anything and the rain came shortly afterwards, which made for a long and uncomfortable night. His stomach was performing somersaults, and every time he drifted off, Rolf's lifeless eyes stared up at him, forcing him awake with a jolt.

What have I become?

As dawn approached, a calmness settled over him. He was surprised, yet delighted at the same time. He didn't want nerves to unsettle either his aim or his thoughts. If he was to die this morn, at least he would die knowing that he had given the best of himself.

Daylight brought with it an early morning mist that hung like a blanket over the Thames and the brewhouses. John could barely see one hundred yards, which was ideal. God was indeed smiling on him this morning.

Shouting and yelling rose from the housing areas near The Bear, and John knew the chiefs would soon be all over London trying to find the German and himself.

"Find them today and get 'em back here," Ren shouted to his chiefs. "Stephen, go and see the lady and find out if they even got there yesterday. If they didn't, assume it was Howard that we had and go find him. Now that we know what he looks like, it'll be easy."

"Yes, boss."

John shuddered. He had no doubts that Ren would make his death a spectacle for the crowds to watch. He couldn't be seen to be losing control and fear was his greatest weapon.

John ran down the lane between the Unicorn and the Barge brewhouse as soon as the noise had died down and hid behind a tree.

He was ready.

Footsteps crunched in the wet mud on Maiden Lane, and he heard the unmistakable voice of Ren Walden getting closer and closer. He clenched his fists in anger and anticipation.

"Try anything funny and I'll rip yer throat out. I've got other business to see to today, so I want to get this over wiv quick."

The girl mumbled something, but John couldn't make out what it was. He felt incredibly sorry for her. This monster had killed her father and was forcing her to work in a brothel. What kind of man did that?

A man like Ren Walden, that's who.

"Get a move on, whore. I don't have time fer yer crying."

When they appeared, Ren was pushing the girl in front of him in the courtyard, heading towards the Unicorn.

John was to the right of them, hidden in the trees and bushes. He aimed his longbow carefully and waited.

When they were about sixty or so yards away, he let loose. The arrow swooshed in the air, burying itself deep into Walden's chest. He groaned and fell in a heap on the ground. The girl screamed and ran a few feet before turning back to watch what was happening. John had never seen such fear etched on someone's face in his life.

He noticed that her hands were tied behind her back.

John rushed over to them, yelling at the girl that she was safe.

"Shut up and stop screaming or they'll be all over us," he yelled harshly. Ren glowered up at John from the ground, not a hint of fear in his eyes.

"You," he gasped. "You're a dead man."

"Wrong. It is you who is the dead man, Ren Walden. Your days of causing misery and suffering to the people of London are over."

Ren started getting up, but John pulled the knife from beneath his cloak and drove it deep into Ren's stomach. Anger and disgust had overtaken any fear he may have had. Ren Walden was not walking away from this.

Walden fell back to the ground. "I didn't think you had it in you, boy," he said.

"Allow me to introduce myself, although I think you already know who I am." John spoke in his best aristocratic accent. "My name is John Howard, and I came back here to kill you and avenge John Two and all the other boys you've killed in my name."

"Stephen will hunt you down for the rest of your miserable life." Ren coughed up blood.

"Stephen knew who I was. It was he who gave me this knife, so he isn't who you think he is. You should have chosen the people you trust better."

Walden lurched forward, but John grabbed him by his cloak and dragged him past the side of the Unicorn. The girl followed, watching John intently as he dragged Ren to the banks of the Thames.

"This is for John Two, and the countless others you have killed without mercy."

Ren struggled as John dragged him to the water's edge. "I can't swim," he gasped.

"Neither could John Two."

One more push and the mighty Thames swept away the Strete Master as if it was cleansing London of his sins. John and the girl watched as he moved faster and faster with the tide until he was out of sight, never to be seen again.

"Who are you?" the girl asked after a long pause. "Why did you save me?"

"You heard my name being mentioned. I am John Howard, the fallen aristocrat everyone in London seems to be searching for. I might add that I am innocent of all the crimes I am accused of. I rescued you because I heard Walden would be alone with you this morning and it gave me the chance I needed to ambush and kill him."

The girl remained speechless, no doubt suffering from the same shock that John was. Walden was the second man he'd killed in as many days, and he didn't feel any better about it, although a weight seemed to lift from his shoulders where the spirit of John Two had been leaning since his demise. For some reason, John felt that John Two was satisfied now Walden was dead.

"What are you going to do with me?" The girl started crying again.

"Calm down. I didn't rescue you just to put you back into service somewhere. You are free to go wherever you feel safest, although you might want to stay with me until we get over the bridge. Walden's chiefs will surely be after us and we must remain vigilant."

The girl clung to John's cloak. She obviously didn't know what to do.

"What's your name?"

"Catherine Devine."

John shook hands with her, noticing for the first time that she was about his age and as pretty as could be. Her long blonde hair flowed down her back, making her features stand out even more.

John shook himself back to the here and now.

"Come on, we've got to get out of here. After that, you're free."

John led the way through Winchester Park and around the priory to Long Southwark, which led to London Bridge. They made their way over the bridge, grateful for the heavy mist that made for poor visibility. On the other side, they headed down Thames Strete and into the walled city.

In the West Fish Market, someone yelled from across the strete. John looked over and saw one of Walden's boys staring at him, struggling through the growing crowd to get to him.

"He's seen us." John grabbed Catherine by the arm. "Come on."

They ran for their lives down Bred Strete.

John had an idea. "This way," he yelled.

He ran through the small churchyard into Gerard's Hall where he'd been with Isaac in what seemed like a lifetime ago. He pulled Catherine into the room at the rear of the hall, closing the door behind him. There was nothing to wedge it with, so he quickly opened the window leading to the yard behind.

The chief crashed about in the hall behind them, shouting obscenities and making as much noise as he could.

"He's trying to frighten us," John said. "Ignore him."

They ran into the churchyard of Holy Trinity the Less where John found the large tomb of the Whittingtons, and, making sure the coast was clear, he pushed the large stone slab to the side.

"What's this?" Catherine asked.

"Our way out," John said. "Hurry."

Catherine went down the narrow steps while John closed the stone slab over the top of them, sealing them in complete darkness.

"What is this place?" Catherine whispered.

"It's a secret tunnel leading to safety. Grab hold of me and keep close."

John edged his way along the long, narrow tunnel until he reached the steps at the other end. They emerged into St Mary Aldermary's graveyard and from there they ran to the busy market stretes of Cheppes Syed.

Reunion

Once John was sure the coast was clear, he pulled Catherine into one of the narrow, dirty stretes that made him feel like the world was closing in on him and took a deep breath, pushing the nauseating trepidation to the back of his mind.

"You're safe now, and free to return to your family."

Catherine stared at her hands. "I don't have any family. My father was all I had, and Walden killed him."

Her eyes filled up and large tears rolled down her face. John felt the emotion and took her hands in his.

"I'm so sorry. Ren Walden and his gang are as evil as they come. He's dead now, but the gang will no doubt find a new leader and carry on like nothing happened. You need to be careful and stay out of their way."

"The one with the scar down his face is just as bad." Catherine held her hands in his, making John's spine tingle. There was something about her that captivated him, but whatever it was, he didn't have time for it now.

"I don't know about him," John said, butterflies dancing in the pit of his stomach. Every time he looked at her, she somehow looked even prettier. He looked anywhere but at Catherine. "He's an enigma. I thought he was evil, but now I'm not so sure."

He put Stephen aside for the moment. "What are you going to do?"

"I have nowhere to go," Catherine said, tears running down her face again.

"Well, you can't stay here."

"Can I come with you? At least until I find somewhere safe to stay?"

John shook his head. "It's too dangerous. I have a lot of things I have to do, and any one of them could result in my death. It's not safe to be anywhere near me."

Catherine stared at John for a long moment. "You're him, aren't you? You're the one everyone's been looking for." It was more of a statement than a question.

John held her gaze. "Yes. I've already told you I'm John Howard, which is why it isn't safe to be around me."

"I owe you my life. You don't act like the monster the cryers make you out to be."

"I'm not. I'm innocent, and I'm going to prove it. You need to be as far away from me as you can."

Catherine shook her head. "Like I said, I've nowhere to go. I want to stay with you, at least for now."

"You can't. It's too dangerous. In any case, I'm not alone. Once I rejoin my friends, they might not want you around."

The look on Catherine's face made John squirm. He jumped to his feet and paced around, muttering to himself.

"Okay." He turned back to Catherine. "I think I can trust you, but what I am about to tell you must remain between us. If I tell you, you cannot leave and must remain with us until it's over. Do I have your word?"

Catherine nodded.

"Do I have your word?"

"Yes. I promise. I don't have any other choice right now."

John sighed. "Andrew will probably be furious, but here it is. Not only am I John Howard, but I am also a member of the Underlings, who I'm sure you've heard of. They're innocent as well, as we will prove. We were leaving London on this very mission when I was captured by Walden's chiefs. If you come with me, you will be in as much danger as the rest of us."

Catherine's eyes widened. "Wow, you really are mixed up in it. I don't have any other choice, do I? I won't survive on the stretes on my own, and it looks like I won't survive long with you either."

"At least you will be amongst friends that you can trust. That's got to be worth something."

"Will they accept me, or will they throw me out like you wanted to?"

"If I explain how I found you, they will understand. I promise to take care of you – at least until you can be safe somewhere else – and I am a man of my word. I would never forgive myself if I cast you aside now and discovered later that something happened to you."

For the first time, Catherine smiled. John's heart jumped in his chest, and he felt as vulnerable as he'd ever done. He quickly shook himself back to reality.

What's happening to me? I see a pretty girl and I turn to mush! I need to get a grip on myself.

They hung around the markets and busy stretes until dusk because John didn't want to be seen approaching the covered bridge in daylight. As soon as the light began to fade and visibility dropped, he led her to Black Friars and their way out.

"Where are we going?" Catherine asked. "Don't you

know that London is dangerous after curfew? What about the watch? I thought you knew what you were doing?"

"Relax. I know exactly what I'm doing. I know a secret way in and out of the city. I was waiting until dusk so we wouldn't be seen entering it. We don't live inside the city, it's too dangerous."

"You know a secret tunnel out of the city? Like the one we did earlier?"

"Yes. Now be quiet before every soul in London hears of it."

The stomach-churning stench of the River Fleet hit John's nostrils long before he could hear it. Ignoring it, he stopped for a moment to make sure the way forward was clear.

It amazed him that Catherine didn't seem to notice the putrid stink of either the river or the city itself. It seemed like he was the only one who even knew about it.

Grabbing Catherine's hand, he guided her through the large bush and into the secret passageway.

"You have to be very quiet when we go under the bridge. Guards are walking all over it above us. One word and we'll be discovered."

Catherine squeezed his hand to acknowledge his words.

John walked around the Old Mill and found the riverside entrance the Underlings always used because it gave them the most cover. He gave the secret knock that told everyone inside all was well – three times, twice, then once, all in rapid succession.

The door flew open, revealing Isaac, who'd been on guard duty.

"John!" Isaac shouted, throwing himself forward towards his good friend. "Andrew told us you'd be okay, but I didn't believe him. Did they hurt you? How did you escape?"

He noticed someone else stood in the shadows and stepped backwards, drawing his sword. "Who's this?"

"Relax, Isaac. She's with me. I rescued her from Walden's clutches."

"John!"

Andrew, Abraham, David and Helena ran up and hugged John. "You're safe! How did you escape? Did they hurt you?" Everyone spoke at once until the figure of Catherine came into view.

Everyone fell silent.

"Who's this?" Andrew asked.

"Everyone, this is Catherine Devine. Walden murdered her father and was taking her to the brothels. I rescued her when I killed him. She has no family and nowhere to go, so I brought her with me. I hope you don't mind."

"You killed Walden?" David asked, raising his eyebrows.

"I heard him telling his chiefs that he'd be taking Catherine to the Unicorn this morning, so I knew he'd be alone. I went back after I escaped and killed him."

David turned to Catherine. "Did he really kill Walden? Is he gone?"

Catherine nodded. "He was very brave. He used a longbow and threw him into the Thames. He's dead."

Respect was etched over the faces of all the Underlings. Even Andrew, who had seen more action than most.

"How did you escape?" Helena asked. "We thought you were done for."

"That's the mystery," John said. "Walden and his gang communicated in German, which they thought nobody but them could understand. It so happens that I'm fluent in German, so I understood every word. I knew Rolf, his

German chief, would take me to see Margaret yesterday morning, so I sat in my cage trying to plan how I'd overpower him and escape."

"What happened next?" Abraham asked. "What's the mystery?"

"You won't believe this, but Stephen of all people came to me during the night and gave me a knife. He told me that Rolf was taking me to see Margaret the next morning. He said he knew who I was and that I had to get away from Rolf if I wanted to live."

"Stephen? The man with the horrible scar?" David shouted. "That man is pure evil. He helped you? I don't believe it."

"I wouldn't either if it wasn't true," John agreed. "I still don't understand why he did it. I was worth a lot of coin to them."

"It could be a power struggle within the gang," Andrew suggested. "Margaret was probably mad at Walden for not finding you sooner, and Stephen might have seen a chance to get rid of him and take over the gang. You killing Walden just made it a lot easier for him."

"Good point," John said. "With Walden out of the way and taking all the blame for my escape, Stephen steps in and takes over the gang. From what I've seen, he's just as ruthless as Walden was."

"Oh, he is," David said. "I know."

"How did you escape from Rolf?" Abraham asked.

"I killed him behind a bakery. Then I went back, robbed a drunkard of his longbow and killed Walden as he was taking Catherine to the Unicorn."

"Very impressive," Isaac said. "Andrew was right when he said we should believe in you. I wanted to go over the bridge and rescue you, but that would have been suicide. We all thought you'd be dead by now, or at least that the cryer would be telling everyone about your capture."

"I got lucky. Without Stephen's help, I'd never have overpowered Rolf. He was much bigger and stronger than me."

"We can't worry about what Stephen's up to," Andrew said. "We've got to get up to Warwickshire and clear our names. Fellow Underlings, John Howard is a hard man to kill, and I'm glad he's on our side."

Everyone agreed.

"Well, then, Catherine," Andrew roared. "Welcome to our home. I'm sure John told you all about us. My name is Andrew, and I'm the leader of the Underlings. I'll allow the rest to introduce themselves. I hope you enjoy living in the shadows because until we prove our innocence, that's what we have to do."

"John told me all about it," Catherine said. "I'd be living in the shadows if I was alone. I have nowhere to go and nobody to help me. John saved me, and he's all I've got. Thank you for letting me join you. I promise I'll earn my keep and won't be a burden."

While everyone introduced themselves and spoke to Catherine, Andrew grabbed John and steered him to a different room where they could talk in private.

"Do you trust the girl?" Andrew asked. "It's not a good time to be bringing anyone to us."

"I do," John said. "I didn't see any other choice. Walden murdered her father, who was her only family, and she had nowhere to go. If I'd abandoned her, she'd have been in terrible danger again. I couldn't do that to her."

"Aye, you're a good man, John Howard. But we'll need to keep a close eye on her until we're sure we can trust her."

"I was planning on it."

John changed the subject. "Margaret will be angry that I escaped, but now that Walden is dead, she might return to Broxley. We have to get up there fast and confront Mark while she's gone."

"Agreed. I'll see Pye tomorrow and arrange the transport. We'll get out of here as soon as we can. Plus, they'll be looking for yea even harder now you've killed their leader."

"I'm still not sure about Stephen," John said, pulling his face. "He said he knew who I was. How did he know, and how could he be so sure?"

"Who knows?" Andrew said. "Maybe he was bluffing and was using you to take over the gang."

"Perhaps. But why me? He could have used any one of the boys Walden sent to Margaret. No, he knew exactly who I was."

"This is far from over."

Broxley

The ride to Cambridge took four uncomfortable days. Stuck between Catherine and salted fish, John could barely stretch or move the entire way and was glad when they finally arrived. The good thing was that the trip was uneventful, which was all the Underlings could have hoped for.

The even better thing was that John got to know Catherine better. He couldn't help but stare every time his gaze fell upon her. Something about her made him short of breath, and whenever the bumpy cart threw them closer together, he felt his body tingling like never before.

I don't have time for this right now. Whatever it is I feel for this girl, it has to wait. I need to concentrate fully on clearing my name. If I fall for her now, I'll make a mistake and we'll all die.

But that didn't change the fact that his heart skipped every time they were close.

The bad thing was that they all stank like fish.

The journey from Cambridge to Coventry took two weeks, and by the end of it, they were all grateful it was over.

"If I have to lie next to a salty fish ever again, I swear I'll throw up all over it," David complained. "Everyone complains London smells, but nothing's as bad as a salty fish that smacks you in the face every time you turn your head."

Everyone laughed.

"That's the easy bit," John said. "Now we have a day's ride to reach Broxley."

John used the coin Gamaliell Pye had given him to hire the horses for the journey.

Daylight was fading when he led them to the rear of St Michael's Church near Broxley. The last time he'd been here was when Mark collapsed from the poisoning and it seemed strange seeing it again now. It was familiar, and yet somehow removed. Whereas it was once a place of worship and peace, now it stood as a forbidding reminder of his past life and the dangers that lay ahead.

John shook himself back to reality.

"You'll be safe here for the night," he said once the horses were taken care of. "I'm going to wait until everyone's retired to their bed chambers and then I'll make my move. If I'm not back here by first light, get away as fast as you can. Get back to Coventry and get out of here."

He handed Andrew all the coin he'd brought with him. "This won't be any use to me if I'm captured. Use it to get back to London."

"Are you sure you want to go in there alone?" Andrew asked for the thousandth time. "It's safer if I go with you."

John shook his head. "We've already been over this. Father has guards on both the outside and the inside. The slightest noise will get us both killed. I know my way around that house like the back of my hand, and I know places to hide the guards would never know. It's better I go alone. I plan on getting out of there long before first light, either with Mark and my sister or alone if I have to. Believe me, I have no desire to be captured."

Catherine approached him and took his hands in hers. Sparks erupted through his body, and he felt like a wet fish flopping around on the ground.

"Please take care, John. I've..." She trailed off and looked away as if unsure of her words. "I've grown fond of you, and I don't want anything to happen to you."

"I'll be—" His head exploded as Catherine reached forward and kissed him on the cheek.

"I'll be back before you know it." John forced the words out, struggling for breath. He pulled away and knelt in prayer.

Late in the night, John slipped out of St Michael's Church and made his way down the short road to Broxley Manor. It looked massive in the clear night sky, and John suppressed the memories that flooded back when he saw it.

Like many mediaeval homes, Broxley Hall was full of secrets, and John knew most of them. After crossing the drawbridge, he stayed close to the walls as he made his way to the rear. Making sure nobody had seen him, he climbed the wall and dropped into the courtyard, being careful to avoid the guards that patrolled at irregular intervals. He entered the empty kitchens and approached the huge fireplace that had made so many great meals for the Howard family.

John walked right inside the fireplace and touched his hands along the wall to the left of where he stood. Finding the small latch, he slid it until he heard a soft click. He pushed, and a large black hole opened up.

This was his way into the house.

Once inside, he closed the door behind him and fumbled around for the recess he knew was there. Eventually, he found it, taking out the candles he and Sarah had hidden there a lifetime ago.

Now he could see where he was going, John made good headway through the narrow, winding tunnel deep inside his boyhood home. He turned his thoughts inwards and examined how he felt about being back at Broxley.

Surprisingly, he didn't feel much of anything, except, perhaps, a twinge of sadness. More than anything, he felt like a trespasser in his own home.

In short, he no longer felt like he belonged to this world. He now inhabited an altogether different world, and strangely enough, he felt safer there than he'd ever done since his mother passed away.

Thoughts of Sarah brought a lump to his throat and his heart jumped when he thought of how she'd react to him waking her up. He'd decided to see her first and tell her all about his plans.

He exited in the large library, and wiping himself down as best he could, he left the secret door slightly ajar so he could make a swift escape if needed.

He crept up the stairs, avoiding a guard that passed close by, and stopped outside Sarah's bedchamber. His heart racing, he entered silently and closed the door behind him.

The curtains were open, and the clear sky sent a silvery light over Sarah's sleeping face. John's eyes filled up when he saw how peaceful and graceful she looked. He almost didn't want to disturb her.

He leant over her, covering her mouth gently with his hand.

"Sarah. Sarah, it's me, John."

Sarah shot up like a squirrel leaping up a tree.

"HELP!" she shouted through the haze of sleep, although it was muffled because of John's hand.

"Sarah, Sarah, it's me. It's John. Please be quiet."

Sarah stopped struggling and stared at him in the moonlight. "John? Is that really you?"

"Yes, it's really me."

They embraced for a long time before Sarah pulled away. "You stink like salty fish." She pulled her nose. "And you look terrible too. What are you doing here?"

"It's a long story." John pulled up a chair.

Mark

"So, Margaret is using strete gangs to round up anyone that looks like you, and then having them killed when she finds out it's not you?"

"I don't know if it's Margaret or the strete gang, but that's what's happening, or it was until I killed their leader, Ren Walden."

"You've changed so much, John. That evil woman has put you through so much."

"Father is no better," John reminded her. "He has guards posted everywhere looking for me, with orders to arrest me and take me to Newgate Gaol. I'm to have a trial at least, but the outcome is a foregone conclusion. From there I am to be taken to Tyburn and hanged from a tree."

Sarah shuddered and gripped her brother tightly before backing away, holding her nose. "You need some new clothes before you leave here. You really do stink."

"No. These clothes allow me to fit in and not stand out. They have saved my life many times. They might stink, but I need them for now.

"Is Margaret here, or is she still in London?"

"Both Father and Margaret are in London," Sarah answered. "I haven't seen either of them for weeks."

"Here's what I need." John leant forward and clasped his sister's hand. "Refuse me if you must, but I really need your help, Sarah. But understand that if you agree, you cannot stay here. You must come with me where life is nothing like what you're used to. It's the only way I can keep you safe."

"You want me to live on the stretes like a beggar?" Sarah asked, her face squashed into a ball. "What would you have me do that requires such a drastic act?"

"Do you want to help me?" John asked. "This is a matter of life and death, and not just for me."

"Of course I do, silly. I hate Margaret as much as you, and I don't recognise Father anymore. Margaret has changed him."

"I know I'm asking a lot, and I wouldn't do it if it wasn't so important."

"I know." Sarah climbed out of her bed and grabbed some clothes. "What are we going to do?"

"We're going to convince Mark to help us, and then we're all going to Norwich to seek Uncle Thomas's help. For some reason, he seems to dislike Margaret, and I'm hoping we can use that to our advantage."

"Do you think Mark will agree to help?" Sarah asked. "I wouldn't count on it. One day he hates his mother and wants to turn her in, and the next he loves her like she's the greatest mother England's ever known. And what of Uncle Thomas? How do you know he'll help? He might just turn you over to Father when you show up in Norfolk."

"That's a risk I'm prepared to take. Good Lord, it's so good to see you again, Sarah. I feared it would never happen."

"Me too." Sarah hugged her brother again. "But you

really do stink. You do realise Father will be on the warpath when he finds out what you're up to, don't you?"

"I know he will, but I have to clear my name, and this is the only way I can think of to do it. Uncle Thomas has to help or I'm a dead man."

"Let's go wake Mark and see what he says." Sarah stepped towards her door.

"Wait," John said. "I need to go to my room and get the coin I hid there."

"No need." Sarah smiled at her brother. "That is no longer your room. It's been prepared for Arthur when he leaves the nursery. I have your coin here with mine."

"How did you find it?" John asked, pursing his lips. "It was well hidden."

"You don't own all the secrets around here, big brother."

"How is Arthur? Is he well?"

"Yes, he's doing very well." Sarah shook her head. "I don't see him much. Margaret keeps me away from him."

John pursed his lips. "Are you ready?"

"I'm ready."

Sarah led the way, sneaking silently along the corridor to Mark's room. She listened for a moment and then slid inside, holding the door open for John.

"Let me wake him," she said. "If he sees you, he'll wake the dead."

John stood back while Sarah gently woke Mark. All he could see was Mark's oversized nose sticking out from Sarah's side.

"Mark, are you awake?" John heard Sarah whisper. "I have someone here who wants to speak with you, but first you must promise to remain silent."

Mark must have agreed because Sarah moved aside,

revealing John's silhouette standing by the bedchamber door.

"Hello, Mark."

Mark fell backwards in surprise. "John? Is that you? I surely thought you would be dead by now."

"If it was up to your mother I would be," John said sharply. "Listen, we don't have much time, but I need your help. If you refuse, Margaret wins, and I will die an innocent man. You know I didn't poison you, and further, you know she is guilty. She did it before when you were young, and she did it again to blame me and remove me from my heritage."

Mark sat silently, staring at John, his mouth opening and closing like a fish in a pond.

"This goes beyond just me. As we speak, your mother is in London ordering a violent strete gang to round up anyone who looks like me, and when they are identified as not me, they are killed. Up to now, at least forty boys have been killed by your mother's actions. This has to stop, Mark."

Mark stared.

"Not only that, but I am with a group of people whose own fates hang in the balance, and if I can clear my name, then I can clear them as well. You need to step forward and do the right thing or many other innocent lives will be lost."

"You want me to turn in my own mother?"

"If you have any conscience at all, you'll do what's right," John said. "Your mother will never stop until she gets what she wants."

Mark shook his head. "What's to stop me from just shouting for a guard right now and handing you over?"

"Nothing," John said. "But you know that you'd be

handing over an innocent man. You more than any other knows this to be true."

"I will not do it," Mark said, speaking louder. "I cannot give up my mother. She loves me, and underneath, she is a kind, caring lady."

"Mark, I need you to understand what your mother is doing to people in my name. Innocent boys are dying because of her, and many more will in the future if you don't do something about it. Even if you don't care about my survival, at least consider all those others who aren't so fortunate. Do you want all their deaths on your hands? Because they will be if you don't do something about it. You're the only one who can."

"I can't," Mark sobbed, forcing John to tell him to be quiet. "I'm afraid of her."

"I understand that," John said, "But you need to be strong and stand up to her. A friend of mine had both his arms chopped off, and they threw him into the Thames. His only crime was that he wasn't me. This will keep happening if you allow your fear to control you. Please, Mark, I beg of you. Please help me stop this."

Mark sat forward, his head in his hands. Sarah sat next to him and comforted him. "I know it's a lot to ask," she said. "But I'll be with you every step of the way. It's as big a risk for me as it is for you. We have to help, Mark."

"Henry Colte." His words stumbled out between sobs.

"Your uncle?" John scratched his head. "What can he do to help?"

"He's the Earl of Farnborough, my father's brother. He always suspected Mother of murdering my father. I heard him shouting at her before he kicked us out of Horsham. He accused her of poisoning me and killing my father. Of course Mother denied it, but he didn't believe her."

John shot a glance at Sarah. "Why didn't he report her and have her arrested?"

"I don't know. I suppose he never had the evidence to prove it."

"Do you think he'll help us now?"

"I don't know. I haven't heard from him since Father died. I won't go against Mother, I can't. But I will agree to travel to London where my uncle lives and tell him what happened to you. Either he will or he won't help you. That's the best I can do."

"That'll do. Grab your clothes and let's get out of here."

Back to London

John led them through the passage in the library to the large fireplace in the kitchens.

"I never knew about this," Mark said. "How many more secret passageways are there?"

"There's a lot about Broxley you don't know," John said.

"Why didn't you show me?"

"We didn't trust you. In any case, every time I went near you, Margaret got angry at me and sent you away."

Mark didn't answer.

Making sure the coast was clear, John ran to the wall at the darkest part of the courtyard.

"Don't we need horses?" Sarah whispered. "Or are we walking to Farnborough?"

John ignored the obvious sarcasm. "There are guards on patrol all over this place. If we try taking any horses, we'll be captured. We have to get them from somewhere else."

"Where?" Sarah pressed John for answers.

"Leave that to me, dear sister. The world out there is

not one you are familiar with. Life is very different beyond these walls."

"It's me, I've got them," John called out softly when they entered St Michael's Church. The Underlings came out of their hiding places and surrounded a wary Sarah and Mark.

"Who are these rascals?" Mark asked. "Has anyone ever told them they smell like piss?"

"We don't have time for formal introductions," John said. "Mark and Sarah, meet the infamous Underlings. These are my friends who saved my life in London. We're going to prove our innocence together so we can all live free."

Mark and Sarah threw questions at them in rapid succession, but John waved them off. "We don't have time for this. As soon as it's daylight they'll discover you both gone. Father's guards and everyone in the villages will be out looking for you. We need to be several hours ahead of them before they find out. There's no way they could know I was involved, and they wouldn't have any idea why you're missing, so we have several advantages in our favour."

"We're off to Norfolk then?" Andrew asked.

"Change of plans," John said. "We're going to Farnborough, which is south of London. Mark has an uncle there who suspects Margaret of murdering Mark's father. We're going to get him to help us."

"Uncle Henry isn't in Farnborough," Mark interrupted. "He spends all his time in London. That's where he will be, I'm sure of it."

"London it is then." John headed for the door. "But first we head back to Coventry."

In Coventry, John used his coin to hire more horses. He took note of the gentleman's name and the stables where they were hired from. He felt guilty because he knew they wouldn't be returning the horses, so he made a note to remind himself to reimburse him for the loss.

They made sure to ride through the towns for resupply during the busy times of the day, and at all times Mark and Sarah were kept hidden from view. John could only imagine the angst Margaret and his father would go through once they heard the news. He was sure no expense would be spared in finding them.

"You, what was your name? Isaac?" Sarah asked the first night they made camp.

"Yes, Lady Sarah. My name is Isaac."

"Good. Please tend to my horse and bring me dinner. I'm tired and hungered."

Isaac stared at Sarah, who looked at him expectantly. Laughter rang out from the Underlings. Andrew was almost bent double, such was the depth of his uncontrollable laughter.

"What do you find so amusing?" Sarah's face flushed red. "Were my orders not clear enough?"

Isaac looked at John for help. John laughed and slapped him on the back.

"Sister, dear, this is not Broxley. Nor is it the Stronde. I know this is strange to you, but we're all equals out here. We take care of our own chores. The Underlings are our friends, not our servants."

Sarah rose to her feet, her face deep red. "You expect me to take care of the horses myself and prepare my own food? You never told me that before I agreed to help you."

"Calm down, Sarah," John said. "I'll tend to your horse, but you need to understand your privilege doesn't work out here. We're all in this together, and we must work as a team if we're to be successful. The same goes for Mark and me as well. You need to put aside your aristocracy until Margaret is convicted. Then you can go back to Broxley and resume your life. Can you do that for me?"

Sarah stared around the small gathering before fixing her gaze on Isaac. "Please accept my apologies, Isaac. I'll try to remember my place here." She walked off to be on her own for a while.

"She'll be fine." John stopped Mark from going after her. "It's a big shock coming from a place like Broxley to this. It took me ages to adjust, and we're asking you to do it overnight. Give her some time and she'll be fine. Sarah is the strongest girl I've ever known."

It took a whole week to reach the outskirts of London, and Sarah stayed quiet most of it. Isaac followed her around, making sure her every need was taken care of and as they neared the end of their journey, she approached Isaac and took his hand in hers.

"Please forgive my poor manners, Isaac. I have a lot to learn about life outside my own walls. I hope I didn't offend you."

Isaac smiled and bowed to her. "Not at all, Lady Sarah. In fact, it's been my pleasure to have ridden with you on this journey. I hope we can remain friends long after this is over."

John smiled at his sister. He'd known she would come around eventually. Now she was learning how the majority of people in England lived without the trappings of affluence and influence, and it was a major shock to her system.

Just as it had been for him when he first broke away.

They made their final camp near the spot where John had spent a few nights earlier in the summer after he'd realised he couldn't stay in the Steelyard. It was as peaceful now as it had been then.

He knew it was the calm before the storm.

"We give the horses to the stables at St Mary Priory

tomorrow morning," he said to the gathered group. "This is where we have to split up. Sarah, Mark and I will enter the city through Bishopgate and try to find Henry Colte. The rest of you split up and enter through different gates. Wait for us at the Old Mill, and if that's not safe, Isaac knows where my secret hideout is, but be very careful if you go there because my father has guards all over it."

"You've taken over as leader now, have yea?" Andrew eyed John, his head cocked to the side.

"No, you're still the leader. But right now, with the people we're dealing with, it's better I take control."

Andrew shrugged his shoulders and nodded. "Fair point."

"Be very careful in the city," John carried on. "Even though my father and Margaret have no reason to suspect Sarah and Mark of being in London, they'll be frantically searching for them everywhere. The gang will be after my blood for killing Walden, so London's especially dangerous for us right now."

"He's right," Andrew said. "The rest of yea go straight to the Old Mill. Me and Helena will call on Gamaliell to get some food. Then we'll join yea."

He turned to John, Sarah, and Mark. "Be careful, and may God be with yea. We'll give you two days, and if you're not back by then we'll assume the worst. We might have to leave the Old Mill, but at least one of us will be at your hideout."

They shook hands, and the Underlings said their goodbyes to Mark and Sarah.

"You look pale, Mark," John said. "It's the same look you always had when your mother caught you spending time with me at Broxley."

Mark forced a smile. "I'm fine but I don't know if I want to do this. I can't go against my own mother."

"We've already been through this many times," John said. "You're not doing it for yourself. You're not even doing it for me. You're doing it to stop her from killing any more innocent boys in her search for me. She might have even killed your father and that's something you can't allow her to get away with."

"I don't believe that," Mark snapped. "Uncle Henry never liked my mother. He's probably just making it up. Otherwise, he would surely have come forward by now."

"He needs to know what Margaret is doing, Mark," Sarah said gently. "You know that she can't be allowed to carry on murdering people like this. She has to be stopped. You're the only one that can do it."

Mark sighed. "I know. I feel so guilty though."

"That's understandable," John said, "but it still needs to be done."

He stood up. "Are we ready?"

Henry Colte

Bishopgate was particularly busy, and although extra guards were posted, they passed through unnoticed.

Sarah pulled her nose and shuddered, pulling her cloak over the bottom of her face. "London stinks so badly, John. How can you tolerate being here?"

"You never get used to it," John said. "You just learn to put up with it."

Mark gagged and heaved a few times as they weaved their way along the filthy, narrow stretes of England's capital.

Eventually, they came to the Thames by the side of the Steelyard and turned right onto Thames Strete.

"Ooh. The river stinks almost as much as the stretes," Mark said.

"Wait until you meet the River Fleet," John replied. "You'll do well to hold on to your stomach when you meet that."

"Can't wait," Sarah said sarcastically.

Crowds were running towards St Paul's, so John stopped and gathered them together. "This usually means the cryer is giving important news. We need to listen to see if it involves you."

They agreed, so John took them to St Paul's Cross, the platform the cryer used when delivering his news.

Oh yeah, oh yeah, oh yeah. Hear this all you good people of London. Fifteen pounds reward for anyone who has information. Runaway murderer John Howard suspected of kidnapping his fourteen-year-old sister, Lady Sarah Howard, and his stepbrother, Master Mark Colte, also fourteen. They were last seen a week ago in their home in Warwickshire. Lady Margaret Colte, the missing boy's mother, has reason to believe that John Howard took them against their will and is holding them somewhere in London. Lady Margaret is offering fifteen pounds for any information that leads to their safe return. Fifteen pounds for any information!

Oh yeah, oh yeah, oh yeah. Fifteen-pound reward…

John gasped at the size of the reward on offer. "Margaret must be furious. That's a huge reward. We'd better be extremely vigilant."

Sarah shrank even further under her hood. "I don't feel safe here, John. Let's go."

Mark was rooted to the spot. "Come on, we can't stay here." John dragged him out of the crowd and pulled his cloak over his head. "Unless you're planning on getting seen, we've got to move."

Mark looked at John with the whitest face he'd ever seen and fell into step behind him.

"I don't like London," was all he said.

"How does she know we're in London?" Sarah asked. "And how does she know we're with you?"

"She doesn't," John answered. "She's just throwing it out there and hoping something happens. We need to be cautious because people all over London will be on the lookout for you with such a big reward on offer."

John took them to Baynard's Castle on the Thames and past the Somerset Inn.

"Stop." Mark brought them to a halt. "That's Uncle Henry's house." He pointed to a large house backing onto the Thames. The gate to the entrance was closed, and guards stood on watch.

"What do we do?" Mark asked. "If I tell them who I am, they might give us up for the reward."

"We don't have a choice," John said. "If we don't get in, then I'm dead in any case. He has to be made to see us."

Sarah squeezed John's arm. "Wouldn't it be better if you stayed out here? We're safe whatever happens, but you aren't."

"I'd thought about that, but if this doesn't work, I'm finished. I have nothing more to give. If this fails, Margaret has won. I'm going in with you."

Mark approached the guards at the gate. "I need to see Earl Henry Colte immediately. This is a matter of extreme importance."

The guards looked him up and down. "And who might you be?"

"My name is Mark Colte." Mark threw back the hood of his cloak. "These are Sarah and John Howard."

The guards' mouths fell open. "D-d-did you say John Howard, sir?"

"I did, and I demand you inform my uncle right away."

"Yes, sir. Immediately."

The guards stared at John, unable to take their eyes off him.

"Wait in the study." A servant guided them to a room, pulling his face at John the entire way. "The master will be with you shortly."

John slouched, feeling the heavy weight of accusations on his shoulders. "I didn't do any of the crimes Margaret accuses me of," he muttered, more to himself than to the others. "She's going to kill me with guilt if I'm not careful."

"You're innocent, John. All of us here know that. We just need to convince Henry." Sarah placed a comforting hand on his arm.

"And what might you need to convince me of, young lady?" A cultured man in his mid-forties entered the room. "To say I'm surprised to see you here is an understatement. You are the talk of the entire country. Especially you." He pointed his finger at John.

"You have a lot of explaining to do. I have already dispatched riders to inform Lord Howard that his daughter and errant son are safe and sound."

"That's not a wise move, Sir Henry." John stepped forward. This wasn't going as he'd hoped.

"And why is that? My nephew, who I haven't seen in over a decade, strolls in off the stretes after he's reported missing and has the entire country looking for him. Not only that, but he walks in with the most wanted man in England along with his sister."

"Did I miss anything?" he added, shrugging his shoulders.

"Uncle Henry, it isn't what it seems." Mark found his voice. John thought he looked even paler than normal if that was possible.

"What am I missing?" Henry Colte wasn't someone that John could like. He came across as pompous and full of self-serving interest. He regretted coming here almost immediately.

"Sir, if you would give us a chance." John stepped back

into the conversation. "Time is very limited if we are to achieve what we came here for."

"And what would that be? I'm assuming you came here to hand yourself in and hope for a fair trial? That's the best I can offer you."

"You don't understand, Uncle. John is innocent. He didn't poison me, and nor did he kidnap us. We came of our own accord to see you. It's my mother who needs the fair trial, not John."

Henry Colte looked at the nephew he hadn't seen for years. His body stiffened at the mention of Margaret, and he stepped back a couple of paces.

"Please, sit down," he said finally. "I'm all ears."

Everyone started speaking at once until Sir Henry held up his hand to stop them. "Please, one at a time."

John took the lead and spent the next hour telling Henry Colte everything that had happened since Margaret Colte arrived at Broxley.

"This is all very interesting, but what does any of it have to do with me?" he asked after listening patiently.

"Sir, Mark told us his father died of the sweating sickness, but he also told us that you suspected Margaret of murdering him. Mark suffered from the same sickness when he was young, but he survived. Don't you think it a coincidence that he suffered a similar sickness years later, only this time I took the blame for it?"

"Should I?"

"Who was the only person present during all of this? Margaret. Who stood to gain the most from your brother's death? Margaret. Who gained from my removal as my father's heir?"

"Margaret." Henry Colte finished the sentence for him. "I see the pattern here."

"Uncle," Mark interrupted. "I don't remember much from my childhood sickness, other than Mother giving me lots of honey that always seemed to make me worse. She did the same thing at Broxley and blamed it on John. We argued about it a lot afterwards, but she wouldn't listen to me."

"Why didn't you come forward sooner? You could have saved your stepbrother here a lot of pain."

"She frightens me." Mark's face turned red, and he looked at the floor. "She threatened to kill both me and Sarah if I ever spoke out about it. I would have gone to Earl Robert, but he would never believe me. He thinks Mother is the sweetest woman in England."

"So why now?" Henry leaned forward in his chair.

"Because Margaret has murdered close to forty innocent boys simply because they look like me," John spoke up. "She uses the strete gangs in London to capture anyone that looks like me, and they kill them when they find out they were wrong."

"And you know this for a fact?"

"I have first-hand knowledge. As I told you earlier, I watched them brutally murder one of my friends when I was there, and they spoke of others." John leaned forward to get closer to Henry Colte.

"She needs to be stopped, sir, before she destroys anybody else. Sarah and Mark are no longer safe because they dare to speak out against her. You are no longer safe because we're here. She is a danger to us all."

"And you can verify all of this, Miss Sarah?"

Sarah nodded. "Broxley for sure, sir. And the fact that she's destroyed my family like she destroyed yours."

"I always suspected that woman of killing Thomas, but I could never prove it. I had her followed at Saddleworth years ago, and she met with some known rascals even back then. When I questioned her, she said she was using them to help her find her mother, whom she'd lost contact with years earlier. I could never prove otherwise."

He stopped and drew a long breath.

"With Mark's knowledge of what happened at Broxley, we can finally bring her to justice. Lord Howard is a very powerful man, and I cannot do this alone. I need the help of someone with an ear to the king."

"Who would that be?" John asked. "My father has that ear as well."

"Not as much as Thomas Cromwell, who I happen to know quite well. He has no love for Robert Howard and his scheming wife. He will stop this once and for all."

"The chief minister?" John asked.

"Yes. He might be the son of a blacksmith, but he has the king's ear like no other."

"So you'll help us then?" Mark asked.

"Yes, nephew, I'll help you. I've wanted Margaret to face justice for years. With your testimony, I believe we can finally make it happen."

"And you can clear John at the same time?" Sarah asked.

"I believe so. If Mark tells Cromwell what he just told me, Robert Howard would have no other choice than to believe his son is innocent. Whether he reinstates him as his heir is up to him, of course."

"I don't care about that," John said. "I used to. In fact, it was all I ever thought about, but now I don't want it back. All I want is to be cleared of the accusations and to be a free man."

"There's no time to waste." Sir Henry jumped up. "Even now Margaret has men searching every corner of London, spreading the word that you are held against your will by the evil John Howard. She means you dead, John Howard, by any means possible."

He looked at John for a lasting moment.

"I cannot promise you the freedom you desire, but I can promise that I will do my very best to stop Margaret. You will stay here tonight as my guests, and we will leave at first light to see Cromwell, who I know is in residence across the city. He will be most delighted to hear the news we bring."

"What about the riders you dispatched to my father?" John asked.

"They are under orders to wait until I'd spoken to you. They will remain here."

John had a restless sleep that night. His life – what was left of it – depended on what happened over the next twenty-four hours.

Ambush

At dawn the next morning, Henry Colte led the way in his carriage. Mark rode with him, along with four of his most trusted guards and John and Sarah travelled a short way behind in a second carriage, along with more guards.

The stretes were quiet and almost deserted, save for a few early morning workers scurrying through the light rain on their way to who knows where.

The two horses pulling Sir Henry's carriage trotted the short distance to the end of Thames Strete and turned right in the direction of St Paul's.

As the carriage turned the corner, John saw a slight movement in the bushes to the left that were a part of Black Friars Dominican.

"Stop!" he screamed. "Stop now."

It was too late.

Several men, way too many to count, burst out of the bushes into the early morning drizzle and unleashed a hail of arrows at the lead carriage. Guards fell, stumbling, trying to protect their master and fight their attackers.

Henry Colte's guards flew out of the second carriage

and joined the fight, but they were mown down by another hail of arrows.

"Sarah!" John shouted. Sarah sat completely still, her mouth gaping wide open. "Sarah."

John grabbed his sister and yanked her out of the side of the carriage. She resisted, unable to peel her eyes away from the carnage playing out in front of her. John pulled her roughly, running into the grounds of the deserted Berkeley Inn and threw her into a muddy ditch where they hid together.

Guards and attackers lay strewn across the road, their blood turning the muddy strete into large pools of dark crimson. Wounded men moaned and cried for help, but there was nothing John could do to aid them.

The attackers vanished as swiftly as they'd appeared. The whole thing lasted only a few minutes, but the carnage was everywhere. Dead bodies mingled with the wounded, and for a moment John's world turned upside down. Everything seemed to happen in slow motion around him.

People rushed from all around to the devastating scene, running past John in slow, methodical strides. Everyone was yelling and screaming, and yet John's world was silent.

He ran towards Colte's carriage, each stride feeling like he was running through waist-deep mud and yelled Mark's name several times, but his ears didn't register any sound.

A carriage trotted past him, and John got a good look at the sole occupant. A sneer, followed by a bark of silent laughter from the wild-eyed woman held John's gaze as her carriage slid slowly by.

Margaret! It was Margaret!

He turned and ran after her carriage, but it was pointless. Her carriage disappeared down Thames Strete as the crowds grew in number, obscuring his view as Margaret slipped away.

John turned his attention back to Mark and Henry Colte. Sarah was leaning over a still body slumped in the carriage seat. He pulled her back to see the lifeless body of Mark, blood running down his neck from the arrow that had gone through it.

Henry Colte lay next to him, barely alive and gurgling through a blood-filled mouth. He grabbed John's arm and pulled him close.

Suddenly, everything burst into life around him. Screams, people yelling and shouting. The volume was amplified, and John's head almost burst open.

Henry pulled John closer. "Margaret," he gurgled. "It's her. You've got to stop her."

"I saw her." John could barely see through the tears that poured out of his eyes.

"Promise you'll avenge us."

"I promise."

Henry Colte's eyes flickered and then closed for the final time.

He was dead.

Large crowds gathered, and John knew it wouldn't be long before the constable, as well as his father's guards, arrived. Sarah was still bent over Mark, shaking him and shouting at him.

"He's gone, Sarah. We've got to get out of here or they'll have died for nothing."

Sarah didn't seem to hear him because she carried on shaking Mark.

"Sarah. Sarah, he's gone. We have to go."

Sarah still ignored him, so he pulled her roughly away and dragged her off, screaming and fighting all the way.

"Father and his guards will be here any minute." John's tone was harsh. "Unless you want us to die here as well, we have to go."

"He's dead. Mark's dead." Sarah's eyes looked empty and lost.

"I know, and we will be too if we don't move quickly."

John dragged his sister away from the horrific scene, and they ran.

And ran.

Town Cryer

They stopped when they reached the wall at Aldersgate. By now, word had spread of the massacre on Thames Strete, and everyone was running in that direction. John and Sarah were the only people running away from it.

The guards at Aldersgate were deep in conversation, talking loudly about the ambush, so John took advantage of the situation. Whatever else they did this day, they had to get out of London. If they didn't, they would surely die.

They slipped past the guards without being noticed.

The small church at St Bartholomew's Hospital on Britten Strete right outside the city gates looked deserted, so they slipped quietly inside and looked for somewhere to rest and find sanctuary.

They found a small, empty room down some stone steps in the church's rear corner where John fell to the ground and closed his eyes, exhaustion and grief enveloping him like a swarm of bees. The events of the last twenty-four hours were too much and he couldn't take any more.

Sarah lay beside him, sobbing softly at first before the

emotion poured out of her in uncontrollable waves. John tried to quieten her, but she wouldn't – or couldn't – stop. She lay next to her brother, shaking and trembling like a leaf in the wind.

"Mark's dead, John. He's dead. He didn't want to do this, and we made him. He's dead because of us." Her cries became louder again.

"We may have talked him into coming with us, but it wasn't us that killed him. You saw her there. It was Margaret. She is responsible for killing her own son."

"How did she know where we were?" Sarah sobbed. "Why didn't she just stop us and take us back? She could have taken you into custody and put you on trial. Why did she have to kill Mark?"

John placed his arm around his sister. "Margaret doesn't want to capture me. I know too much about how she operates and who she deals with. She wants me dead at any cost. I'll wager that when she discovered Henry Colte was involved, she took the opportunity to kill him at the same time. He'd suspected her of poisoning his brother for a long time, so by killing him at the same time as she killed me, she got rid of all her problems at once."

"But she didn't kill you. She killed Mark instead."

"I suspect that was an accident. I don't think even she would kill her own son like that. I bet she didn't know Mark was in the front carriage with Henry Colte."

"Why didn't she kill us? Why did we get away and Mark didn't?"

"Luck," John said. "We were in the carriage behind them, and they took the brunt of the attack. The guards in our carriage died trying to protect Henry. We were lucky to get away."

"Do you think she knew they'd killed Mark?"

"I doubt it, but I'm sure she'll know by now. I bet she's going mad at this point."

"How did she know where we were?" Sarah asked.

"I don't know," John said. "But I'd wager that one of the guards outside Henry's home turned us in. The reward was too large to ignore. That amount of coin will turn most heads, even the most loyal ones."

Footsteps outside the door made him jump. "We've got to hide," he whispered.

There was another door in the room behind them, down a few steps. John berated himself for not noticing it when they had first gone in there, but he had been too emotional to look. The door was locked, so he reached up and ran his fingers around the top of the door frame, hoping a trick he'd learned at St Michael's Church in Warwickshire applied here in London.

His fingers closed around a long, cold metal object. "Got it," he whispered. The key turned, and the door swung open, revealing stone steps leading down into a large black hole.

Sarah hesitated.

"We're too exposed out here," John said. "At least we'll be safe down there."

Sarah shivered.

John was about to go into the abyss when a thought struck him. He turned and walked back to the outer door leading into the church and inserted the key into the lock.

It turned!

The same key worked on both doors. John closed the door to the darkness and sat beside Sarah in the now secure room.

He had a plan.

"I have to get some supplies. It isn't safe for us out there, and everyone will be looking for us, but I have a few supplies hidden away, so I'm going to get them and bring them back here. You'll be much safer here, so please lock the door behind me and don't open it for anyone. I'll knock three times, wait a moment, and then knock twice, and then once. Like this." He demonstrated on the floor.

"That way you'll know it's me."

"I'm coming with you."

"No. I know several secret ways in and out of the city, and it's safer and faster if I go alone. If I'm caught, I don't want to worry about you as well. Stay here, and I'll be as fast as I can."

"What happens if you're caught? What do I do then? I don't know anything about London or this new life that you're living."

John grasped his sister's hands. "I'm really sorry I dragged you into this. If I'd known any other way to clear my name I would have taken it. I regret doing it even more now. I cannot fail, Sarah. Margaret has to pay for her crimes."

"I agree, and I'll forgive you for involving me. I'm not so forgiving about Mark though. He didn't deserve to die like that."

John bowed his head. "I know, and I regret my actions involving both of you. I'd take it back if I could. I should have died back there, not him. All I can do now is make sure he didn't die for nothing."

"So what do I do if you're caught?"

"Give me until first light. If I'm not back by then, assume I've been caught. Go to the guards at the city gates and tell them I kidnapped you and forced you to go with me. You got away when I left to get supplies. That's what I'll tell them if I'm caught, and it should be enough to guarantee your safety. But once you're free of me, make sure you go to Norfolk and seek safety with Uncle Thomas.

Margaret will kill you if you don't because she knows you saw her this morning."

"I can't tell them that, John. They'll kill you." Sarah hung her head.

"They'll kill me anyway if I'm caught. Please promise me you'll save yourself if that happens. I can't die peacefully if I know you are in danger as well, especially as it's all my fault you're involved in this."

Sarah nodded.

"Promise me."

Sarah nodded.

"Say it, Sarah. For me. For Mark."

"I promise," she said. "But I can't lose both of you. Get back here, John, and put an end to this nightmare."

"I promise to do my best."

They hugged, and John was gone, although he waited until he heard the sound of the key turning in the lock behind him.

He slipped outside into the early afternoon bustle and walked through the gate without incident. His stomach churned the entire time he was crossing into the city, and he felt as though all eyes were on him.

He hurried towards St Paul's intending to cross the River Fleet and the city wall using their secret passage, but he was knocked to the side by people rushing past him, running towards St Paul's.

Realising they were racing to hear what the cryer had to say about the murderous ambush, John joined them, making sure he stayed at the rear so he could escape quickly if he had to.

St Paul's Cross was packed with the people of London, all eager to hear about what had happened earlier.

Oh yeah, oh yeah, oh yeah, hear yea good people of London. Underlings captured after brutal murder on the stretes of London. Oh yeah, oh yeah, oh yeah. Underlings captured after a bloodbath on the stretes of London.

The kidnapped children of Lord Howard and Lady Margaret Colte escaped John Howard and the Underlings last night after they'd kidnapped them from their home in Warwickshire.

The two children sought safety with Sir Henry Colte, Mark Colte's uncle. This morning, Sir Henry was personally delivering them to Lady Margaret Colte to reunite them with their family.

As they left Sir Henry's home, they were ambushed by the Underlings. Both Sir Henry and Mark Colte died in a hail of arrows. Sir Henry's guards fought valiantly and captured the Underling leader and most of his gang. John Howard got away, forcing his sister, Lady Sarah Howard, to go with him. The few Underlings who got away will be captured shortly.

Lord Asheborne has joined Lord Howard in demanding the safe return of Lady Sarah Howard. They offer anyone who captures John Howard ten pounds a year for life if they deliver him, along with the safe return of Lady Sarah.

Oh yeah, of yeah, oh yeah. Ten pounds a year for life for the capture of John Howard and the safe return of Lady Sarah Howard. Underling leader captured after a bloodbath on the stretes of London this morning.

Sir Henry Colte and his nephew, Mark Colte, murdered in a hail of arrows...

John pulled the hood of the cloak tightly over his head and backed away from the baying crowds. His clothes were soaked from the cold sweat covering his body.

Grimacing, he forced himself to think about what he'd just heard.

What has she done? What happened to Andrew and the others?

Then he ran.

He ran down Thames Strete and into the grounds of Black Friars, straight past the scene of the grizzly crime.

People were still there, deep in conversation about the day's events.

He ran to the bush next to the wall, and looking around to make sure nobody was watching, he disappeared inside and walked into the darkness.

He had to find out what had happened.

Crypts

Guards were swarming all over the Old Mill, so John gave it a wide berth.

What happened? How did they catch them so fast? More importantly, how were they linked to Henry Colte and Mark's deaths? Whatever it was, Margaret had to be behind it.

John jumped over the wall at Milford Lane and hid, watching for any sign of activity. His father was sure to have increased the guards at the Stronde after recent events in Warwickshire and more recently Sir Henry Colte's residence in London.

He watched as guards working in pairs patrolled the grounds of his father's London home. He timed them as best he could, and watched them for several circuits to make sure he had enough time to reach the treehouse.

Finally satisfied he could make it, he made his move, running to the large tree and scaling it as fast as he could. He emerged into his hiding place, relieved to see scared faces staring back at him.

"John!" Isaac yelled far too loudly. "We thought they'd surely caught you."

His eyes were red and swollen, and John knew he'd been crying.

"Be quiet," John ordered, putting his fingers to his lips in a show of silence. "Father has extra guards all over this place."

"We know," Isaac said. "We see them all the time. We're stuck up here and can't get out."

John looked around to see who was there. His heart skipped a beat when he saw the beautiful features of Catherine Devine sitting in the corner.

"Catherine, I'm so glad you're here," he said, trying to stop his voice from cracking with emotion.

"Hello, John." The sound of her voice made him shiver. Her smile melted him. "I'm glad to see you as well, but I'm sorry about your friends."

"Is this all of you?" he asked, pulling himself from his trance.

Isaac's head drooped and his eyes filled up again. "Yes, we think so. We can't be sure though."

"What happened?"

"After you left us, we split up as we always do," Isaac said. "Andrew went with Helena, Abraham with David, and I took care of Catherine. We took our time going through London so we wouldn't all get to the secret passage at the same time. I'm guessing we were the last because when we got to the Old Mill it was swarming with guards. Lots of them."

Isaac's jaw quivered and his voice wavered. Catherine wept quietly in the corner, and John felt sorry for them.

"Go on," John said. "What happened next?"

"It was horrible. They had Andrew and Helena, and they gave Andrew a good kicking. I wanted to help, I really did, but there were too many of them."

Isaac broke down again. John placed his hand on his arm to comfort him.

"You did the right thing. There was nothing you could do. There's no point in giving yourself up for no reason. Andrew wouldn't have wanted that either."

Isaac nodded. "I know, but it doesn't make me feel any better."

"Then what happened?"

"We hid and watched them drag David out. He fought them all the way. He was hysterical, yelling at them the whole time."

"What was he saying?" John asked.

Isaac looked at Catherine.

"It's okay," she whispered. "Tell him."

"He yelled over and over that it must have been the girl that gave them away." Isaac wrung his hands together. "He kept yelling the girl had betrayed us, that she was one of them all along and that it was your fault for bringing her to us."

John looked at Catherine, who stared at the ground, crying softly.

"It wasn't me. I swear I had nothing to do with it."

John stared at Catherine. "What then?"

"More guards came, and we knew we couldn't stay there. I'm sorry, John, I didn't know anywhere else to go."

"How long have you been here?"

"We came here yesterday, right after we left the Old Mill. We've been here ever since."

"Did David say how they caught them?" John asked. "Did they follow us? Or did someone give us away?" He looked back at Catherine.

"I swear I had nothing to do with it," she said again, tears pouring down her face. "I know why you think it's probably me, but it wasn't. If it were, why is Isaac still not caught? They'd have followed me and caught us in here."

"They could have lost you after you ran." John's face was ice cold. "If you did it, Catherine, tell me now. I won't harm you, but you must tell me the truth. I saved your life, so you owe me at least that much."

Catherine's eyes looked dull and full of tears. "I promise you on my life, I had nothing to do with it. After what they did to my father, I wanted to get as far away from them as I could. I owe you everything, and I wanted to stay with you."

She lowered her head.

"I like you, John Howard, and I want to be with you. I'll leave if you want me to and I understand why you would. But I didn't do it."

John's chest skipped a beat, and the coldness fell from his heart.

"I believe you, although I'm not letting you out of my sight from now on."

"Thank you."

"What happened to you?" Isaac changed the subject. "Where's Mark and Sarah? Did you get the earl to agree to help?"

John sighed loudly and slumped to the floor.

"You're not going to like what I'm about to tell you."

They sat in silence for a moment after John finished telling them what had happened on Thames Strete.

"In God's name, is there nothing that woman won't do?" Isaac bit his lip. "She's the devil herself."

"I don't think she intended for Mark to die," John said. "I think she'll be devastated when she finds out he was killed in the attack, especially as she knows Sarah and I got away."

"What do we do now?" Isaac asked. "We can't stay here for long."

"I found a place where we can hide for a while," John said. "Or at least I think I did. Sarah is there waiting for me, and if I'm right, we could have a place where we'll be safe until we decide what to do next."

"Can't we just stay here?" Catherine asked. "It's been safe so far."

"Do the others know about it?" John looked at Isaac. "Did you tell any of them where it was?"

Isaac shook his head. "I never got the chance. They knew you had a safe hiding place, but I never told any of them where it was, not even Andrew."

"Good," John said. "It's still safe, but not right now. Father has this place teeming with guards. Sooner or later they will hear us up here. We have to go somewhere else."

They gathered what supplies they could, which didn't amount to much. A few clothes, some candles and blankets, and most importantly, John's sword.

He knew sooner or later he would need it.

One by one, they left the treehouse and hid behind the stables. When they were clear of the Stronde, John took them as far to the north of London as daylight would allow. He wanted to get as far away from prying eyes as he could.

None of the city gates would be safe from now on, and even their secret passage in and out of the city was dangerous. If one of the captured Underlings revealed its location under torture, it could be used as a trap. From now on it was out of bounds.

They crossed the Fleet over a deserted cow bridge somewhere near the Priory of St John Jerusalem. Daylight was fading as they went past Smithfield Market onto

Britten Strete, and entered the church where Sarah was waiting for them.

John gave the secret knock and stood back, his heart pounding.

Lord, please let Sarah still be here.

After a long, uneasy pause, the key turned in the door, and Sarah stood before them. She flew into John's arms.

"John, thank the Lord. I was scared they'd caught you. Where's the rest?" Sarah looked around for the missing Underlings.

"They're gone," John said, his voice flat and bitter. "Margaret somehow found them after they left us yesterday. Isaac and Catherine are the only ones left."

"How?" Sarah asked, fumbling with the key. "How could she know about them? Colte's guard could have told her about us, but there's no way he knew anything about your friends."

"That's what I have to find out," John said. "Give me the key. I want to look at something."

He took the key and opened the door to the abyss down the stairs at the back of the room. "I want to see what's down here."

He lit a candle and led the way into the gloomy darkness.

Sarah's Safety

Sarah shivered. "I don't like this place," she whispered.

"I don't either," John said. "But it might be an escape route for us."

He led the way down the wide stone steps until the ground opened up in front of him then lifted the candle high in the musty air and looked around in the dim glow.

He was in the church crypt!

Catherine let out a stifled scream. "This place is horrible!."

John squeezed her arm. "There may be another way out, so we have to keep looking."

Catherine sighed and held on tightly as John stepped forward, following the passageway.

They crept past several tombs, sealed long ago by people of a bygone age. After what seemed like an eternity, they reached another thick door like the one at the other end. John inserted the same key that opened the door at the other end and made a silent prayer.

It worked!

It was dark outside, but it looked like daylight

compared to the pitch darkness they'd just witnessed. He shielded his eyes for a moment until they adjusted, and peered out to see where he was.

John staggered back in amazement. They'd come out of a doorway hidden behind closed gates in a large family tomb in the cemetery at the side of the large church of Grey Friars. The church was to their left as they emerged.

What shocked John was that not only were they back inside the walled city, but they were at the entrance to the Shambles, an area John knew very well. He couldn't believe his luck.

"Where are we?" Isaac emerged from the back of the group.

"We're at Grey Friars, next to the Shambles. This is perfect."

"Wow," was all Isaac could muster. "The good Lord giveth and the good Lord taketh away."

"Isaac, take Catherine back to the room inside the church and wait for me there. I'm going to take Sarah with me and get some supplies from Gamaliell."

"Are you sure?" Isaac looked worried. "It's not safe to be out after dark."

"It's not safe for us anywhere at any time," John reminded him. "In any case, his house is right around the corner from here."

"Please be careful." Catherine squeezed John's hand, sending shivers pulsating through his entire body.

What's happening to me? All she has to do is look at me and I turn into a wet fish. I don't have time for this now.

"I'll see you back in the church."

John locked the door after Isaac and Catherine walked through.

"Where are we going?" Sarah asked, squinting at John. "What are you up to?"

"Nothing. I want you with me so I can keep you safe. We're going to a good friend's home. He saved my life once, and he's the best friend any man could ever wish for."

Sarah started to speak but John grabbed her arm and strode off, keeping to the shadows to avoid the Watch.

A few minutes later, John rapped on the door at the rear of Gamaliell Pye's large home. He shuddered as he remembered the state he'd been in the last time he was here.

The door slowly opened, and a gaping mouthed Gamaliell Pye stood staring at them.

"Come inside, quickly," he said. "You'll get us all killed if anyone sees you."

"Do you know what happened?" John asked, doing away with any pleasantries.

Pye shook his head. "Nothing more than strete gossip. I haven't heard anything officially, if that's what you mean."

"What have you heard?"

"I'm guessing this is your sister?" Pye pointed at Sarah.

"Yes, sorry. Sarah, this is my good friend, Gamaliell Pye."

They shook hands.

"What have you heard?" John repeated.

"Only that you kidnapped your sister and stepbrother from Warwickshire and brought them under duress to London. Sarah and Mark Colte managed to escape your evil clutches and ran for help to Mark's uncle, Sir Henry Colte. You ambushed them early this morning, killing both Sir Henry and Mark Colte. The guards captured most of the Underlings, including Andrew, but you escaped with your sister. That's about all I've heard."

"None of that is true," Sarah glowered, her face bright red. "I don't know who came up with that, but it's nonsense. For one, John didn't kidnap us. We came here of our own accord. We went to Henry Colte together for help in defeating Margaret. I don't know who ambushed us but it wasn't John's friends."

"That I can believe," Pye said. "All the above came from Margaret Colte. She's told the same story to everyone who'll listen, including the king, from what I hear. It is said the king is furious and wants you captured at all costs."

"Margaret is behind all of it," John said. "I doubt she meant to kill Mark, but she's the one behind it all."

"I heard she is distraught about the death of her son. I believe you when you say his death was an accident. That arrow was no doubt meant for you."

"How did she get Andrew and the others?" John asked.

"That I don't know. There is a veil of secrecy regarding the Underlings. I'm sure word will get out eventually, but right now there's nothing but silence."

"I have to get them out."

"That might prove to be too much even for you."

"I have to," John said. "All this is my fault. Everyone who has died has been because of me. I have to stop it." John was visibly sweating.

"How can I help?" Pye asked softly.

"Sarah can't stay with me," John started. "It's too dangerous for her."

Sarah backed away from John, her eyes wide. Her face flushed again. "You brought me here to get rid of me? I won't allow it. You brought me here, and I am staying with you."

"It's too dangerous for you, Sarah. You don't belong in this world, and I'm the most wanted man in England right now. If you stay with me, I'll get you killed, and I can't do that. It's my fault Mark's dead, and I can't have your death on my conscience as well."

"So, what? You'll send me back to Broxley where Margaret can take her time killing me instead? Father is never there and now Mark's dead do you really think she'll spare me? Especially after she saw me leaving that terrible scene with you this morning."

"No." John shook his head and looked at Pye. "Can you keep her safe and arrange for her to go to Thomas Howard in Norfolk? He'll keep her safe until this is over."

"If it's ever over," Sarah added.

John pursed his lips. "Yes, if it's ever over. But even if she wins, you'll be safe with Uncle Thomas."

"I can do better than that." Pye looked at them both. "Sir Thomas is in London as we speak. Not far from here, in fact. I can have a message sent to him this evening."

"Can you keep Sarah safe until he gets her?" John asked. "If I don't do anything else in my life, and if I die tomorrow, I want to make sure my sister is safe from that evil woman."

"You have my word," Pye replied.

Sarah's eyes filled with tears and John knew he was not far behind. He grabbed her and hugged her as hard as he could.

"I'm sorry, Sarah, but I have to make sure you're safe. Please do this for me now, even if you never speak to me again. Promise me."

Sarah looked at her brother, tears falling down her face. "None of this is your fault. This is all Margaret. She blamed you for her crimes and then pursued you when you ran away, murdering anyone that got in her way. I don't want to leave you, but I'll do as you ask. If I am to die, it won't be on your conscience. You're right when you say I don't belong in this world. I don't."

"Thank you." John hugged his sister one more time. "I'll come and get you when this is over."

Sarah looked at John, wiping her nose with her sleeve. "Please be careful, brother. I demand to see you again, do you hear?"

"I promise to do my best." John gave them both one more harrowed look and then vanished into the night with the supplies Pye had made ready for him.

Hiding

Shadows danced on the walls under the dim candlelight around the ancient tombs. It was an eerie setting, but at least they were safe. Nobody would ever find the Underlings there.

John, Isaac, and Catherine sat in a small circle discussing the day's events. This was all that remained of their beloved group of Underlings.

"We stay down here where it's safe," John said. "It's scary and dark, but nobody will ever find us. Even if they do, we have an escape route."

"What happened?" Isaac asked. "How did Lady Margaret find Andrew and the others?"

"I don't know," John answered curtly. "I'm hoping to find out soon so we can decide what to do."

"Decide what to do?" Isaac raised his voice. "We're finished, John. Andrew's gone, Abraham's gone, and Helena and David. Mark was the only one who could stop her, and he's dead too. We're all that's left. We have to get out of London if we have any chance of staying alive."

"We can't leave London until we know what happened to Andrew and the others," John replied. "I have to prove Margaret was behind the murders this morning. Perhaps then my father will believe me and do something about her."

"And how are you going to do that?" Isaac asked.

"I don't know yet," John answered. "I'm still thinking about it."

Catherine, who had remained quiet up to this point, chimed in. "She might make a mistake because of her grief over killing her son. If she didn't mean for him to die, she'll be praying to God for mercy."

John looked up at her. Her features softened in the warm glow of the candlelight, and he felt the goosebumps all over his body. He resisted the urge to touch her hand and forced himself to look away.

"You have a good point. Let's see if she makes a move. She must be desperate to catch me after I escaped again."

"We can't stay down here," Isaac said. "This place gives me the creeps. It's scary and I don't like it."

"Neither do I," John said. "But we're safe, and unless you know somewhere better, we have no choice. My father and Lord Asheborne are offering ten pounds a year for life for anyone that turns me in. That's going to make everyone in London be on the lookout for me."

"Which is why I said we need to get out of London." Isaac's eyes danced in the candlelight. "We're dead if we stay here."

"We're dead no matter where we go if we don't stop Margaret." John stood up. "She will pursue me for the rest of her life if I don't stop her."

He looked at Isaac and Catherine. "It's me she's after, not you. As long as you stay away from Asheborne's guards, you'll be safe. I'm the one she wants."

Isaac jumped to his feet. "You want me to abandon you after all that's happened? Andrew and the others got caught trying to help you, and I'm not going anywhere."

John clasped hands tightly with his best friend. "Thank you for standing with me, my friend. I shall not forget this."

During the night, John woke up with a start with Isaac shaking him gently. "What is it?" he asked, struggling to clear the mist from his brain.

"Shh, I don't want to wake Catherine. Listen, John. I know you like her but think about it. All of this happened after you brought her to us. Before that we were fine. She has to be the one who gave us up. How else could Margaret have found Andrew and the others so quickly?"

"I don't know," John said, "and I'm not ruling it out. She's been very quiet since we've been here. She's hardly spoken a word, but I'm not convinced it's her. Think about it, Isaac, why would she help them? Walden murdered her father and was taking her to work in a brothel. She has no reason to help them."

"Ten pounds a year for life will sway anyone's mind."

"Possibly," John answered. "But that wasn't offered until the attack on Mark and his uncle. Until I rescued Catherine , she wouldn't have ever heard of Margaret. She had no idea who I was until I rescued her, and she's been with us ever since. She didn't have a chance to tell anyone even if she'd wanted to. It can't possibly have been Catherine's fault."

"So what happened then? How did she catch them so quickly?"

"I don't know," John said. "Maybe it was just bad luck and one of her guards or one of the strete chiefs saw them on the way to the Old Mill and followed them. That's what I think happened."

"I don't trust her," Isaac said, the anger in his voice apparent in the darkness.

"You don't need to trust her. Just keep an eye on her until this is over."

"What are you going to do?"

"I'm still thinking about it." John lay his head down and tried going back to sleep, but the visions of recent days tormented his soul. He tried thinking of better times.

What will I do after Margaret has been hanged for murder and Father has taken me back into the family? How can Sarah and I move on from this?

He sat up with a jolt. For the first time, he realised that he didn't want to go back to Broxley and the way it was before. He had changed. Into what, he didn't know, but whatever it was, he knew he would never be the same again. He felt at home on the stretes of London.

He shook himself. *Don't be stupid. I had everything I could ever want in life, and I want it back.*

He forced himself to stop thinking and close his eyes.

The next morning they shared the food and ale Pye had provided the previous evening in the small storeroom inside the church.

"We can't stay down there unless we have to," Isaac stated for the fiftieth time that morning. "It's scary, and so dark we don't even know if it's day or night."

"I agree," John said. "As long as we keep that door locked there's no reason we can't stay in here." He pointed to the door leading to the church. "We can't go out that door though."

"We can't stay here forever," Isaac said. "We have to do something."

John looked at Catherine, who had barely spoken a word. "What do you think, Catherine?" He tried bringing her into the conversation.

Catherine looked at John. "It doesn't matter what I think. Isaac believes it was me who gave you all up, and he won't change his mind. It wasn't me, and I'll do anything to prove it. He wants to kill me. I can see it in his eyes when he looks at me."

Isaac sighed. "I don't want to kill you. If I did, you'd be dead already. I don't trust you, and there's nothing wrong with that, but I won't hurt you. Not unless we find out it was you who gave us up."

"Enough of this," John said. "We're stuck together whether we like it or not. Let's get along and get through this. I had an idea last night that might work."

"What?" Isaac and Catherine asked at the same time.

"Pye's home is close to the entrance to the crypts. I can go there every night to find out the latest news. If I can find out what's happening to Andrew and the others, I might be able to get to them and get them out."

"That's not a plan," Isaac said. "That's suicide."

"Maybe, but it's the best I can come up with for now."

After dark, John crept out of the family tomb and slipped quietly to the rear door of Gamaliell Pye's home. He rapped several times on the door and held his breath. If Pye had been caught, he was done for.

Pye opened the door and beckoned him inside.

"I was expecting you," he said, pointing to a bag of supplies he had readied for him.

"Thank you, Gamaliell. I owe you a debt of gratitude I fear I may never be able to repay. I come here eager for news as much as supplies. Did Sarah get away safely? What have you heard?"

"Please, sit." Pye pointed to a set of chairs.

"Your sister is safe. I met with Sir Thomas myself and he was more than happy to help. In fact, he requested a meeting with you if you're willing."

"Uncle Thomas wants to see me? Why? Does he want to help me or turn me in?"

"He didn't tell me his thoughts, but he doesn't like Margaret Colte. He knew of the allegations Sir Henry made against her years ago, and he never liked it when your father announced his marriage to her. I'm assuming he's wanting to help you in some way. If you're willing that is."

"Yes! Yes, please arrange it for me." John's spirits lifted for the first time in days. "This might be the only way I can get anyone to believe my word against hers. When do I meet him, and where?"

"Leave it with me, and I'll try to arrange it while he's here in London. Come back tomorrow night when I should be able to tell you more."

"What of Andrew and the others?"

"Not so good news, I'm afraid. The cryers have been all over the city telling everyone how the Underlings murdered Sir Henry and his nephew. They are to face a trial in three days' time."

John sighed heavily. "We all know how that's going to go. They're as guilty as Anne Boleyn was, yet they executed her. If they can behead a queen, Andrew and the rest have no chance."

"I fear you are correct," Pye said. "There is nothing either I or you can do about it, so stay hidden in your crypts and don't do anything stupid. I'll arrange the meeting with Sir Thomas and I'll see you tomorrow evening."

John thanked him for the supplies and slid back into the shadows of the night.

John, Isaac and Catherine stayed in the storage room that night and the next day. Nobody tried the door, so they felt safe enough where they were. The door to the crypts was open just in case, and they would bolt down the stairs and lock the door behind them at the slightest sound from inside the church.

None of them wanted to spend another night down there unless they had to.

Thomas Howard

Gamaliell Pye ushered John into his house bearing good news.

"You are to stay here tonight in my safety room. Sir Thomas will send a carriage here after curfew has lifted to take you to a meeting with him."

John nodded. "I can agree to that."

"I have laid out some new clothes for you in the room. The one's you're wearing stink so bad I fear your uncle will refuse to see you."

John smiled for the first time in days. "I can see him doing that. My uncle isn't used to meeting rascals from the stretes of London. Is Sarah still there?"

"I don't know where she is. Your uncle promised to keep her safe, and I have no reason to disbelieve him. Other than that, I have no place questioning the Duke of Norfolk. You should understand that more than most."

"Do you have any more news of the Underlings?"

"No." Pye shook his head. "I won't hear anything else until after the trial. Your uncle might know more. Will your friends worry if you don't go back tonight?"

"I told Isaac not to worry if I didn't return. There's nowhere else better for them to hide, and I told him I'll be back when I have news."

Pye pressed a hidden lever on the dark wood-panelled library wall, and as if by magic a room appeared that was big enough to hide one person safely.

"Stay here until I come to get you. There are candles, food and ale in there, so you will be refreshed for your meeting tomorrow. And don't forget to change clothing."

"I won't. Thank you once again, Gamaliell. I owe you a great debt and I hope to repay it one day."

"I'm just glad to be of help," Pye replied. "Now get in there and get some sleep."

John struggled against the ropes that bound him. The more he struggled, the more he became entangled in their grip. Margaret stood over him, laughing maniacally at his hopelessness.

She opened the sack she was holding, staring at John the entire time. "This is all your fault, John. None of this would have happened if you'd just got on that boat and gone to France."

John thrashed and fought against the ropes that burned deep into his flesh. His heart pounded inside his chest as he looked up at Margaret staring down at him triumphantly.

She opened the sack and slowly pulled out its contents. John screamed as the severed head of his sister emerged into view.

John screamed again, thrashing for all he was worth. His body convulsed in uncontrollable fits of rage and grief.

"It's all your fault, John."

The sound of grinding wheels echoed around the room, drowning his screams. Cool air hit him, and the sound of Gamaliell's voice dragged him back from the abyss.

He woke up, drenched from head to foot in a cold sweat.

"You were dreaming again?" Pye asked.

"It's the same dream I've had every night since Mark's death. Margaret attacks me even in my dreams."

"She is an evil woman," Pye said. "You will never be rid of her as long as she is alive. The carriage is here to take you to see Thomas Howard, so you'd better hurry."

John thanked Pye once again and stepped out of the rear door into daylight. The weak morning sun felt good on his face, and he paused for a moment to enjoy it. This was the first time in many days he'd dared go outside in daylight.

The guards remained silent and stern faced the entire journey. John tried making conversation by asking them where they were going, but they remained tight-lipped and didn't say a word. John was glad when they eventually reached their destination, which was a large house in the Austin Friars area where many of the senior aristocrats had homes. Thomas Cromwell himself lived somewhere around here, as did many of the dukes like his uncle.

He was shown into a plush study where he waited impatiently. His stomach churned and he shivered uncontrollably.

What if he'd misread the situation and given both Sarah and himself up for slaughter?

He sighed and shook his shoulders. *There's nothing I can do about it now, so try to relax and see what happens. If guards burst through the door, I'll know I failed. I just hope it's my uncle and not Margaret who's waiting to see me.*

The door opened, and John braced himself for what was about to happen.

Thomas Howard, 3rd Duke of Norfolk, strode into the study looking every inch the powerful man that he was. His silk shirt and fine woollen doublet alone would have cost more than most people in London make in a year. His hair went down to his collar, and his dark velvet hat stood proudly on his head.

"I never expected to see you again, John. I hear you have been running around murdering anyone that gets in your path."

"Thank you for seeing me, Uncle. You know I'm not guilty of any of it, or you wouldn't have agreed to see me today."

"Your manner is more abrupt than I seem to remember, but that is understandable given your situation. Please, sit." Thomas gestured for him to sit down.

"So, please tell me what happened."

"Where do you want me to start?"

"At the beginning, when Margaret Colte married your father."

"I will tell you everything gladly, Uncle, but first, please tell me that Sarah is safe and well."

"Your sister is in my custody and is safe. Nobody knows she is here, and I intend keeping it that way."

"You won't send her back to my father and Margaret?"

"You think me a fool, boy?" Thomas Howard's voice raised several notches. "I know exactly what would happen to Sarah if I did such a thing. No, she is staying with me until this sorry mess is over."

"I'm sorry, Uncle. I meant no disrespect. After all that's happened recently I've forgotten my manners."

"After what you've been through, it's understandable. Now, tell me what happened."

John spent the next hour telling his uncle everything that had happened to him since the day Margaret Colte walked into his life. He held nothing back except the current hiding place of Isaac and Catherine. If he was going to meet his end here, he would not take them down with him.

John looked down to show respect for his powerful uncle. "Uncle, I got the impression when I saw you at the wedding that you knew Margaret and didn't like her too much. Is this correct? How did you know her?"

"I knew her. I met her when she was married to Farnborough's brother. Sir Henry and I were friends, and he confided in me after his brother died. She was bad news then, and she's even worse now. I warned Robert, but he wouldn't listen. I told him she would bring nothing but misery to our family, and unfortunately, I have been proven correct."

"I didn't poison Mark, I swear. If I'd gone to France as Father arranged, I'm convinced Margaret would have sent assassins after me and killed me. I had to get away and somehow prove my innocence."

"I never thought you capable of such deeds and I told Robert my feelings. He didn't believe any mother would ever poison her own child, and it seems he hasn't changed his mind because he's believing everything she's telling him now about the assassination of Henry Colte and her son."

"Uncle, how can I prove my innocence? What can I do to show my father the truth? How can I clear my name? Can you help me with that?"

Thomas Howard sat back and crossed his hands together. "Unfortunately, there is so much hatred pointed towards you that I, as a lone voice, can do nothing to persuade them differently. Margaret has other duke's like Asheborne believing her every word, and I hear the king himself is on her side. I'm afraid I can't do anything to help you prove your innocence."

"Please excuse my bluntness, but why am I here then? If it's only to tell me that Sarah is safe then surely you could have relayed that to me via Gamaliell Pye."

"Because there is a way I can help you though I cannot

be seen to have any involvement in this matter. The king is already angered at me because I was the uncle to Anne Boleyn, and I dare not risk his wrath any further. Your father has the close ear to him, and even I cannot override that."

He stared at John for several moments. "Before I tell you how I can help, there is something you should know."

John raised his eyebrows and waited.

"Your friends, these Underlings, as they are known. They have been wanted for the murder of Asheborne's brother for a long time. Their leader's capture has been Asheborne's priority for as long as I can remember. Did you know about any of this when you met them?"

"Yes, Uncle. They told me all about it. Andrew saved my life, and he is a good man. They are as innocent of their crimes as I am of mine. They didn't do it, Uncle. Asheborne's brother was murdered by Ren Walden and his gang, and they blamed it on the Underlings."

"Ah, Ren Walden. His death is no sad loss to humanity. From what you say, Margaret has – or had – close dealings with him. You did the country a great service when you killed him. However, now he's dead, there is no way to prove your friend's innocence."

John was about to speak, but his uncle waved him off. Thomas Howard leant forward in his chair.

"Your friends will be tried in two days' time. I have been ordered to sit on the jury by the king, and as such I must comply. I can tell you that Lord Asheborne has already arranged the guilty verdict and there is nothing I can do to stop it."

John stared at his uncle, his breath uneven and shaky.

"If I am the sole dissenter, questions will be asked of me at the royal court. As I am already in a state of disregard with the king, I dare not be the one who stands against Asheborne. I must comply and find them all guilty."

"But they're not guilty. They're innocent."

"So were my niece and nephew, but the king made sure I sat on the jury and found them guilty. When the king tells you to do something, you do it."

John swallowed hard. "What about Helena? She is a young girl and deserves to be shown mercy."

His uncle shook his head. "I'm sorry, John. There will be no mercy."

"What will happen to them?"

"It's already arranged. The Underling leader will be hanged, drawn, and quartered at Tyburn, right after the other two are hanged. I wish there was more I could do to help, but I can't. I must confess, I always believed them guilty, but from what you tell me, I now believe them to be innocent. It doesn't change anything though, no matter how wrong it may seem to you."

John put his hands on his face. "Uncle, I implore you. Lord Asheborne has got it wrong, and innocent people are being put to their deaths. You have to stop th—"

He stopped mid-sentence and stared at his uncle. "Wait, tell me again what you said. Andrew is going to Tyburn, along with the other two? Is that what you told me? Who are the other two, Helena and David?"

"Yes, if that's their names."

"What about Abraham? What's happening to him?"

"Who's Abraham?"

"He's the same age as Andrew, the leader. The Underlings have two adult leaders, Andrew and Abraham. What happened to him?"

Thomas lowered his head. "I assumed you already knew. The older one was the one who gave your friends up to Margaret. He is getting the reward and is guaranteed safe passage out of London after the executions. He's been kept around so he can help recognise you and anyone else who's still out there."

John held up his hand and watched it trembling in front of him. "Abraham gave us up? He's the reason Andrew, Helena and David are being murdered? Where is he?"

"I don't know where he is being held. Asheborne has him somewhere in London. If it soothes your conscience, I can make enquiries and find out where he's keeping him."

"Yes, I demand to know. He cannot get away with this. Do you know when the executions will take place?"

"The trials are in two days. The executions will be two days after that. I'm sorry, John. I wish I could do more to help you."

John got to his feet. "Uncle, I need you to find out where Abraham is being held. Please relay the whereabouts to Pye."

"He will be well guarded. You will die if you try anything."

"I cannot stand by and allow him to betray us and do nothing, Uncle. He's murdered his best friend."

John walked towards the door.

"There's one more thing." Thomas paused. "Even bigger than what I've just told you. It's the reason I brought you here."

"Go on."

"There is no way you will ever prove your innocence to your father. Margaret has him feeding out of her hands. You know that by now. No matter what evidence you gather, nobody will take your word over Robert's. If they catch you, they will kill you. That I can promise you."

"I already know this, Uncle."

"Margaret will never stop coming after you. Until

you're dead, she's always going to be worried that one day you will come back and reclaim your destiny as the heir to your father's title and estates. That's the one thing that scares her above everything else. Through Arthur, she will retain control of everything your father possesses, and she wants it all."

"I knew that also, Uncle. I hope she is rotting away inside knowing she murdered her own son in the process."

"Oh, she's beside herself with grief over her son's death. Except she said you did it, and that's made even more people want you dead."

"Thank you, Uncle, you've been most helpful."

"I haven't finished yet. The only way you can ever stop this is if you get to her before she gets to you. You understand what I'm saying, don't you?"

John nodded. "But then Father will be after me. And Asheborne. Then after that, I'm sure Arthur will want me dead. It will never end."

"That is true, but nobody will ever hunt you as relentlessly as she does. If you ever want to live in peace again, you have to take care of Margaret Colte."

"I'm not a murderer, Uncle, no matter what you have heard about me. I wanted to prove my innocence and clear my name. If she is to die, I wanted it to be the king who decreed it, not me."

"I have no doubts about that, John. I'm only telling you she will never stop until you are found and killed. Whatever hope you had of proving your innocence died with Colte and his nephew. All you can do now is protect yourself from her wrath. She is well protected at the Stronde, so I suggest you keep away from there."

"And? What are you holding back from me, Uncle?"

"Margaret Colte is going to a celebration party at Asheborne's home outside London, close to the Charter

House Priory the evening after the execution of the Underling leader at Tyburn. She will be guarded, but only by a few of her guards. That's when she will be at her most vulnerable, and if you are to ever get to her, that is when it should be."

"Why are you telling me this? Couldn't you send someone after her? After all, you have many men loyal to you who could do it much more efficiently than I ever could. As I said, I'm not a murderer."

"Yet you readily admitted to killing two people in recent days. I cannot allow myself to be involved. If I were found to be entertaining you here today, the king would have my head. Unlike you, I cannot just vanish into the stretes of London. I'm too well known, and frankly, I'm too old. I can have no involvement in this. But I am willing to help you if you want me to."

"The night after Andrew's execution, you say? And that's going to be four days from now?"

Thomas Howard nodded slowly.

"Thank you, Uncle. I am glad of your help."

"One last thing." Thomas Howard got up and pressed a bag of coins into his nephew's palms. "You will need this if you are to escape after it's over. You were always my favourite nephew, John, and I'm here if you need any advice or information. Just tell Pye what you need and he will get word to me."

Flames danced in John's eyes, and for the first time since all this began, he knew exactly what he had to do. Even if he died in the process.

Tyburn

The crowds were already large when John and Isaac joined them, mingling in, fighting for a good spot to view the day's entertainments.

The cryers had done their jobs well and had whipped up the fervour in the city to a crescendo in anticipation of the execution of the hated leader of the Underlings.

The other two were just a bonus.

Public hangings were big business, and the brewhouses enjoyed significant trade on days such as this. It made John sick. He jostled to get a suitable position outside the White Hart on Holbourne Road. Three horses and carts would pass by here on their way to the gallows hanging over the trees at Tyburn.

Andrew.

Helena.

David.

There would be others. The Underlings weren't the only ones being hanged today. The people of the city loved days like this because they executed several criminals at the same time.

Murder, thievery, treason. These were the crimes the poor souls meeting their ends were accused of. Some of them had had a trial at the Old Bailey, even though the verdicts were sealed before they ever set foot in the courtroom.

The Underlings were a special case. They'd had a trial in the King's Hall in the Tower of London. Lord Asheborne had led the proceedings along with Thomas Howard, Duke of Norfolk, and Robert Howard, Earl of Coventry.

The murder of a duke's brother and an earl demanded a special kind of justice. The Underlings had no chance of a fair trial, and the outcome was always going to be a foregone conclusion. Membership of the Underlings was already forbidden, which meant execution with or without a trial.

The trial was nothing but a showpiece designed to whip up the excitement even more than it already was.

Andrew was further accused of sorcery and devil worship. They even accused him of treason against the king, but for what, John had no idea. But these were the charges yelled out by the town cryers as the crowds grew larger and larger and the anticipation heightened.

John waited outside the White Hart, standing alongside drunken men fighting for a better vantage point. He and Isaac had split up in case they were seen, and took different vantage points. Catherine decided to stay inside their hiding place. She had no interest in watching people die.

John's anger burned at their betrayal, yet all of this was overshadowed by his great sense of helplessness and loss. Andrew was his friend, his mentor and his saviour.

Life would never be the same.

Shouts erupted, and the crowds swelled as men and women emboldened by alcohol came out of the brewhouses to watch the terrible spectacle. John stood in subdued dismay as the procession approached. He counted eight horse-drawn carts, one following the other. The accused sat on the backs of their solitary carts with their hands tied behind them, facing the baying crowds.

Women threw food at the prisoners while others threw stones, cutting their faces and bodies. Some men threw ale, while others threw stale urine.

Everyone jeered as the horses ambled the two miles to the gallows. Those at the front used their fists to hit the prisoners in the head as they rocked past them on their horse-drawn death carts. John looked down at the ground. He couldn't believe how cruel humanity could be.

One by one, the carts made their way past the blood-thirsty crowd. The Underlings were at the very back. David first, followed by Helena and Andrew. Their carts had fallen behind because they were getting special treatment. Asheborne's guards were shouting as Andrew approached, his head bowed in what looked like a silent prayer.

"Give 'em a good send-off," a guard shouted. "Make sure it's one to remember."

John stepped forward when the carts got level with him. David never saw him, but Helena looked right at him, her eyes full of pain and acceptance.

Andrew came next, and when John looked at him, he looked straight into the face of his beloved leader. Andrew's eyes widened with recognition. He smiled and winked as if to say everything was okay, although John could see he'd been badly beaten. When Andrew smiled, his front teeth were missing. They had either been knocked out or more likely pulled out during torture.

John gagged and found it difficult to breathe. His chest was heaving and his heart pounding. He couldn't even imagine the terrible suffering they'd forced his friends to endure since their capture.

Girls blew kisses at Andrew, while others hit him with food. One man ran forward and struck him in the face. John was furious and turned to attack the man, but whoever it was had vanished back into the dense crowds.

Another man threw a handful of excrement over Andrew's head. Roars of laughter erupted as the crowd bayed for more. Someone else washed it off with a bowl of stale urine that soaked John as he tried to shield him.

"Don't blame yourself, laddie," Andrew spoke through broken teeth. "My time is up. Do what I couldn't and take care of the others."

John was pulled back into the crowd as people rushed forward to throw more things at him. Their eyes locked as he drifted slowly into the distance. John fought his way through the crowd, following the carts. He couldn't let them die alone.

Finally, the procession reached the trees at Tyburn. Each cart stopped underneath a hangman's rope, which was tied around the necks of the condemned.

"Do you have anything to say for yourselves before you answer to God?" one guard sneered.

A few mumbles came from the accused, but John was transfixed on the Underlings. David said nothing. He stared straight ahead, his face and eyes emotionless as though he'd already died inside and was just waiting for his physical body to catch up.

Andrew looked around the crowds as if searching for a friendly face, but with so much hatred on display, there was none to be found.

John got a closer look at Helena. She didn't seem as badly beaten, but the harrowing look on her face told him they had tortured her in other ways. He forced himself not to scream at them and charge their attackers. The cruelty was undeniable.

"Ladies and gentlemen," the announcer began. "Don't feel sorry for these filthy Underlings. They are guilty of murdering an esteemed duke's brother as well as an earl and his young nephew. They are vermin that deserve no place on this earth."

The crowd shouted and yelled at the Underlings strung out in front of them.

"Even more," the announcer continued, "these filthy Underlings have robbed, beaten, and murdered people on the stretes of London for years. They have made our stretes unsafe and unclean, and now they must pay for their crimes."

The crowds bayed and yelled loudly, and John sensed the rising tension.

The announcer put his hand up to silence the angry crowd. "They have betrayed God himself. They have admitted to devil worship. The filthy, dirty, criminal Underlings are traitors to humanity, traitors to the good people of London, and traitors to God."

He roared as he reached the end of his speech and the crowd threw whatever they had in their hands at the three forlorn figures stood before them.

"That's it, Underlings. Repent your sins in front of God and pray for his mercy," the announcer said. "This one wants to speak." He pointed to Helena.

"The only thing we're guilty of is stealing small items so we could live." Helena's voice cracked with emotion, but she held herself together.

The crowd screamed and yelled at her, blocking the sounds of her voice. John stared in disbelief, his heart wrenched from his body.

"We are neither murderers nor devil worshippers,"

Helena continued, although John could barely hear her over the noise of the roaring crowd.

"These are made up charges against us by our betrayer. Those of you out there who know the truth will know who the evil one is amongst us."

John heard her loud and clear.

"We go to our Lord innocent of all the charges against us," Helena finished her speech. "We go to our Lord in peace."

John watched in helpless misery as the carts holding Helena and David slowly moved forward until their feet slid off the back. He watched wide-eyed as they thrashed and jiggled around before softly falling still and quiet.

Helena and David were dead.

Stephen

Now it was Andrew's turn.

"We've saved the worst until last. This one is Andrew Cullane, the leader of the Underlings. It was on his orders they murdered Lord Asheborne's brother. It was on his orders they murdered the Earl of Farnborough and his nephew, Mark Colte. I want to remind you that John Howard, the other murdering son of an earl, is still out there somewhere and needs to be found so he can face the same justice his friend faces today. He might even be here watching right now, so if you see 'im, bring 'im in."

John shrank back and pulled his head as far back into his hood as he could. He needn't have worried though, everyone was fixated on Andrew and what was about to happen to him.

"Cullane here is going to know what it feels like when you cross the line and murder our superiors. He's goin' to be hung, drawn, and quartered. Nice and slow for your entertainment."

John couldn't take any more. His stomach churned,

and he retched inside his hood. He'd seen enough. He forgot to breathe through the tension he felt inside his chest, and the bile burned the back of his throat.

He wanted to scream and attack everyone around him. Frantically looking around for someone to blame, his eyes locked onto a shadowy figure hidden behind the hood of a cloak. He studied the eyes glaring at Andrew's tormented body.

It was Abraham!

John resisted the urge to charge and kill him and instead sank back into the crowds to get nearer. He might not get to him now, but he wasn't going to let him get away. He watched as several of Asheborne's guards flanked Abraham. There were five of them, and they were easily recognisable because of their light blue uniforms.

He turned his back on the brutality and inched closer to Abraham. He felt his body's heat rising higher and higher, and the sense of betrayal and revenge consumed him.

All sense of purpose deserted him, and his body coiled tight, ready to explode. He moved closer and closer towards Abraham, his hand touching the handle of the knife hidden inside his cloak.

All thoughts of others, including himself, vanished. It was just Abraham and himself.

So what if I die today?

He was going to die in any case. It was only a matter of time. It would be worth it if he could take the traitor with him.

Today was as good a day as any to die.

A scream rang out that ripped through John's heart like an arrow, pulling him back out of his trance and stopping him dead in his tracks. Andrew screamed again, and John shuddered, throwing his hands to his ears.

He couldn't hear any more of this.

He pushed his way out of the baying crowds and crawled away like a crab reaching for the safety of water. He reached the Antelope brewhouse and collapsed to his knees, convulsing and sweating like never before.

He struggled to his feet, feeling weak and useless, and staggered towards Holbourne Bridge, oblivious to everything going on around him.

Until someone shouted.

"That's him! That's John Howard."

John snapped out of his trance and scanned the opposite side of the road to see who was shouting at him. It was one of Walden's chiefs.

John recognised his face immediately. It was Patrick, and he was part of the gang that held John Two down when they murdered him. Two more boys were with him.

He ran.

He ran across pastures and fields with no idea where he was heading, knowing he had to get away from these murderers and clear his head. He was as vulnerable as he'd ever been.

His plan didn't work for long. His legs were weak and unsteady, and the three boys quickly caught up to him.

They pommelled him to the ground and began kicking the life out of him. They shouted and screamed, but John couldn't hear them. He lay on the wet, muddy ground protecting his head and praying his death would be quick, unlike Andrew's.

A grunt, followed by one of the boys collapsing in a heap on top of him brought him back to his senses. Another one fell next to him, blood oozing from the place his throat had been moments earlier.

John uncoiled himself and turned over to see what was

happening. Patrick was in a fierce battle with a stranger hidden inside a hooded cloak.

"You're a traitor. The boss trusted you and you've betrayed us. The lady will want you dead almost as much as Howard." Patrick screamed, fighting for all he was worth.

He was no match for the bigger, stronger boy, and John watched from the ground in morbid fascination as his unknown saviour stabbed Patrick through the neck and stood over him, watching his life slowly fade away.

When he turned around, John's veins turned to ice.

"Stephen!" was all he could say.

He recoiled trying to get to his feet, but Stephen got to him quicker and reached down. John covered his head again, but the blows he was expecting never came. He peered through his fingers and saw Stephen's scar glistening with sweat as he leant forwards, offering his hand to help him up.

John took it, still disbelieving what he was seeing.

"Stephen. Why are you helping me? Why did you help me the first time?"

Stephen helped John to his feet. "It's not safe for you out here. I found you before you even spoke to Andrew on the cart, and I've been following you ever since, making sure nobody went after you. I was about to stop you from attacking Abraham until Andrew's screams stopped you in your tracks."

"Why? Why are you helping me? Who *are* you? And how do you know who I am?"

Stephen led John to a barn where they were safe from prying eyes. "I helped you because I made a promise."

He sighed and looked at John, his scar glistening inside his hood.

"I made a promise to Andrew that I'd protect you and help you escape. He told me who you were."

"Why would Andrew do that?" John asked.

"Because he's my brother. My name is Stephen Cullane."

Revelations

"I don't believe you." John gripped the handle of the knife hidden beneath his cloak. "Andrew hates you just as much as he hated Ren Walden."

Stephen shook his head. "We had to protect each other, or we'd both have been killed."

"Stephen, you beat me half to death when you caught me. You sneered and taunted me, and you're as cruel as Walden was. You're lying."

"The only language Walden ever understood was violence. I had to do those things to you so I could get close to him and get him to trust me. I didn't know who you were when we caught you. At the time you were just another possible."

"Another possible?" John shouted. "Another possible murder victim whose only crime was that he wasn't me?"

"I didn't kill any of them. That was Rolf. He enjoyed killing as much as Walden did."

"So what happened? How did you end up in Walden's gang?"

"We were both runners for the strete gang when we

were young boys. Walden had just taken over the gang and was proving himself by killing anyone who got in his way."

"I was faster than most of the other boys so Ren took a liking to me. He wanted me to work for him all the time and train me to be one of his chief's."

John listened intently, unsure what to make of Stephen's story.

"I refused because Andrew was all I had. Our parents were dead, and as the oldest, I took a vow to protect my little brother. Life was hard for us, and we'd take stuff from the dockyard that we weren't supposed to. You saw for yourself what the boss did to anyone who stole from him."

John shuddered at the memory of Walden brutally murdering Catherine's father for stealing his bread.

"How could I ever forget such barbarity?" he said flatly.

"One time, Andrew and his friend Abraham got caught stealing. I wasn't there, but I heard about it pretty quick. I knew what was going to happen, so I made a deal with the boss."

Stephen stopped and looked away. For the first time, John saw emotion in Stephen's cold, lifeless eyes.

"What deal?"

"I told the boss I'd work for him and do whatever he asked of me if he'd show mercy to Andrew. I didn't care about Abraham, but I made him promise he'd not hurt Andrew if I stayed."

"Walden showed mercy?" John looked sceptical. "He wasn't capable."

"He might have been cruel, but he wasn't stupid. He knew I was the fastest and strongest boy in the docks, and that I knew all the boys who were stealing from him."

"So he agreed and let Andrew and Abraham go?"

"Yes," Stephen said. "He let Andrew go without a

mark on him, but Abraham got a good kicking before he left. I thought the boss had killed him, but Andrew dragged him off and he's still here, so obviously he didn't die."

"Is that why Abraham betrayed us? Was he getting revenge for his beating when they were boys?"

"I doubt it. He knew you'd be caught eventually so he took the easy way and betrayed you. That's a lot of money for anyone, and Abraham could live like a king for the rest of his life if he turned you in. That's why he did it."

John nodded in agreement.

"I didn't trust the boss would keep his word, and I was scared he'd just kill Andrew once I'd agreed to work for him. So I had to get close so I could find out what he was up to. It was the only way I could protect my brother."

More emotion flickered behind his eyes.

He is human, after all.

"I had to be cruel and ruthless to prove myself, and eventually it became easy. Andrew thought I was dead, and I kept it that way because I was ashamed of what I'd become."

"Why didn't you leave after Andrew was safe?"

"You think he was ever safe from Ren Walden?" Stephen sneered. "He used that against me all the time. He reminded me every day that he knew where Andrew lived, and if I gave him even the slightest doubt of my loyalty, he'd make me watch as he skinned my brother alive in front of me."

"Did he know where Andrew lived?"

"I could never be sure but I had to believe him. One thing I learned was never to doubt his word. If Walden said he'd do something, he did it, no matter who got hurt."

John pursed his lips. He could see the anguish on Stephen's face, and he was beginning to believe him.

"As we got older, Andrew thought I was dead, but I was

always watching him from the shadows to make sure he was safe. He never knew how many times I hurt people to save him. It was better that way."

"If he told you who I was, he obviously knew you were alive," John said.

"Everything was fine until he started saving a few young ones from our gang and calling themselves the Underlings. It got really bad when they stole from the aristocrat's homes that we protected. The boss wanted them killed on sight. Luckily, he didn't know Andrew was the leader."

"Did you?"

"I'd kept an eye on him for years, and I knew it was him. I hated the Underlings, and I still do. They caused me no end of trouble. I wanted them dead as much as the boss did, but I had to stop the boss from finding out Andrew was their leader or he'd have killed us both. He'd have used me to get to Andrew."

Stephen stopped and turned away. It was obvious that recalling what happened was painful.

"Go on?" John prompted.

"The boys protecting the houses sometimes helped themselves. It was easy to blame the Underlings, so Lord Asheborne had the boss put word out that the Underlings had a price on their heads. Especially the leader."

"Why are they wanted for murder?"

"The duke's brother came in when he wasn't expected and caught Rolf and some others helping themselves to his stuff. Rolf killed him and blamed it on the Underlings. The duke went mad and made Andrew the most wanted man in England."

"Until you arrived in London," he added.

"Why didn't you come forward and clear his name?

That would have made Andrew's life so much better if you'd done the correct thing."

Stephen frowned. "You still don't get it, do you? If I'd told him, the boss might have killed Rolf, but he'd never admit to the aristocrats that it was one of us that had done the duke's brother. All he'd have done was kill me to keep me quiet."

John nodded. "I can see that. So what did you do?"

"Things got really bad for them, so Andrew tried getting them out of London. I followed to make sure they were safe because the boss had been going to meetings with the duke, and I didn't trust him. So I followed Andrew until he was safely out of London."

"What happened?"

"They were ambushed. I saved Andrew's life and told him I was alive. We agreed to work together to keep ourselves safe. That's it."

"That's it?" John asked.

"That's it, yea. I told him I'd help him, but I hated the Underlings and I wanted them dead as much as the boss did. We both agreed to keep them out of it because I'd never help any of them. Only Andrew."

"So why did you help me?"

"After we caught you, Andrew found me and told me who you were. He told me you could prove they didn't kill the duke's brother and clear his name. He begged me to help you."

"Why did you agree? You've already said you hated the Underlings as much as Walden did."

"I knew if I gave you the knife and told you what was happening, you'd have a chance of killing Rolf. He was starting to suspect me of working against the boss, and he wanted my position as leader of the chiefs. It was a good way to get rid of him, and if you failed, there was no way it could be traced back to me."

"So you didn't do it for Andrew."

"Yea, I did. If you killed Rolf, I knew you'd find Andrew again and help prove it wasn't him that killed the aristocrat. I didn't expect you to come back and kill the boss, but I was glad you did. You saved me the job."

"You were going to kill Walden?"

"Eventually, yea. I always knew I'd have to kill him one day. You doing it made it a lot easier for me to take down the gang."

"Why did you just save me again?"

"I promised Andrew I would do everything I could to protect you. After you killed Rolf, I knew you were as strong as Andrew said you were. You have been a loyal friend to my brother, even in his final moments. I couldn't stand back and let the boys take you down after that. I saved you, even though it means the rest of them will be after me now. They'll know what I did, and someone else will take over the gang. I'm a dead man walking, but it's worth it. Andrew loved you and trusted you with his life. That was enough for me."

"What will you do now?"

Stephen shrugged his shoulders. "Help you kill the woman, clear Andrew's name, and rid this city of the strete gangs. That's the least I can do for my brother. I hate that bitch as much as you do. Meet me here at noon every day. We're going to end this."

Stephen stood up and left the barn, leaving a stunned John Howard staring after him.

Plans

John was surprised to find his fellow Underlings huddled together in the gloomy darkness of the crypts. A solitary candle burned slowly, casting their shadows onto the tombs of important people long forgotten to history.

"Why are you here? Did something happen?"

"Someone tried to open the door to the room when you were gone," Catherine said. "I thought they'd caught you, so I ran down here and prayed for you."

Catherine surprised John by jumping up and kissing him softly on the cheek, sending lightning bolts down his arms and legs.

"What happened to yea?" Isaac asked. "I lost you when the carts came past. I tried to find you, but I couldn't watch them butcher Andrew. Did you hear Helena's last words? Did you hear her? I wanted to rush in and kill them all, but I knew I didn't stand a chance. It was horrible."

John bowed his head. "I heard her, and I wanted to attack them too, but it was useless. I couldn't get anywhere near them."

"Where have you been?" Isaac asked. "I've been back here for ages."

"I was seen by some of Walden's chiefs. They chased me and beat me to the ground. I'm sure they were going to kill me, but out of nowhere, a man covered by a hood appeared and killed them all. It was…"

John hesitated and looked at Isaac and Catherine.

"It was Stephen."

"Stephen saved you? Again?" Isaac shouted.

"Stephen?" Catherine looked dumbfounded. "Why is he helping you? That man is evil."

John sank down against one of the tombs and told them everything that had happened, except for one small detail. When he finished, there was an astonished, disbelieving silence amongst the Underlings.

"Do you trust him?" Isaac asked. "I don't. I hope you didn't tell him where we're hiding."

John shook his head. "He never asked and I never told. He just got up and walked off after he told me to meet him at the barn at noon every day."

"Are you going to meet him?" Catherine interjected. "What if it's a trap?"

"Why would he kill his fellow gang members if it was a trap?" John threw his hands in the air. "He could easily have killed me himself, or taken me to Margaret, but he didn't do any of those things. He saved my life for the second time. I believe him."

"I still don't trust him. Did he say why he is helping you?" Isaac asked.

"He's Andrew's brother." John dropped the final bombshell and watched as Isaac's and Catherine's jaws fell to the ground.

"What? No way he's Andrew's brother." Isaac finally broke the silence.

"He said he was and I believed him."

John told them what Stephen had revealed.

"I still don't trust him," Catherine said.

"If he can help us get to Margaret and Abraham, then I'll be happy, and I think he will," John countered. "If he doesn't, then we're dead anyway, so we have no other choice than to trust him. We either kill them or die trying."

John crossed his arms and thrust his chin forwards, fixing his gaze firmly on Isaac's disbelieving face.

"You have a plan, don't you?" Isaac's tone told John it wasn't a question.

"I might have. But it's risky."

"Can't we just run away and forget all of this?" Catherine asked.

"No." John and Isaac spoke at the same time.

"Margaret will never stop, and she's killed too many innocent boys in my name. I can't run from her anymore." John was steadfast.

"Andrew and the others will have died for nothing if we run away now, and Asheborne will never stop searching for us either. We have to stop this." Isaac folded his arms and looked as determined as John had ever seen him.

"Even if we die?" Catherine asked again.

"Even if we die."

"What plans do you have?" Isaac asked.

John huddled them close together and told them about his plans to stop Margaret the following evening.

Revenge

John rapped on Gamaliell Pye's door in the usual manner after darkness fell and the curfew bells rang out.

"I need three longbows and quivers." John didn't mince his words.

Pye shrugged. "I have those on hand, and you are welcome to take them. It's a terrible thing what happened to Andrew and your friends. I was there to witness the executions, and I saw you headed towards a group of Lord Asheborne's guards with a fury I've never seen before."

"I caught sight of Abraham and a red mist fell over me. I wanted revenge, and I was prepared to die for it."

"I'm glad you realised your quest was fruitless or you wouldn't be here this evening."

"Andrew's cries of agony pulled me around. I couldn't bear to hear any more, so I left to fight another day."

"Speaking of which, I have word from Lord Howard," Pye said. "He said the Lady Margaret will travel to Lord Asheborne's home at dusk this evening. She will go past Smithfield Market along Long Lane before turning up Golden Lane to Lord Asheborne's home across the fields from the Charterhouse. She will be in a carriage with only six guards. Lord Howard pressed the message that you will never get a better chance of confronting her."

"What about Abraham? Did my uncle discover where he is hiding?"

"Indeed, he did. He is under heavy guard at a house on Woodstrete, which is inside the city near Cripplegate. Lord Howard told me he is located opposite Curriers Hall, in a house next to the Almshouses. You can't miss it because it's full of Lord Asheborne's guards."

"Thank you, Gamaliell. I'm deeply indebted to you for everything you have done for both myself and Andrew. If you give me the longbows, I promise not a word of your assistance shall ever pass my lips should I be caught."

Pye grabbed John's arm. "Your uncle insists it's too dangerous to attempt revenge on Abraham. He is too well guarded and it will be suicide if you attempt it. He wants you to stop Lady Margaret and leave Abraham alone."

"You know I can't promise that. He betrayed us, and it's because of him that Andrew's blood was spilt along with Helena's and David's. I cannot allow him to get away with it."

"Your uncle made me promise to make you see sense."

"I have to get past Margaret first, and that will most likely be my final act in this life, so tell my uncle you did your duty. Tell him I understand the risks, and whatever happens next is all on me."

Gamaliell Pye bowed to John. "It has been a pleasure to know you, John Howard. I wish you God's speed and protection in your quest for righteous revenge. I will be ready to assist when it's all over."

"Do you have any news of my sister?" John asked.

"Lord Howard assured me she is safe and well in

hiding. Your father doesn't know he has her, and he wants it kept that way."

The two men shook hands one last time before John slipped back into the night.

Darkness fell as the Underlings approached Lord Asheborne's magnificent home at the edge of Golden Strete, across from the Charterhouse priory where Stephen was waiting for them. John recognised it as soon as he saw it. He'd been there before on several occasions when he lived a different life.

The night skies were clear, and the full moon made visibility good. John prayed in thanks for such a clear night.

Carriages of all shapes and sizes cantered along Golden Lane before turning into the long, heavily gated entrance to Asheborne's home. John recognised the liveries of nearly all of them, but the one he was waiting for hadn't yet arrived.

Thomas Howard had told Pye that his father would arrive separately from Margaret because he was travelling from Whitehall Palace after attending to the king. Margaret would be one of the last to arrive because of a meeting she'd called at the Stronde with some uninvited dignitaries.

The nature of the meeting was unknown to his uncle.

Happy with his plans, John led the way through the muddy fields to the junction with the Red Cross, which is where Margaret would soon approach before turning left onto Golden Lane.

They moved into position past the row of houses further up the lane, and split into two groups. Isaac and Stephen crossed the lane and lay in a muddy ditch for

John's signal, which would be a stone thrown across the lane towards them. As soon as they heard the thud of the stone in the bushes behind them, they would know it was time to act.

John took up his position opposite Isaac and Stephen. Catherine lay next to him, waiting for his command.

The rumble of the carriages died down as their numbers dwindled. John watched every one of them pass, checking the liveries carefully as they went by.

Nothing.

After a while, doubt began to creep into John's mind.

Had she used a different livery to fool them and ensure she arrived safely?

John didn't doubt her cunning for a second, and he began to think she'd outfoxed him.

A slight rumble caught his attention. The sound of horses trotting towards them made his palms sweat. His hands started trembling as he listened to the sound of the horses getting closer.

The carriage turned up Golden Lane, the glow from the moon making it easy to see the large livery painted on the side. The unmistakable shield-like shape of the Howard livery reflected back to him.

This is it!

"That's her," he whispered to Catherine. "Go." He picked up the stone he'd kept next to him and hurled it into the bushes across the strete.

All fear left him as he sprang into action. He stood up and readied his longbow.

Catherine stumbled into the middle of the road, weaving from side to side like an injured animal. She put her hands up in front of her as the carriage got close.

"What ails you, miss?" the driver – also one of the

guards – shouted down as he brought the carriage to a stop.

"Sir, I fell from my horse and I fear—"

A hail of arrows from both directions pierced the night sky, shredding the driver, and the guards surrounding a huddled figure inside the carriage, to pieces.

Catherine ran to the horses and grabbed hold of the reins to stop them from bolting. What was left of the guards jumped out of the carriage and ran towards their attackers.

John was waiting for them.

Another arrow pierced the heart of the guard rushing towards him, and he fell to the ground in a heap, his blood mingling with the mud at John's feet.

The same was happening on the other side as John heard the guards screaming as they fell.

The screams died to a whimper before they ceased altogether.

Silence.

John ran to the carriage where the one remaining guard stood over the huddled figure of Margaret with his sword held high.

John stopped dead in his tracks.

"Willis!" he yelled, piercing the silence. Memories of the guard helping him escape rushed through his head, clouding his judgement and his focus.

"Master John, is that you?" Willis brought his sword down to his side. "I didn't believe the stories I was hearing about you. What are you doin—"

He stopped and lurched forward as the tip of a sword ran through his body and out the other side. Willis's blood splattered all over John as he lurched into his arms.

"No, stop." John was too late.

Stephen stood on the sides of the carriage, blood dripping from his sword. Isaac was next to him, holding his sword over Margaret, who was huddled on the floorboards like the coward she was.

"We don't have time, John," Isaac panted. "We've got to kill her and get out of here. Asheborne's guards will be here soon."

"I'm so sorry, Willis." John cradled him for a moment. "I never meant for any of this to happen."

He looked up at Margaret and locked eyes on her. "This is all your fault. You have ruined my life and so many others. You have murdered without remorse and even killed your own son. Your time is over, Margaret."

Margaret Colte rose from the floor, pushing Isaac away as she moved. The hatred in her eyes made John shiver, and she sneered as she spoke.

"You haven't got the guts to kill me. All you've ever done is run away, and that's what you'll do now."

John raised his sword. "Not this time. Your time is over."

"Sarah." Margaret raised her hands.

John stopped in his tracks. "What did you say? Sarah is somewhere safe where even you can't get to her."

"Don't be so sure about that, John Howard. I have people everywhere, and I know where she is. If I don't arrive at Lord Asheborne's party intact, they have orders to kill her. That will be your fault, and your father will hunt you for the rest of your miserable life."

"John, we've got to hurry." Isaac pressed him.

"Kill the woman or I will," Stephen spat the words out.

The sound of horses made Margaret's smile look even more sinister in the moonlight. "See? They're coming to rescue me right now. Run, John Howard, like the coward you are."

A flash of light glinted from her hands as she lashed

out with a knife she had hidden in her cloak. John staggered back and fell to his knees, blood streaming down his arm from the wound in his shoulder.

Margaret's wild eyes glowed like a demon rising from the depths. She jumped down from the carriage towards John, away from Stephen and Isaac, death mere feet from the point of her knife. From out of nowhere, Catherine jumped in front of her, ramming her knife deep into Margaret's chest.

"No you don't, bitch. Get away from him."

Margaret's eyes changed from wild fury to stunned surprise. Her mouth fell open, and she jerked her head back. Catherine withdrew her knife and slammed it as hard as she could into Margaret's neck, almost severing her head with the fierceness of the blow.

"This is for Andrew, Helena, David, and all those others you've killed in cold blood. Even your own son."

John staggered to his feet and caught Catherine as she fell backwards in shock at what she'd done.

Margaret fell back, dead before she even hit the floor.

The sounds of horses drew nearer. "Come on." John clutched his shoulder. "We've got to get out of here."

Isaac and Stephen ran around the carriage to join them. Willis reached up and gurgled, his hand scrambling for John in the blood-soaked moonlight.

"Willis." John knelt next to him. "I'm so sorry." He took his hand for a brief moment. Willis pulled him towards him and whispered in his ear.

"Don't worry about Lady Sarah. Margaret didn't know where she is. That much I know, Master John. It has been a pleasure serving you. Now leave before they get here."

John nodded, thanked him, and got up to leave.

"Run. Let's get out of here before we're caught."

"Go," Stephen said. "I'll see you at our usual place. There's something I have to do."

John didn't have time to argue. He shoved Isaac with his good arm, grabbed Catherine, and ran.

Stephen turned and hunched himself over Margaret's dead body.

London Bridge

The Underlings remained in the crypts the next day to avoid the inevitable backlash from the elites of London. They knew they would be blamed for it even if nobody knew for sure it was them that did it.

Catherine remained isolated behind one of the tombs, and whenever anyone tried speaking to her, she ushered them away. Finally, after several hours, John sat beside her, holding his injured shoulder tenderly as he sat down.

"You saved my life last night and what you did was very brave. If you hadn't done what you did, Margaret would have killed me, and I am glad you were there. Thank you, Catherine."

"I don't want to talk about it."

John was sure he could see tears falling down her face in the dull light reflecting softly on her face from the candle by his side. His heart sank and he reached out for her hand.

She pulled it away.

"It'll never go away," he said softly. "Believe me, I know. I'm haunted every night by the look on Rolf's face.

Even Walden's when I can bear to think about it. Killing another person does terrible things to us, but if you hadn't killed her, it would be me that was dead and not Margaret. She was as evil as any woman could ever be, and she had to die. England is a safer place with her gone."

"Yes, but I wish it hadn't been me that had to do it. I've never killed anyone before, and it's haunting me. Every time I close my eyes I relive what I did, and it's tearing my soul out of my body."

"Would it help if we pray together?"

"Would you? I would like that."

John bent his head forward and clasped his hands together. Quietly, he began reciting the Lord's Prayer in Latin. His words echoed off the hallowed walls of the crypt and penetrated every fibre of his being. It was as if the Lord himself was forgiving them for their sins.

Pater noster, qui es in caelis,
sanctificetur nomen tuum.
Adveniat regnum tuum.
Fiat voluntas tua,
sicut in caelo et in terra.
Panem nostrum quotidianum da nobis hodie,
et dimitte nobis debita nostra,
sicut et nos dimittimus debitoribus nostris.
Et ne nos inducas in tentationem,
sed libera nos a malo.
Amen.

By the time he finished, Isaac had joined them in prayer, and all three of them sat together in a circle praying in silence for their souls.

"Thank you." Catherine finally broke the silence. "I needed that."

She reached out and touched John's arm, causing him to pull back and yelp in pain.

"I'm sorry, I didn't mean to hurt you. Let me look at that and see if I can't make it feel better."

"An arm for a soul," John said. "I like that."

Catherine got to work on John's shoulder, smearing it with honey from Pye's offerings to protect it from infection. Her hand seemed to linger on his skin, sending involuntary shock waves through his body.

He reached up and pressed her hand into his skin firmly. "You saved my life yesterday, and I will never forget it."

Their eyes locked, and for the longest moment, he felt like his heart had stopped. He placed his uninjured arm around her neck and gently pulled her towards him, her hot breath teasing him, making him want her even more.

Their lips pressed together, and for a brief moment, John Howard forgot everything. All his problems melted away until the only thing that mattered was this girl, kissing him right now, making him feel like the banks of the Thames had burst open and all the power of the mighty river was rushing through him.

Catherine pulled away and looked deep into his eyes. Without saying another word, she lay her head on his shoulder and sobbed quietly. John felt the rhythm of her heartbeat and he held her as tightly as he could.

They sat together in silence for a long time, neither speaking nor moving. Feeling her warmth next to him made everything feel right, and he never wanted it to end.

John waited until deep into the night before making the short but dangerous journey to the home of the only friend the remaining Underlings had in the entire city – and probably the only true friend they had in England – Gamaliell Pye.

He'd barely rapped on the heavy wooden door when Pye opened it quickly and ushered him in. "You've caused a furore the likes of which I have never seen. London is no longer safe for you. You have to get out of here as fast as you can."

"Not until I take revenge on Abraham."

A shadow appeared from the doorway to John's left. He spun around, drawing his knife from under his cloak.

"Relax, John. It's me, Stephen."

"Stephen?" John took a few steps backwards. "What are you doing here?"

"It's dangerous out there. Asheborne and your father have guards searching for you everywhere. I came here to warn you of the dangers."

"How did you know about this place?" John asked, still stunned by his presence.

"Gamaliell has known who I am for years. He was the contact point between me and Andrew. It's how we passed information to each other."

"You've known about him for years and never told me?" John glared at Pye.

"We don't have time for this right now," Pye said flatly. "I don't reveal all my secrets to you, John Howard."

"What happened after we killed Margaret?" John changed the subject, his face a deep crimson.

"You obviously don't know what he did after the ambush," Pye answered, shooting Stephen a dirty look.

"I don't know anything that happened afterwards. How could I? I suppose you told him where we are hiding as well?"

"Calm down, John." Pye placed his hand on John's shoulder, causing him to flinch and move away. "Whether you believe it or not, Stephen is not your enemy and never has been. He's faced many serious risks to his life to protect Andrew, and now he's taken even more to help you. He's on your side and it's a good thing he is, so stop this nonsense and listen to what I have to say. Your life depends on it."

John slumped into a chair. "I wish you'd told me, that's all."

"You're not privy to all I know. Let's just leave it at that."

Pye gathered them at a wooden table and passed around the wine he had waiting for them. John gulped it down, surprised at the thirst grabbing the back of his throat.

"What did you do after the ambush?" John fixed his eyes on Stephen.

"I did to the lady what she would have done to you after your execution." He looked at Pye and then fell silent.

"What did you do?" John asked again. He cast his mind back to the blood-soaked scene then shot up in his chair, clenching his fists at Stephen.

"You didn't…" He couldn't finish his sentence.

Silence.

Pye nodded slowly. "He cut off her head and hung it on a spike over London Bridge. The aristocrats went wild when they heard. Even the king got involved. It would have been bad if you'd left her for dead, but a commoner – even a fallen aristocratic one like you – doing something like this is treasonous. King Henry is on the warpath and he's demanding your head be removed. Nowhere is safe for you anymore."

Spittle bubbled from the corner of John's mouth. "Why did you do that?" he raged at Stephen. "That was never a part of our plans. Now my father will never listen to the truth, no matter who tells it to him. He will hunt me until the day he dies."

"She killed countless boys simply because they looked like you." Stephen stood up, scowling at John. "You know what she had us do to those boys. Especially the one that looked most like you. You were there. You saw what she had Ren make us do. She deserved what she got."

Pye pulled Stephen back to his chair.

"Was that Margaret?" John retorted. "Or was that Ren and your friends just enjoying themselves?"

Stephen sighed. "Ren and Margaret agreed it between them that the boys would die. How they died was down to the boss. But it's her fault. If she hadn't ordered their deaths, none of them would have been killed."

Pye slammed the jug of wine onto the table. "Enough. Whether or not she deserved it – and let there not be a single doubt that she did – it happened and now you have to live with the consequences. Your uncle sent word earlier this day that your father wants your head delivered to him personally. The king made the same order. Whatever else you do, you cannot stay in London. Your uncle has a house in the country that will be safe until this dies down. He wants you to lie low until arrangements can be made."

"I can't leave until I avenge Andrew and the others." John clenched his fists again.

"Your uncle also told me that Abraham has been moved for his safety to a secret location, and his guards have been quadrupled. He is the only person still alive that knows what you look like today, and Asheborne will protect him for as long as it takes until you are caught. Even the king couldn't get to him at this point. Abraham is out of your reach, and you must let him go."

"I can't."

"You must, if not for yourself, then for Isaac and the girl. If you go after him, you'll be caught, and when they torture you – as they surely will – you will be forced to give up their locations. You know what awaits them if that happens. Let Abraham go, if only while you escape and allow the situation to calm down."

John scowled. He knew Pye was correct, but he didn't like it never the less. "Where is this place my uncle has for me?"

"I don't know," Pye answered. "His messenger merely told me of its existence. He said you are to stay in hiding until the arrangements are made."

"We can't stay in those crypts much longer. They're depressing and frightening, and no place for us to live."

"They are keeping you alive while your uncle – at great personal risk, I might add – is making arrangements to get you out of London safely. He ordered you to stay there and keep out of sight. If you disobey him, he will abandon you, and you will be on your own. I will do the same. If that happens, I give you a week at most before you're caught getting food somewhere."

Pye looked beseechingly at John. "I implore you, John Howard, for the safety of you all, you must obey your uncle this one time."

He hesitated. "He also said that if you didn't do as he requests, he would send your sister back to her father and wash his hands of the both of you."

John bowed his head in defeat. "I will do as my uncle asks and please convey my gratitude for his help. I am aware of the significant risk you are both taking for us."

"Come here for supplies. Do not go anywhere else for any reason. Is that clear?"

John exhaled loudly. "Yes, Gamaliell, you have made it perfectly clear."

"Thank you," Pye said, flashing John a withering look. "There is one more thing."

"What would that be?"

"It isn't safe for Stephen to stay here. I have already

had Lord Asheborne's and Lord Howard's guards pay me a visit. He must return to the crypts with you and remain there until you leave."

"I don't think—"

"It's better you don't think," Pye interrupted. "Now go."

New Life

"What's he doing here?" Isaac jumped up and drew his sword when he saw Stephen in the dim candlelight. "I thought we agreed he wasn't to know where we were hiding."

"I still don't like him, even if he did help us," Catherine said. "I don't want to be down here with him."

"He knew all along." John slumped to the cold ground and rested his back against an ancient tomb. "Pye was the go-between between him and Andrew, and he knew everything about us."

Stephen spoke up. "You have good reason to not like me. Hell, you have good reason to hate me. I've never hidden my hatred of the Underlings because you made my life difficult. I vowed many years ago to protect my little brother, and I lived up to that vow until the day he died. I'm not sorry for what I did because I did it to protect Andrew."

"Stop." John held up his good arm. "Stephen put himself at great risk when he helped me escape. He saved my life again when I was attacked by Ren's boys after

Andrew's execution, and we couldn't have stopped Margaret without his help. Even if we don't like him, we owe him a debt of gratitude. We're stuck together anyway, so I say let's give him a chance and see how it works out. Andrew would have wanted it this way, so if we don't do it for any other reason, let's do it for him."

"I saw you beat John to the ground." Isaac spat on the floor at the side of Stephen's feet. "What would you have done to me if Andrew hadn't saved me?"

"Do you think I didn't see Andrew pulling you away?" Stephen bared his rotten teeth. "I shielded you from the sight of the others so Andrew could get you away safely. I'll admit I did it for him and not you, but I saved your life as well that day. In any case, I don't plan on being around very long. As soon as it's safe, I'm off. I have unfinished business with the rest of the strete gang."

"That's settled then," John said. "He stays until we leave London, which won't be long. My uncle is making the arrangements for us to hide in one of his country estates. When we leave, Stephen can have this all to himself."

Isaac grunted, clearly not happy.

For the next few nights, John and Stephen joined the homeless and the destitute, trying to avoid the evil side of London's dangerous nightlife as they made their way to Gamaliell Pye's large home close to their secret entrance inside the inner city walls.

Each night they returned with nothing but news regarding how badly the elite wanted them captured and hanged for their terrible crimes. Robert Howard, John's father, offered a further ten pounds a year for life to whoever brought about his capture. Twenty pounds a year would make anyone very wealthy, and from what Pye told them, families were turning on one another in their quest for wealth.

Nobody was safe, and the sooner the Underlings could get away from the city, the better it would be. Living in the dark, damp, cold, eerie crypts day after day was taking its toll, and John knew they couldn't stay there much longer if they were to retain their sanity.

Stephen entertained them with stories about his youth when he and Andrew had acted as runners for Ren Walden. Slowly but surely, John warmed to him.

He even began to like him.

Finally, Pye had some news.

"Lord Howard has arranged for you to stay at one of his country homes in Oxfordshire. You are to be at the horse pool at West Smithfield Market at first light the day after tomorrow. A man will wear a white cloth around his arm. He will have a covered carriage waiting for you."

"Where in Oxfordshire?" John asked. "I don't recall my uncle ever having any property there."

Pye shrugged. "I don't know. All he told me was it's somewhere near Banbury. I knew better than to ask any further questions. I shall not see you again after this, so I wish you all the very best, and may God watch over you. Maybe one day when this has all been forgotten we may meet again, but until then take care of yourself, John Howard."

They shook hands and Pye pressed a bag of coins into his hands. John went to say something, but Pye cut him off.

"Something tells me you will need this before it is all over."

"What—"

Pye waved him off and turned to Stephen. "Whatever road you may take, I wish you God spede." They shook hands, and John was sure he saw a bag of coins being handed over as they shook.

"This is the last night we shall see each other," Pye said. "Questions regarding my affinity to help the poor are being asked in the royal court, and I cannot risk the king's wrath. You cannot come here ever again, is that clear? I have done what I can for you both, and now I must take my leave."

"You have done more than I could have ever hoped," John said. "I will be forever in your debt."

"As shall I. What you did for me and Andrew will never be forgotten."

John felt a lump in his throat as he walked away. This strange, kindly old man had risked his life many times over helping him, and he still didn't know why. Gamaliell Pye helped many of the city's poor, but he had gone overboard with John, and he knew he would have been dead by now without his considerable help.

"One day." John turned around to face Pye one last time. "One day I shall return to repay your kindness. My sister and I shall not forget you, Gamaliell Pye."

Stephen followed him into the darkness of the night.

Leaving London

John Howard stood at the top of the stone steps and looked back into the pitch blackness of the crypts one last time. He shivered, relieved to be done with this cold, lifeless place that had given them safe refuge from the sprawling city above.

He shook himself as he locked the door and secured the key inside his cloak. "I'm glad we're getting out of here, but I can't help but have feelings for this place. It's kept us safe during our time of need.

"That's because nobody in their right mind would ever want to go in there." Isaac stood behind him. "But I admit to feeling it too."

"Not me," Catherine said. "I never liked that place. I always felt I was being watched by ghosts from the past who didn't want to be disturbed."

"They probably didn't," John said. "And I don't blame them."

They stepped outside the church in the pre-dawn drizzle and waited, listening intently for any signs of human activity. Satisfied they were alone, John moved towards Britten Strete and the West Smithfield Market.

Stephen didn't move. He stood still, staring at John's back.

"What's wrong, Stephen?" Catherine whispered. "Did you see something?"

"This is where we say goodbye. I wish you well, John Howard and the Underlings, and I hope our paths cross again in the future. Take care of yourselves and stay alive."

John turned around. "I wish you would come with us. Andrew would have wanted it, and I think you'd agree that together we make a formidable team. London isn't safe for any of us."

Stephen shook his head. "You're the one they're after, not us. Me, Isaac and Catherine could walk away and live safely because hardly anyone knows what we look like. The aristocrats all know who you are, and you're the one they all want."

"What are you saying?" John asked.

"I'm saying I'll be safe here. I have unfinished business with the strete gang. If I don't stop them, they'll carry on doing the same thing Walden did, and all those innocent people would have died for nothing. I'm the only person who can stop them, and I can't leave knowing they're still out there. I have to stay."

"They'll kill you," Isaac said. "London isn't safe for any of us anymore."

"I'm going to stop them. Pye knew what I was planning, and he gave me enough coin to make a run for it after I've taken care of the gang. That's what I'm going to do."

"Perhaps I should stay as well." John looked at Catherine and Isaac. "Stephen is right. It is me they're after, not you. If you leave London, you'll have the chance of a good life, but as long as I'm around, you'll always be in danger. Besides, I'm still angry that Abraham got away. I need to stay here and find him."

"No." Catherine ran to his side. "If you're staying then so am I. I'm not going without you."

"You're not getting rid of us that easy, John." Isaac strode up to him. "Nobody wants Abraham to suffer more than I do, but right now we've got to get out of here and lie low. We've been over this a thousand times. We wouldn't get anywhere near him, and we'd die for nothing. If we wait a while, I'm sure fate will allow us another chance to get to him. We have to do it on our terms, not theirs. For now, let's live. We've taken out the worst of them in Margaret, so let's not get greedy."

John sighed. "You're both as stubborn as mules. But you're right, we need to leave Abraham for another day. I pray every night that God gives us another chance to kill him. If he does, I'll be ready."

"You'd better get going if you're going to get there before dawn," Stephen said.

"I wish you would come with us, but I understand." John shook hands with Stephen. "I never thought I'd say this, but you have become a good friend, and I wish you all the best. I hope our paths will cross another day when the circumstances are much better for all of us."

"Where will you stay?" Isaac asked. "Are you going to stay in the crypts?"

"Hell, no," Stephen shivered. "That place is haunted. I hate it in there. I'm not going back there alone."

"Where will you stay then?" Catherine asked.

Stephen backed away into the shadows. "I heard there's a good treehouse sitting empty."

"Wait. What?" John stepped forward, but Stephen had vanished into the darkness. "Did he mean…"

"Never mind," Isaac said. "It's too late to worry about that now. We've got to go."

John shook his head and pursed his lips.

Stephen must have known about my treehouse all along. That means Andrew must have known about it as well.

He cast it to the back of his mind. He had more important things to worry about.

They reached the horse pool just as the sun cast the first rays of dim light on West Smithfield Market. The drizzle came down, soaking the Underlings to the skin. The day was going to be wet and miserable.

It was a good day to be leaving London.

John noticed a man standing near a covered goods carriage wearing a white cloth around his arm. Making sure nobody was watching, John signalled for Isaac and Catherine to remain hidden while he approached.

When the man saw him, he pointed to one of the carriages without saying a word before walking off to talk to his colleagues, probably as a distraction.

John signalled to the others, and they silently climbed inside the carriage, pulling the cover over their heads. Then they waited for what seemed like hours before the sounds of horses and sudden movement jolted them awake.

They were moving! John's heart beat out of his chest as the carriage made its way along the rough roads towards its destination somewhere near Banbury.

John's pulse soared every time he heard a shout, or whenever the horses stopped. He expected the covers to be pulled back at any moment, revealing them to the guards searching for them on their way out of the city.

But nobody disturbed their carriage, and as the day went on and the sun finally rose, John relaxed as they moved farther and farther away from their would-be executioners.

His mind turned back to Stephen and the treehouse. *How did he know about it? Had he seen him climb into it? Had he been there? Did Andrew know about it? Who else knew about it? Pye?*

All these questions swirled around his mind, and he wondered if he would ever find out the truth. He thought of Sarah and what had become of her. *Where had her uncle placed her? Was she safe?*

He was sure she was, but it bothered him just the same.

Would he ever see her again? What about his father? Would he ever forgive him for killing Margaret?

He doubted it.

Then what about Arthur? He will grow up hating his older brother for crimes he never committed.

Anger coursed through his veins once again as the image of Abraham betraying them entered his mind for the thousandth time that morning.

He may think he's going to have a good life with all that coin, but I'll hunt him until the day I die. Abraham is going to regret the day he betrayed his best friend.

As the carriage trundled towards Banbury, John continued reflecting on his life and how he'd reached the point where he was now at.

Maybe I should have gone to France after all. I wouldn't have been in any less danger that's for sure, and poor Mark would still be alive.

He shook his head.

He squeezed Catherine's hand next to him, enjoying the tingling sensation that raced through his body. Whatever the future held for him, he knew it would involve this beautiful girl that held his heart like no other.

John Howard looked forward to the future.

Yes, he even dared to believe they had a chance of a normal, quiet life.

But not yet.

As long as Abraham was alive, this wasn't over.

Not yet.

THE END

Get a FREE Book!

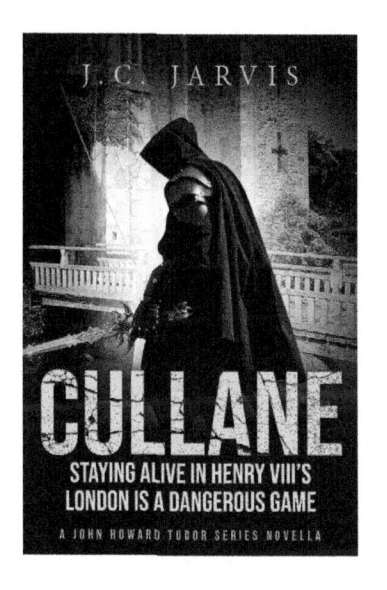

Before John Howard found sanctuary on the streets of London, Andrew Cullane formed a small band of outlawed survivors called the Underlings. Discover their fight for life for free when you join J.C. Jarvis's newsletter at jcjarvis.com/cullane

PLEASE LEAVE A REVIEW!

If you loved the book and have a moment to spare, I would really appreciate a short review.

Your help in spreading the word is gratefully appreciated and reviews make a huge difference to helping new readers find the series.

Please visit the appropriate link below to leave your review:

Amazon USA: https://geni.us/UnderlingsReviewUS
Amazon UK: https://geni.us/UnderlingsReviewUK
Other Amazon Stores: https://geni.us/underlings
Thank you!

MORE BOOKS BY J.C. JARVIS

John Howard Tudor Series

John Howard and the Underlings

John Howard and the Tudor Legacy

John Howard and the Tudor Deception

Fernsby's War Series

Ryskamp

Alderauge *Coming Soon…*

About the Author

J.C. Jarvis is the author of the breakout John Howard series.

He makes his home at www.jcjarvis.com

Email: jc@jcjarvis.com